Madeline's Protector

Vanessa Riley

Happy Mother's Day
Beverly!

Thank you for all
your support!
VR

Madeline's Protector

Contact Information: titleadmin@pelicanbookgroup.com

Scripture quotations, unless otherwise indicated are taken from the King James translation, public domain.

Cover Art by Nicola Martinez

White Rose Publishing, a division of Pelican Ventures, LLC
www.pelicanbookgroup.com PO Box 1738 *Aztec, NM * 87410

Publishing History
First White Rose Edition, 2013
Print Edition ISBN 978-1-61116-226-4
Electronic Edition ISBN 978-1-61116-225-7
Published in the United States of America

Dedication

I dedicate this book to my First Copy Editor, my mother Louise, my loving hubby Frank, and daughter Ellen. Their patience and support have meant the world to me.

I also dedicate this labor of love to critique partners extraordinaire: June, Mildred, Lori, Connie, Gail, Ada, Sarah, Angela, and Faye.

My mentors, Laurie Alice, Debra R. & Linda W. for answering all my endless questions

My editor, Lisa, for seeing the vision.

And my team of encouragers: Sandra, Michela, Deb, Sharon, Panya, Kelly, and Ellecia

God, I thank You this day for birthing these characters and Your arms of refuge. Psalms 71

Praise for *Madeline's Protector*

These characters, this story, and Riley's skillful prose captured my attention from the first line and held me captive to the end. ~ Award-winning author, Laurie Alice Eakes

Ms. Riley's novel is a sweet treat with stolen kisses and a sense of intrigue where her gallant characters discover God has the answers for their lives. ~ Author, June Foster

Throughout the entire book, I was kept on the edge of my seat as the author led me through an exciting journey filled with gentleness and love born of distrust and uncertainty. This is a touching look into the past that will grip your heart as it takes you on a well described, exciting, and fulfilling ride that leaves you satisfied when you reach the end. I highly recommend *Madeline's Protector*. ~ Author, Mildred Colvin

1

Shropshire, England, Iron Country, August 5, 1821

"Stop, thief!" Madeline St. James grabbed the coarse sleeve of the man who stole her guineas, but he shook free and dashed away.

"Give those back, this instant." Mouth open, pulse racing, she stopped her pursuit. A scream bubbled in the pit of her stomach, but she pursed her lips. A St. James never made a public scene or conceded defeat.

The thief reached the other side of the vacant courtyard, well ahead of a wagon rumbling up the cobblestone lane. He shot her a toothless grin and traipsed to the main building of Tilford Coaching Inn.

The dray and its lumbering horse team swerved closer, but if she waited one more second, the thief would escape her view. Another man would've taken advantage of her. Not again.

Picking up her weighty skirts, she sprinted onto the slick rocks of the road. The silver hem of her long carriage dress slapped at the mud. Better to be dirty than a victim. Cupping her palm to her eyes, she scanned for the thief.

The man bounded up the stone entree. He'd vanish like her driver, amongst the sea of gaming travellers.

She lengthened her stride to intercept him.

One high step too many, her boot heel caught in

the sagging silk, tripping her. The air pushed from her lungs as she fell flat. The soggy earth saturated her layers to the shift and petticoat. Her injured elbow stung anew.

Wheels squealed. Hooves clomped the cobbles. Soon the horses would be on top of her, stomping and kicking.

A couple of tugs and yanks couldn't fish her boot free. No escape this time. *Abba Father, forgive.* She turned her head and braced for the onslaught.

A band of iron gripped her stomach and hauled her from the muck. She went limp, sprawled against the hard chest of a rescuer. He pulled her off the lane and under one of the overhanging galleries of the inn.

Wind slapped her cheek as the horses swept past. No one held the reins. The wagon swung wide, crashed into the inn's main building, and flipped to the ground. Ejected barrels hit the whitewashed wall and sprayed foamy liquid.

Madeline's breath came in heaves, and she clutched the titan arm sheltering her. *No fainting. No need to lose more dignity.*

One of the draught horses loosed from its tether and galloped to the emerald pines scalloping the surrounding hills. The other roan remained with the wreck, lifting its crooked leg. Poor lame creature.

An old man rushed out of the inn and cut at the horse's strap. "Bring my gun. This one needs to be put down."

With an awkward hold on her middle, her rescuer spun her, perhaps to keep her from seeing the cruelty. He needn't be concerned.

The past two weeks had numbed her to violence. Yet, God kept her as He did again today. "Thank you,

Providence, but please…spare the roan."

"You're welcome, but it's Devonshire, Lord Devonshire." The low voice kissed her ear, heated the pulsing vein along her throat.

How could this man sound calm? They both could've died.

He flung open the door to an onyx carriage and eased her onto the floorboards. "Are you injured, miss?"

"No." She rubbed her arms and gazed at her rescuer. He was very tall, enough to make her feel dainty even at her Amazon height. With broad shoulders and a solid chin, she couldn't have sculpted a more perfect hero. "The horse, sir? Can you help it?"

"Stay put. This mere mortal will see what can be done." He grabbed his top hat from the seat and marched away. His elegant form, straight posture, disappeared into the growing crowd.

It didn't matter she sat on the floor, chilled in her clothes, imposing demands of a stranger. Even against this errant horse, Death shouldn't win. She'd seen its victories too often, with Mama's passing seven years ago and Cousin Thomas dying this past spring.

She squeezed her throbbing elbow. Falling aggravated the sprain.

A quick shake of her foot didn't release her trapped kid boot but tore the lace trim on her gown, Mama's carriage dress. A lump formed in Madeline's throat. She missed Mama so much.

A few choice words shouted from the crowd and a round of loud snickers interrupted her woolgathering.

Lord Devonshire returned and rubbed the scruff of his neck. "It cost three guineas, but your nag will be kept by the innkeeper's daughter."

"I'll repay you, sir. My abigail has my reticule." She swallowed gall. The thief took most of her money, but surely three coins were left.

He waved his hand. "I'd rather not be a paid fool." Leaning along the door, he stared at her with irises bluer than a summer day.

What could Lord Devonshire learn from her disheveled appearance? She didn't mind his gaze. Since travelling to Shropshire, grey ash painted the clouds, no doubt from the ore foundries. No sunny skies like Hampshire.

"Now to be of true assistance." He reached under her hem, gripped above her ankle, and freed her boot from the tangle of silk. The warmth arising from his gloved hands seared her thin stockings. "Not broken." He released her foot to dangle through the entrance.

Shocking and bold. Though dressed as a gentleman in buff buckskins and an azure tailcoat, this definitely wasn't someone with whom to be alone.

Her wits returned, and she bounced out of the carriage. "I'll get your payment."

"Wait." Deep and commanding like Father's voice, his words stopped her. "I saw you trip trailing the miner."

She pivoted and clasped her hands across her ruined pelisse. Mud covered the delicate puce rosettes embroidered on the bodice.

"You were very brave to run after him."

"Bacon-brained would be a more apt description." A raindrop splashed her forehead. Her bonnet must have fallen in the commotion. She wiped her brow. The cold balm of mud smoothed against her skin. Her heart sunk, and she wrenched off her soiled gloves. If her cheeks weren't already scarlet, they should be.

He shortened the distance between them, a smile tugging at his full lips. "In mining country, the strikes have set everyone on edge. Some resort to crime. There's a would-be highwayman on every corner. You must take care around Tilford."

A fortnight ago, his concern might've warmed her, but not now.

"Father of Heav'n!" Mrs. Elsie Wilkins, Madeline's abigail, ran to her.

"Y' weren't to leave the livery." The good woman wrapped her stubby arms about Madeline's hips. "Too much for m' heart."

In vain, Madeline pushed at Mrs. Wilkins's indigo redingote to keep it from soiling, but no force could stop the woman's bear-like embrace.

Madeline's trampled bonnet peeked from the motherly woman's reticule. Dredged in dirt, the hat's ostrich plume lay crooked. Even in haste, her abigail took care of Madeline.

With another clench, Mrs. Wilkins finally let go. "Y' face?" She yanked from her pocket a crimson cloth and scrubbed Madeline's chin.

Madeline clasped her friend's wrist. "Dear, hand me my scarf. I'll do it."

Mrs. Wilkins shook her head and kept swatting the mud. She didn't want to come on this adventure, but how could Madeline be without her strongest ally? It must be the Irish blood bubbling in the abigail's veins, making her so loyal.

"First a broken wheel, now this." Mrs. Wilkins added a spit shine to Madeline's cheek then pivoted to Lord Devonshire. "The stable boys said ye saved her. Bless ye."

"I…I saw the lass fall in the path of the wagon. I

am the Earl of Devonshire. Very glad to be of assistance." An unreadable expression set on his countenance as he flicked a rain droplet from his sleeve. "Are there others in your party?"

"There's me—Mrs. Wilkins—and my lady, Miss Madeline St. James." She stretched on tiptoes and picked at Madeline's unraveling chignon, reseating pins and tucking tresses. "And m' lady's driver, but he disappeared, the no good lout."

Great. Mrs. Wilkins just confirmed they were alone. Now he'd be obliged to help. Indebted to a man. Could this day get any worse?

The earl rubbed his jaw. His gaze seemed locked on the colourful scarf.

Another drip from the overcast skies splattered and curled into the sable-brown hair peeking beneath Lord Devonshire's brim. He was too fine looking, too virile to be trusted. Step-mother's nephew, the handsome Mr. Kent, imparted that lesson before Madeline left home.

"Mrs. Wilkins, hand me my coins. I need to repay his lordship."

"No, miss. 'Tis my duty to escort you to your destination."

Madeline shook her head. "'Unnecessary."

"Cheshire. Please take us there." Mrs. Wilkins dabbed at her coat. "Like a divine appointm'nt, the earl being here."

"I can't speak for divinity, but you might say I've been waiting on a sign." He slipped the cloth from Mrs. Wilkins and waved it like a flag. "Someone brave to show me the way."

"I suppose we have no choice." Madeline snatched it from him with trembling fingers. She may be bacon-brained but not helpless or a plaything.

"There's always a choice. Like should I chase a scoundrel or let you freeze?"

She stilled her shaking palms.

He stepped near, removed his tailcoat, and draped it onto her shoulders. With his thick thumbs, he flipped the collar's revers to cradle her neck. His touch was gentle. "This should stop your shivers. I'll have my Mason get blankets."

Hugging herself beneath the weighty wool, Madeline gaped at Lord Devonshire. "Sir, we haven't agreed."

"The drizzle will get worse." He rotated to Mrs. Wilkins. "The young lady was just in my Berlin. Perhaps the visit was too short to attest to its comfort."

Trimmed in gold, the carriage could overshadow her father's. Either the earl possessed great wealth or liked the appearance of it. In her experience, both conditions made men pompous or cruel. She rubbed her elbow again.

Mrs. Wilkins curtsied. "My lord, we've two trunks in the stables with our brok'n carriage."

The earl nodded, opened the door to his Berlin, and then plodded the long lane toward the livery of the coaching inn. Was it confidence or arrogance squaring his shoulders?

He didn't pivot to check on them, not once. Arrogance.

"Come along, Lady Maddie. Don't get stubborn. Remember *your* plan."

Madeline raised her chin, grasped Mrs. Wilkins's forearm, and lumbered toward Lord Devonshire's carriage. "Another obstacle to peace."

Her friend's cheeks glowed. "The beginning of

peace, child. It's the beginning."

If only Mrs. Wilkins could be right. The unease in Madeline's spirit disagreed.

&

The temptation to look back almost overtook Justain Delveaux, the Earl of Devonshire. He strode faster to the livery. The girl had been spooked. If he seemed anxious, she'd run.

A fire of independence burned in her jade eyes. He'd have to placate Miss St. James and win her trust. Then she'd lead him to the killer.

At the entry of the hay-filled livery, his driver brushed Athena, Justain's filly. "Sir, are you ready to give up? The informant isn't going to show."

Justain stroked Athena's thick ebony coat, a shade lighter than Miss St. James's raven locks. "He didn't. *She* did. Look behind me. Are ladies entering my Berlin?"

Mason squinted. "Yes."

"The young one possesses the red cloth signal. She's the informant."

Furrowing his brows, Mason shrugged. "You and your jokes, sir."

"I'm serious. We're taking them to Cheshire, probably a clandestine meeting. Never thought to look for a woman. Well, not for an informant. The lass will lead me to lynch—"

"Must you wax poetic?" Mason chortled. "Genteel women shouldn't be left here, but…"

"Just say it."

"We need to leave, sir. Something's afoot." Mason wiped water from the brim of his tricorn. "The miners say a blood vengeance rides tonight."

"We'll leave soon, with my new acquaintances." Why was Mason hedging his words? Since Justain was knee-high, the man never held his tongue.

Rain fell in buckets. Justain moved under the stable's roof.

Mason and Athena followed. He searched his blue-black flap coat and retrieved his treasured silver flask and Justain's bottle of tincture. "The filly's cut is sealed."

"Superb, but no more of this." Justain pocketed the tincture. "Put away your spirits and say your peace."

"This chase won't bring Lord Richard back." His driver's voice grated like a rebuke from the old man, Justain's father. "You've other things to contend."

Justain concentrated on the steady rhythm of the shower. It blocked the memory of Richard's last breath and Justain's mounting guilt. He was to blame for Richard dying. Nothing took precedence over avenging his brother.

"Send blankets to my guests. Have the stable grooms load Miss St. James's trunks." He trudged toward the Berlin. This couldn't be a fool's errand. He hated being a fool.

Madeline forced a smile at Lord Devonshire as he leapt into the Berlin. He sat in the opposing seat, tossed his sodden top hat and gloves onto the floorboards, then pushed wet hair from his face. The rain poured hard minutes after she and Mrs. Wilkins entered his carriage, and it hadn't lessened.

Seeing him soaked eased her slight agitation at

him.

"Thank ye, for savin' m' mistress." Mrs. Wilkins snuggled into the corner of his carriage, her greying red curls rested upon the creamy silk lining the walls. "Ye gen'rous to escort us to Cheshire." She yawned then winked at Madeline. "So noble and so handsome."

Heat crept up Madeline's neck. She didn't need to be reminded of his looks or his bravery. "We are grateful."

"Be at ease. It's not often I play the hero these days." His sable-brown mop shadowed a lean nose and tanned cheeks. "The escapade gave me needed exercise."

At least, he remained humoured. Gratitude should weigh on her spirit, but was his deed happenstance or had he followed her? Miles and miles from Hampshire, and the feeling of being chased refused to quit.

A servant stuck his head inside the carriage. Rain drizzled down his uniform causing the braiding on his mantle to droop. "To Cheshire, my lord?"

Twisting a signet ring, Lord Devonshire glanced toward Madeline and Mrs. Wilkins and then turned to the opening. "Yes, Mason, I haven't changed my mind. My guests have gone to great lengths to find me. I shan't forsake them."

What? Why did the earl think she sought him? What tales men must feed each other.

"Yes, my lord." The frowning servant nodded and shut the heavy door.

Madeline smoothed her bodice, trying to calm the tickle in her stomach. Father told her every kindness held a price. She'd paid enough for trusting Mr. Kent. The pain from his blows to her side persisted.

"Lord Devonshire, we haven't departed. Pray help us hire a post chaise to ferry my abigail and me to my aunt?"

"No. I will see this through." He cleared his throat. "I look forward to our conversation."

Though the earl's countenance appeared pleasant with his lips curling, he fidgeted his wilted cravat. Dried, the neckcloth might've held a little height in a fashionable sense. Was he one of those pompous dandies? Her scarlet handkerchief did hold his interest.

No. If he were, the earl would've let Madeline die than risk wrinkles to his clothes. The parade of fortune hunters Step-mother marched through Avington Manor surely would've made no effort. The shrewish woman probably hoped the flock of peacocks supping at their home could convince Madeline to accept her nephew for a mate, a lesser of evils.

The carriage lurched forward. Lord Devonshire reclined as if he posed for a portrait. His steady gaze set upon her.

Did he want his jacket returned? Did her slipping bonnet offend him? She righted it and smoothed its bent feather. "May I at least reimburse the livery expenses for my carriage?"

"Keep your precious gold coins. 'Tis my honour to serve you, Miss St. James." He grinned. Smooth white teeth peeked. "The opportunity to pull a headstrong beauty from harm's way is something I relish."

"Would you let a thief abscond with your coins?"

His smile dissolved. "No. I protect what is mine, and I'll avenge what is stolen."

Few had the patience for her opinions. She rolled one of the silver buttons of his jacket along her thumb.

"Praise be unto Prov…" Mrs. Wilkins snorted a

harsh noise, her chin bobbling in the throes of sleep. With a fold and a tuck, Madeline secured the dear woman's blanket then tugged a book from the abigail's reticule.

"You two are my first guests in this new coach." The earl's tone was low.

He needn't be concerned about awakening Mrs. Wilkins. After this harrowing day, wild elephants couldn't rouse her.

Slumping near the window, Madeline glanced at the retreating landscape, the evergreens reflecting in the puddles. She'd enjoy nature now, before they crossed the Severn Gorge. Seeing the bottomless chasm would rattle her frayed nerves. The last time, ten years ago, she took this route with her parents and had curled next to Mama and hid within the folds of her shawl. *Abba Father, please allow each of my steps to be surefooted. Tell Mama I miss her.*

Lord Devonshire inched closer. Though the carriage rocked with each clip-clop of the horse team, he didn't sway. His tall frame sat erect like a sleek marble sculpture. "Is there anything I can do to make you comfortable?"

Mrs. Wilkins's bonnet fell onto her lap, her snores bleating to an embarrassing high pitch. The symphony of snoots quieted, but not before one protracted trumpet.

"No, sir." Madeline's cheeks warmed. Explaining her hasty exodus from Avington would lower his opinion of her, not that she needed his good opinion.

Egad. Step-mother was right. Madeline did over think things. She yanked her bookmark, flipped a few pages, and tried to lose herself in the passage.

He rapped the book and lowered it. "You'll ruin

your sight, reading all the way to Cheshire. At our next stop, I'll have a lantern set down, unless I can capture your interest."

Another opportunist. Yes, he'd saved her from being trampled, but he was still a man. Did they do anything but seek their own pleasures? Like Mr. Kent.

Kent's sibilant whispers turned to yells ringing in her ear. He threatened to kill her for refusing his proposal. What type of life would she have if she'd eloped with a man of such vile temperament? She shuddered. Shoving her novel in Kent's eye darkened it and helped her escape.

"Miss St. James? Are you well?"

"Yes." She glanced at her wet hero. "You must be cold. I should return this." She lifted the tailcoat an inch and an ache rippled along her elbow. She clenched her teeth and let the jacket fall back to her shoulders.

"Just damp." He whipped his sleeves, rustling ivory buttons. "You seem to favour your right arm. Did I injure you in our last embrace?"

"No…no, my lord." Her breath hitched, and she sniffed an odour similar to fresh dye. It reeked. She huddled deeper in the tailcoat and swathed her nostrils. The mild fragrance of sandalwood lingered in Lord Devonshire's jacket. Peace reined in every storm, and this one smelled of safety, like her father's robes.

The earl shifted his boots hard onto the floor. "Some say confession is good for the soul. Do tell. Why were you at Tilford—a gaming den, no less?"

Madeline wobbled on the tufted cushion. "My carriage broke down. One usually has no choice where this happens."

"And your driver's missing? Such a fanciful story.

I love a quality Banbury." He folded his arms like a solicitor in the midst of an inquiry. "Are you running from or to someone?"

"*To* my aunt in Cheshire, Lady Cecil Glaston. She's to tour Italy with me." Well, it would be the plan once Madeline convinced the art patroness. Madeline intended to sculpt such a stirring picture, Aunt would be anxious to see Michelangelo's *David* and abandon holding a matchmaking season. After Mr. Kent's betrayal, Madeline wasn't ready to belong to any man.

"I think you are running from someone whose wrath you fear. Don't lose courage. So much trouble is wrought from silence." For one second, the earl's sky-blue pools seemed to ripple with hurt before he blinked them clear. "We mustn't allow this."

She squinted at Lord Devonshire. Could he know she'd kept quiet about Mr. Kent?

"Help me, Miss St. James, my brave lass?"

Madeline's heart responded to the plea, thundering within her ribs, but could she be of aid without inviting Kent's revenge?

Lord Devonshire reached for her hand. "Tell me your secret. My dear, you can trust me."

2

Madeline peered at the earl through her dark lashes. Confession bubbled on her tongue until he spewed the awful sentiment. "Trust? It's the most misused verb in the king's language. People treat it as witchcraft, to force others to do what they want."

Lord Devonshire seemed to wince at the acrid statement, but then nodded. "You're too young to be disillusioned. Typically this comes later in life. Are you one and twenty?"

"Almost twenty."

He slouched and scratched the small scar on his chin as if rethinking his course of action.

What did the earl want? She tapped her nose. Father would find a way to test this man. She clutched the book to her bodice and whisked the sagging feather of her bonnet to the side.

"Tell me, lass, what has you engrossed? Poetry or a romantic tale?" The phrase slipped his full lips.

She loosened her tight grip on the pages. "A spy's tale."

Lord Devonshire straightened, returning to his statuesque pose. "Humph. A spy's tale? Are King and country safe?"

"Yes, because of a harlot's…a woman's bravery." She covered her mouth.

His countenance glowed with laughter. "Reading

of harlots? I suppose fairytales are out of fashion." He leaned forward and adjusted her bonnet, tugging the ostrich's plume from her face. "There, now you may peruse your prostitution in peace."

Madeline heard a murmured "*ma cherie*." Had she given him license to be familiar? The sandalwood lacked enough zest to calm her. She bit her lip and slid out of the jacket. "My lord, I hope I haven't creased it."

With his long limbs, Lord Devonshire reached across the carriage, took his tailcoat, and imprisoned her hand. The heat of his calloused palm thawed her chilled fingers.

"Sir, release me."

He lifted their union to his jaw but stopped short of kissing her fist. "You are injured. May I?"

It wasn't a question for he gave no time for response. Instead, she became captive to a feather-light massage. Each stroke brought more comfort than the last.

"Tilford was unsettling, but you're free, and you've found your champion." The words kissed her skin as the cold band of his ring skidded along the lifeline of her mitt. The sensation jolted as it cajoled.

Brazen *ma cherie*. Madeline should jerk free, but somehow, the kneading circles drained the tension from her strained muscles. She stopped resisting and let the artisan sculpt.

Now, his motion tickled, and she suppressed a giggle. Thank goodness, her long sleeves hid Kent's bruises. If Lord Devonshire saw the markings, no telling what he'd do.

The earl dimpled then connected her freckles as if jotting with an imagined quill. "*Trust* I can take the pain away. That I can ease your conscience."

He must have knowledge of Mr. Kent, but how? "Are you here to protect me?"

"Yes." The earl blew steamy air along the valleys of her knuckles. Unlike her father, Lord Devonshire didn't need to yell to have his way.

"Miss St. James." He stroked the silver threads of her cuff. "Tell me who sent you."

"My fa—" The consonants caught in her windpipe as his thumb slid beneath the silk. He'd see the raw marks. "My father." She tried to push back upon her seat.

As if sensing her anxiety, Lord Devonshire retreated but maintained an easy grip. She could withdraw.

"Such a gallant lass to brave all to find me. Was it too dangerous for your father to come?"

"I couldn't have him with me. I asked to leave." Not for a come-out, a lavish season given by Lady Glaston. Father and her aunt rarely spoke since Mama passed. "What does—"

"Let me be plain." He swept her palm flat upon his chest, hiding it deep within the folds of his cravat. "I'll safeguard you and your family, if you admit all now."

Madeline's pinkie lay against the soft linen. The earl must be in league with her father, one of his many agents. She choked back a sob. Father used his connections to force someone to watch over her. Judging from today's progression, she needed the help, but she'd rather be sick than mention out loud Mr. Kent laid hands on her.

The carriage hit a bump, and the earl steadied her. The handle of a gun peeked from his velvet waistcoat. He drew her attention away and tucked a wispy tendril of her hair behind her ear. "I'll make things right."

Lord Devonshire glided closer, his mouth inches from hers. "Tell me, Miss St. James. Where do I find the fiend?

"Will you have him make amends quietly, without tarnishing my reputation?"

"Why are you protecting him? He's hurt you, your family…?" The word 'too' seemed to fall silent on his lips.

With bullets or his bare strength, the earl could avenge her shame, but she wanted peace. She cast her gaze to the floorboards.

Lord Devonshire lifted her chin. His touch felt as if he'd taken the ostrich plume from her hat and stroked her face. "I understand and shall protect you. Say where the killer hides."

Those murderous threats Kent spat upon her neck were true. "What can be done?"

"Lead me to find Barrow, and I'll do anything you want."

"Barrow?" She shook her head. Lord Devonshire hunted his own fiend. "Who is he?"

The earl squinted, and his pupils narrowed to dots. "You don't know him, his location?" The strain in his voice was palpable. He craned his neck toward the ceiling. "Then why were you at Tilford, bandying a red cloth?"

She tried to shake free, but he clamped her hand. "Our driver stopped there and disappeared trying to fix a broken wheel. Please don't be angry. Barrow, I know him not."

The grimace on his countenance cleared. "You, you speak the truth."

With a small peck to her palm, Lord Devonshire released her then threw his jacket about his potent shoulders and stretched out on his seat.

Mrs. Wilkins moaned and stole closer to her corner. She might as well sleep to Cheshire.

His voice melted, returning to smooth baritone notes. "What draws you north?"

The mercurial change from hero, to lover, to stone made Madeline dizzy. This was a game to Lord Devonshire, and she'd almost swooned. How could she continue to be so gullible to men? It was time to stop this and announce checkmate. "My father the Duke of Hampshire will reward you for your good deeds. And so will my aunt. She's Lady Cecil Glaston, wed to the second son of the Duke of Cheshire."

His brow rose, then he leaned further in repose. His large Adam's apple bulged above his snowy cravat. "Why would the duke allow his daughter to journey unprotected?"

"Arrangements were made in haste, and my step-mother thought one attendant sufficient."

"And your father, the duke, would allow you to be transported in this manner? I'm astounded, Lady Madeline."

She balled her fist beneath her book. "My lord, I am the duke's daughter. Should I ask for proof of your peerage?"

"I never seek for anyone to prove themselves. I wait for their character to be revealed." Lord Devonshire shrugged. "It seems odd to allow a cherished daughter to travel far from home with little regard."

With a snap of a page, she fingered the lines of ink. She never questioned her father's love, but his heavy-handed judgments and bitterness filled her with anguish. She flipped to her bookmark and waited for the peace of the verses to quiet her soul.

❧

Another empty chase. His driver was right.

Justain Delveaux, the newly ascended Lord Devonshire, used every ounce of his composure and his practiced commerce face to keep his disappointment contained. It wasn't the skittish lamb's fault. What were the odds the young lady's red-haired servant would carry a red scarf, the agreed upon signal, the day he was to meet the informant?

The weather or Barrow subverted the person with the knowledge he sought. Blast it. No justice for Richard. He'd failed his brother again. Justain peered through his casement. Rain slapped the glass. "My Mason will drown if this continues."

The slight reflection of the lass's frown tinted the pane. His driver's plight concerned the girl. Good character. Miss St. James was no servant, not used to hard labour. Her skin felt too soft and her nails too clean even for a governess. But a duke's daughter? "When I deposit you and Mrs. Wilkins to Lady Glaston, retell our story with kindness. Wouldn't want her upset with me. Are you upset?"

"No, it's a common practice to be questioned about murderers." Her jade eyes clouded, perhaps with disappointment.

Most women seemed to enjoy his attention. Since he returned from the war, no one was impervious to his charms. Even his childhood love, Miss Caroline Lavis, now sought him out at parties.

"Who is this Barrow? Why do you seek him?" Miss St. James's pouty lips were worthy of worship.

"We shall speak no more of this." No need to heap more salt upon his wounds.

"Very well." She frowned and returned to her book.

Curiosity was a woman's undoing, but no matter how beautiful she was—slim build, raven hair, pert nose—an alleged duke's daughter was off limits. Well, his brother, Richard would make an exception. As if the man knew his life would be short, Richard courted mistresses and scandals across England.

Miss St. James dropped her puce bookmark.

He retrieved the ribbon and extended it to her as if she'd dropped a handkerchief.

"Thank you." The words sounded begrudged, and she avoided the touch of his fingers.

He dug into his leather satchel, his overstuffed correspondence pouch from the war, and retrieved the crop rotation plans for Trenchard Park and thumbed some pages.

Perhaps he should go to Lancashire and propose to Miss Lavis? The family ring, another trinket of Delveaux tradition, travelled in his saddlebag. Miss Lavis would attend him in the parlour. The lavender adorning her wrists would swirl about him, conjuring up every one of his inadequacies. Had he done enough to win her hand?

He still had four months before his twenty-eighth birthday. Why would his great-grandfather perpetrate a crime upon the males of their lineage and tie inheritance to marriage? Justain adjusted his cravat. He'd wallow in pity tomorrow. A distraction for his ego sat too near.

"Madeline St. James, or better Lady Madeline, you seem enthralled with the agony of the harlot."

She put down her book. Those kissable lips parted. "Enthralled? I do like reading."

"Odd, I've found most young ladies prefer other entertainments, crafts, and music, not the lyrics of the demimonde."

Her pupils grew wide at the comparison. "Is there no better way to pass the time?"

"We could hold hands." He smothered a chuckle. "And please remove the headpiece. I'd be able to listen more intently without a feather covering your eye every other second."

The girl stared at him, maybe searching his face, hunting for something. She unpinned her bonnet and placed it across the curve of her knees. "You have more puzzling questions? You'll find I'm not like your other ladies, these acquaintances that prefer music or crafts."

A gut-wrenching laugh broke free, in spite of his need to maintain control. "No, you're too honest. Refreshing."

She brushed aside the ebony tendril escaping the austere knot topping her head. This raven beauty would look well in broad skirts with the winds of his moors tousling her curls.

"My father has taught me to hate hypocrisy. He'll flay a man over it."

"It's his pre-prerogative." Justain exercised his jaw. His stutter often got the better of him. He still hadn't learned how to reflect upon his father, the old man, without a wave of sadness lapping at his spirit. He folded his arms and fingered the old scars on his side. "I'll keep that in mind. Have you gathered any tips from your reading?"

She coddled a page and flipped it. "From the courtesan, the strumpet?"

A sweet vision of the lass wrapped in bright satins filtered into his brain box. "Such words on your tongue. Perhaps you should read to me over dinner?"

The lass waved her arm, stopping him from signalling his driver. "I'm reading of Rahab, the harlot of the Old Testament who was redeemed by her faith." She rubbed her elbow and giggled. "Sorry to go on about it, but it's been awhile since I've laughed."

The black book wasn't Byron's latest Turkish tale, but a Bible. He envisioned her sitting in the pew of his cousin's church, singing hymns, readying for a missionary tour. Was it wise to flirt with a religious miss, an alleged missionary duke's daughter? The girl's drenched skirts outlined the longest legs he'd seen since Spain. No, it wasn't wise.

"I hope my attention, Lady Madeline, hasn't caused you discomfort."

She tilted her heart-shaped face to the side. Her expression softened to a smile. "Have you, in some odd way, tried to make me comfortable?" She could beguile with her large jade eyes.

He slumped onto his bench away from temptation. "Miss St. James, I—"

The wild sound of hooves rattled the walls. Guttural commands flew outside.

The shouts became clear. "Stop the carriage!"

The cabin jolted as the horses surged forward.

Miss St. James dropped onto his feet. He hauled her from the floor. "Seems we have more takers for your remaining gold coins. Perhaps mine, too."

"You think that, that…" The girl shivered within his hold.

Raising her onto the seat, he offered a smile. "We'll outrun this."

Gunfire crackled in the air.

Justain pressed to the glass.

"Gut the reins or die!" The demand came from a rider twenty paces behind. The man pointed a flintlock rifle. At least three other bandits chased, gaining on the dirt highway.

"We're surrounded!" Miss St. James clasped her chaperone's arm, awakening her.

"Press forward!" The rally slipped through Justain's teeth.

"Father of Heav'n!" Mrs. Wilkins clutched the seat.

Hard items, probably rocks showered the roof. Men must be in the hills, hiding amongst the lush pines. This was an ambush. Barrow's doing?

A bullet exploded outside the window.

Elbowing the glass open, he peppered the chamber of his blunderbuss, took aim, and got off one shot.

A villain fell to the ground. His rearing horse kicked up a dust storm.

Justain readied caps for another pass. The carriage hit a rut. His hand slammed against the casement, knocking away his gun. He clamped his lips, buttoning his anger from his passenger's delicate ears.

His carriage team whinnied. Perhaps pelted by more stones. *Let there be no torches. No firestorm like my beloved Trenchard.*

"Provid'nce, be with us." The companion folded her hands in prayer.

Miss St. James rocked back and forth. "Yes, please, Abba Father."

Justain wanted to stifle their cries. He couldn't

think with the noise, but he was in no position to take away their hope. Without his pistol, they all needed help.

Another gun belched.

A shriek answered overhead. A large object crashed onto the roof and rolled to the ground. A lump wearing a dark flap jacket stretched across the gravel road. Justain turned from the window not wanting to see his man, his friend, trampled. Poor Mason, his loyal servant.

Justain clenched his fist and punched the ceiling. Tomorrow, he'd mourn his friend. Today, this soldier needed to focus on the mission, protecting the women. The carriage swung to the left. Pellets of metal ripped into the cabin. He wrenched his charges onto the floorboards and straddled them, shielding them from the next spray of rocks and bullets.

The girl squealed.

"Skittish miss, please. I'm not taking liberties, but I should suffer the slug first." Justain splayed his arms to cover them.

She grabbed at his lapels. "S-s-sir."

He shifted his weight as the carriage rocked, almost tipping.

"Father of Heav'n!" Mrs. Wilkins kept screaming into his ear.

Another weapon discharged in the distance. By some miracle, had they outrun the bandits?

Justain moved closer to the lass. He shut his lids and counted the seconds between rocks hitting the sides.

The acrid smell of gunpowder leached from the seats. A warm palm nuzzled his ear, obscuring his count.

The girl's lovely mouth lay inches from his. She gritted her teeth. "Please."

Mrs. Wilkins clapped. "Don't hear anythin'. We'll be fine!"

The coach veered. Justain's gut slammed against his ribs. "I wouldn't stop praying yet. We're going too fast." The wheels banged down an incline.

Miss St. James punched his chest, and released a scream. She fainted.

"What? I've not—" Justain pressed his fingers to the limp girl's throat. A rapid pulse!

"Lady Maddie? Oh, Provid'nce, protect her." Mrs. Wilkins sniffled. "Save the earl."

His newly purchased Berlin toppled to its side. A window shattered, showering his back with glass. Justain wedged between the perfectly dyed seats as the carriage pitched and rolled. The faint odour of glue still pervaded the coverings. Papers from his satchel filled the air. The smell of raw earth poured through the seams.

"Where's the bot-bottom?" Every muscle in his body clenched.

"Father of Heav'n!" Mrs. Wilkins's tears sprayed his hand.

He held his breath and braced to strike the rock bed of the Severn Gorge.

3

A ray of light penetrated the shadows. Justain tried to move to it, but something buried him, his face, his legs. He worked a hand free and slid his fingers against his prison. Rough planks pinned him to the ground.

A stream of water snaked through the pile and pelted his forehead. The weight seemed to increase and the pressure caved his chest. He gathered as much air as he could, then shoved with all his might.

He broke free. Flying carriage floorboards crashed with a mighty thud. The motion wrenched a stake from his shoulder. Formed from gilded trim, the shiny stick lacerated more skin than it penetrated. If it left a mark, he'd add the scar to his collection.

The steady rain helped him regain his senses. He took stock of the steep cliff bearing down upon him. The memory of a gunshot echoed in his ear. Mason!

A bullet had assailed his friend, nearly twenty feet up. The man lay injured, dumped on the road. Justain slogged to his feet. He clawed the rock, but his boots couldn't gain footing. He fell back. Justain couldn't save him.

Rain filled his eyes. Another life taken. All Justain's fault.

Horses pounded to the edge of the ridge. He lunged out of sight and hugged the rock.

"All dead!" one shouted.

"No, I seen movement!" The yelp boomed before washing away in the rain. The man must've seen Justain.

"Must be sure! Ride this way. The path down is safer." The bandits' horses pounded away.

"A hiding place, a plan?" Justain squinted and spied a series of shafts along the Severn Gorge's floor. He crawled in that direction.

The iron dust of the gorge blended with the downpour, creating an acidic stench. It burned the lining in his nostrils. *Focus. Forget the pain.*

Breaking from the shadows, he stumbled over a carriage bit. It must've separated as they sped down the hill. At least his horse team escaped. "Better for Athena to be captured than lame." He pushed to stand, but his fingers sank into a book. The rain smeared its ink, but the burnish of the golden pages still shined.

"Bible?" He remembered the frightened prayers of his guests. "The girl and the chaperone?" Justain shook his head. He couldn't fail them, too.

The dormant soldier within awoke, crystallizing his course of action. He'd get the ladies to safety and defeat the scoundrels. The task seemed impossible without weapons, but his luck had to change. Justain started sifting through the remains of his pretentious Berlin carriage. It littered the terrain.

A kid slipper protruded from a mound of debris. He lunged to it, tearing away roofing and seatbacks, anxious to liberate his passengers. "Mrs. Wilkins, speak to—"

She lay silent, crumbled against a boulder.

Justain placed a palm to her nose. No breath left her body. The dislodged bones along her throat confirmed the worst. "Poor woman." The mounting death toll gripped him. Mrs. Wilkins, Mason, both killed because he'd parked at a den of thieves. "And what of the girl!" Justain slipped about the battlefield, crawling betwixt crags and smashed travel boxes. He raised his gaze to the ridge. The enemy could descend any second. "Miss St. James!"

Clothing and chunks of wheel flew from Justain's quaking hands. His crazed actions inflamed his shoulder. He ignored it, for a warrior was only concerned with the mission. "Call out to me so that I may find you!"

The wind howled, sounding of old Wellesley's deep-throated commands, *'keep low in the brush.'* Justain dropped to his knees. His field marshal would've found her by now.

The rain would douse the sights of the villains' rifles and yield more time to locate the girl. Justain flipped whisks of wet hair from his face.

The storm spat rain in horizontal clips, but the gusts unfurled a swirl of silver fabric. "Miss St. James!" It had to be her, trapped underneath a section of shattered carriage wall close to the cliff. He ran to the pile, hefting the framing and metal and unearthed the woman's silent countenance. Grabbing her wrist, he felt for a pulse. *Please be alive!*

A chaotic rhythm coursed, and Justain released his breath. "Just have to shove this door and you'll be free." He strained to move the monstrous thing. With a burst of energy, he pitched the splintered wood to reveal the sea of silk taffeta painted with a red spot. A spreading red spot. "No, lass!" He hoisted her high into his arms but took small comfort in her shallow vitals.

The girl stirred. Her palms slipped beneath his jacket as she swatted at the velvet of his waistcoat. "No, Kent! Release me!"

Justain pressed her hard to his chest. "Miss! It's Lord Delveaux Devonshire. Let me protect you. Don't fight me."

She fainted.

"I'll aid you." He turned and marched toward the openings. Mason's silver flask shined amongst a swell of smashed possessions. He scooped it. "Pity you weren't a brandy drinker." The levity he sought couldn't soothe the ache in his abdomen. Every instinct forced him to acknowledge that his constant ally didn't survive. He'd still make Mason proud. Justain couldn't wallow in the sense of loss; he kept moving.

❧

Something pulled on her skirt.

Fabric snapped and ripped. Madeline's eyelids fluttered open. A haggard beam hung overhead. The smell of iron and damp earth assaulted her nostrils. She gagged; her stomach cramped. Where was she? Did Death make one wait in a cave before judgment?

A groan fled her lips. Everything ached, so she couldn't be dead. She strained to focus on the timber, studying the flecks of amber and garnet etched in the grains and pretended it was rose marble. She'd dream of what to sculpt. Her lids drooped.

Icy, wet fingers yanked off her stocking.

She couldn't breathe, as if Mrs. Wilkins had bound her tight in an ill-sized corset.

Ripping of more cloth.

A tremor vibrated through her. "Kent, no. No!"

She let out a high-pitched wail to shoo the vermin hunched over her, fumbling with her skirts. "Help! H—"

A hand clamped upon her mouth. She flayed her arms in vain. *The Lord is my Shepherd, I shall not want.*

"Be still now, lass," the beast admonished. "Miss St. James, it's not what you think." He moved his palm from her lips to cup her chin.

A faint hint of recognition bloomed as she examined his troubled countenance. Sky-blue eyes. "Not you, too. Let me be!"

"Miss St. James, you've been shot!" He jerked his head toward the opening as if he expected someone to be standing there.

The earl turned back and released a tight breath. "I've carried you from the wreckage to an abandoned mineshaft. If you scream, the villains shall set upon us. They're still close, hunting us even with the storm. You must trust me."

She rocked her head, "no." Moving her foot sent a wave of pain.

"Young woman, you're in no position to refuse my assistance. I've taken no liberties. Your leg's injured."

His explanation didn't prevent her flesh from cringing at his touch. She stared at her beam. Perhaps if she concentrated, she could hide in one of its cracks.

"'Pon my honour, I've been your servant." He wrenched off his coat flinging it beyond her head. "I've sacrificed my cravat, though it's not enough. I need more rags to stem the bleeding." The man peeled off his waistcoat, then undid his shirt, and tore them both into strips.

Madeline pivoted her head from the disrobed man. She decried her limbs for shaking. Her abigail would protect her. "Mrs. Wilkins?"

No answer.

"Mrs. Wilkins? My lord, she went for help? But she'd never leave me."

"I'm here. You're not alone." He applied more weight to the wound.

Madeline attempted to sit. Agony! Everything hurt. "There's a lump on my crown. What have you done to Mrs. Wilkins?"

His brows flew together. "You're tensing, Miss St. James. I can't patch you up if you continue to thrash about." Lord Devonshire helped her ease to the ground. "What can I do to make you calm?"

"The truth. Where's my abigail?"

"Mrs. Wilkins." The folds of her hem muffled his voice. "She and my Mason…"

Dread enveloped her. Her stomach knotted. "Hide naught."

"Your servant will always be in your heart," the earl said. "The woman prayed feverishly for you to be preserved. You have to cooperate to honour her last request."

Madeline sucked in her tears. With the sounds of guns, the impact on the roof, she'd assumed Death took the poor driver, but Mrs. Wilkins? A new wave of loss rippled through her. "Was she shot, too?"

He ripped at his lining. "I can't upset you further."

"Tell me the whole of it." Madeline choked up. "Please."

The earl elevated his sable mop. "It was a violent crash. My poor Berlin litters the terrain." He seemed to be stalling, perhaps searching for words. He licked his lips then met her gaze. "Mrs. Wilkins broke her neck. With that kind of injury, she surely knew no pain. I'm sorry." He continued his ministrations, hiding his eyes.

Her throat tightened, strangling in sobs. Mrs. Wilkins was gone, taken like Mama. "I shouldn't have made her come."

"Please, Miss St. James. Self-doubt will add to your misery." His voice sounded guarded, but peppered with sadness. "Hold still."

Loss must hurt men, too. She wiped a thousand salted drops from her cheeks. Silent cries were her practice. She took a deep breath. "Where are we?"

"We've fallen into a mined tributary of the Severn Gorge. I saw an opening and hid us."

His words tumbled in her ear. "Villains…still seek us?"

"Yes. Our best chance is to wait out in this—Miss St. James." Lord Devonshire perched above her, caressing her face to draw her from her faint. His calloused fingers stroked circles around her mouth. "Stay with me, lass. I need you to be awake. Keep talking."

The man was so close, but his touch so gentle. "You forget your gloves when you ride."

"My lady thinks I should? Any other recommendations from the duke's daughter?" The sensitivity in his tone fled, leaving teasing notes. He moved back to her injury.

She balled her fist. "I'm funny?"

"I thought I was more interesting to you as a rake." His words sparkled with challenge.

"You won't hurt me, will you?"

"No, but I should be more afraid of your intentions." The earl shredded more fabric.

She spread her palm flat. "Frightened of me?"

"You shamelessly flirt with me about harlots, and

in the middle of chaos, you take the opportunity to caress my ear."

"What?" She relaxed the muscles in her leg. "I tried to get your attention."

"Well, you have it, my dear, so full of spirit."

"Sir, you're deceived, you, you libertine."

His head reared up. "Today, the only pleasure this Lothario will have is seeing you live."

She'd misread the earl again, and became her father, discounting Lord Devonshire's motives for evil. "I should be more agreeable."

"You're doing fine. Keep that fire and stay awake." He lowered his countenance and continued binding her leg. "This is far from a normal predicament, and I'm not in the habit of baring myself…well, not in mineshafts."

A streak of dust matted his hair. If she could, she'd brush it away. She wished she had something to offer to show her support.

The earl took another strip and pressed it to the gash. He seemed different from Mr. Kent and Father: neither beast, nor bully. "Your composure is exemplary. Nothing like adventure off the page, my bookworm."

Thunder clapped, and Madeline convulsed. "The mine, the rain, the makings of a gothic tragedy."

He whipped his head to the entrance again then peered back at her. His eyes sparkled. "That would make this a romantic interlude. Shall I drink of your beauty?"

"Yes. Tell me my eyes are rare emeralds." That's what all the fortune hunters saw.

He peered at her for a second. "Not like emeralds. They're too included with specks."

"Sir, my eyes are dirty?"

"No, but like cat's-eye jade. They too are rare, and the mystics say they have healing powers. I think they're lovely."

This young man was different. Maybe he truly saw her.

His gaze darted to the opening for a second. "No one has yet intruded." He sighed as if relieved then winked at her. "Shall I quote you poetry to complete my seduction?"

She shook her head, ignoring his jest. She wasn't ready to laugh, not without Mrs. Wilkins. *Abba Father, help us. "He leadeth me beside the still waters. He restoreth my soul."*

Lord Devonshire's voice became thick like caramel, drowning out her Psalm. *"If yet I have not all thy love, dear, I shall never have it all."* He shifted his hands, applying more pressure. *"I cannot breathe one other sigh, to move."*

Her cheeks warmed from his poem. Lord Devonshire attempted to ease the pain in her heart. God had sent a strange shepherd to lead her from the shadow of death. She recited, *"Nor…entreat one other tear to fall. And all my treasure, which should purchase thee."*

"A cultured bookworm who's partial to Donne's *Lovers' Infiniteness*; you don't disappoint. I'm glad your reading encompasses more than religious fare." He returned to her countenance. "Things are well, but I've got to get that bullet out before it poisons you."

The earl winced as if he hadn't meant to say she could still die. He didn't know her life.

Lord Devonshire cleared his throat. "In Burgos, I learned that the sooner the bullet's out, the sooner you'll be dancing at a ball." For a few seconds, his sandalwood banished the odours of the mine and the freshness of her injury. "I've helped men endure worse," he said. "Forgive this." He cut trim from her dress and tied it above her knee.

"You know medicine?" The band constricted with each passing second.

"I learned a few things in the Peninsula, which will serve us well." He retrieved his jacket and pulled a glass jar and a silver flask from interior pockets then made his jacket into a loaf-shape and propped her neck. He opened the flask and poured a measure on the strike. The liquid felt cold, and yet, it burned.

"Mason loved Scotch. Good man. This will cleanse." The earl dumped the contents of the jar into the flask and swirled the solution. With his buckskins, he looked like a cat, an Egyptian sphinx moving about its lair. A gash marred his golden shoulder.

"You're hurt?"

"A minor scratch." He frowned and drew her gaze to the flask. "We'll use this concoction of horse tincture and spirits to dull the ache. Drink this."

Madeline gritted her teeth. Her leg hurt so much, but she turned away from the shiny container. "I can't. Father wouldn't—"

"Before we lose all light. Maybe the moon's glow will help us." He raised her off the bunched jacket. "Take three large sips."

Her body felt broken. Her leg throbbed, and she lacked vigour. "Will I sleep?"

He brought the flask to her lips. "No, just ease the ache. I know you're hiding the pain."

Madeline didn't want to hurt anymore. She allowed liquid fire to ignite her throat.

Before she could protest, the earl made her drink more of the foul brew, but nothing would wash away all the torment. The orange circles of her beam seemed to spin and picked up speed as he counted down from a hundred. "You carry…these tinc, these things?" She slurred her words.

"Habits from the war." The earl closed the bottle. He fished a buckle from his boot. "Some serve better than others. Bite down on this metal as I start. Trust me, my lady."

Lord Devonshire placed it in her palm, and Madeline laced her fingers with his. She did trust him. "You believe me, not chiv…chival—"

"Chivalrous. It takes practice not to stutter. I've used mirrored glass." He patted her arm.

"Your eyes, like a knight's or a beautiful marble warrior." She pulled his hand to her chin, modeling what Mrs. Wilkins always did to encourage her. "God's made you the vessel to protect me."

"A vessel? Like a flowery vase?" He scowled for a moment. "Even Providence could employ a chamber pot. I'll not abandon your trust."

He slipped back to the bullet wound.

Madeline took the buckle and held it in her mouth. The large loop rested on her tongue. It tasted as hard and as bitter as the iron in the air.

The earl lit a smelly sulfur match. He cleansed his knife in the yellow-orange flame. "I'm starting."

Sharp, piercing metal now surpassed the ache of the bullet. She covered her mouth and screamed into her hand.

"The slug has dug deep, but I'll remove it." He strengthened his grip as the knife struck again.

She yelled, louder than she'd ever done before,

then gnawed the metal. *Father of Heaven, forgive me. Please, let my life mean more than this.*

"I have it! The ball is removed!" He threw the slug against the cavern wall. He poured the last few drops of his elixir onto the gash.

Darkness.

"Stay with me!" Lord Devonshire sounded angry as he squeezed her leg.

Madeline opened her eyes and nodded.

He took fresh pieces of his shirt and tore a strip from her outer silk to form a bandage. "You have to stay awake. The tincture has laudanum, and it has strange effects if you sleep." He wiped the knife and stashed it and his supplies in his jacket. "Lady Madeline."

She dislodged the buckle from her teeth. "Y-yes."

Lord Devonshire paused and studied her ceiling beams as if he searched for clues. "Tell me about your harlot."

With heavy lids, she peered at him.

"Tell me about the harlot in your Bible." His mouth seemed wry with humour. "Unless my little bookworm is too shy to recount the details of the tale."

Her tongue couldn't form any words.

Lord Devonshire pushed close; his lips almost touched hers. "Obey and fight, Miss St. James. You can't quit me for one minute. The bandits intended for us to die. We won't let them win."

She concentrated on the ant-like scar on his chin. He was a knight, battle-hardened and strong. "Madeline; address me as Madeline."

He settled behind the bunches of taffeta. "Tell me, Madeline." A sense of urgency vibrated in his voice.

The intensity touched her. She pushed to counter.

"Rahab was a great listener."

"The piece of fluff had ears?" He tied more material in place; the bands pulled on the wound's sore flesh.

Fighting the pain, she clenched the buckle within her fist. "Rahab's not fluff. Her faith made her worthy of redemption."

"I've read that passage before, and I don't recall anything of what you're talking about."

"Sir, you've studied the Bible?"

He arose above the tattered fabric, Mama's poor dress. "Don't be shocked, miss. I have." His arms twirled about; he must've tied hundreds of knots. "And I'm sure my cousin has preached about it in some sermon."

She awaited his attention, wanted the reassurance of his warm gaze, but he focused upon his work. "Rahab let the spies lodge at her house, hid them from danger."

"Done." He crawled alongside her and steadied her whitening knuckles. He opened Madeline's hand and retrieved the buckle. The edges had started to prick.

Her chest constricted as if a pile of books or a block of marble sat upon her. She forced air into her nose. "Ever wondered why, why she hid the spies?"

"No." The earl refastened his boot. "I assumed that was the way it was supposed to be." He leaned over her and centered Madeline on the makeshift pillow of his jacket.

"You don't appear the kind to"—she inhaled more comforting sandalwood—"to examine only the surface."

He twisted his full lips as if to rejoin, but Madeline

shook her head. "Rahab used faith as her guide. Risked her life for others."

Thunder crackled like gunfire. Her muscles contracted of their own volition.

"Just more bad weather." The earl placed a thumb to her wrist. "Your pulse is strong. Well, the harlot got to live for her trouble, did she not?"

"Her whole family lived, and she married into the royal lineage of Judah. Imagine, one decision changing the lives of gen…generations." She tried to smile but even her cheeks throbbed. "If you hadn't decided to help, the wild carriage at Tilford or the bandits—"

"With that reasoning, you wouldn't have been shot if you hadn't accompanied me." Lord Devonshire furrowed his brows. He released her arm and bounced to his feet. "About this Rahab business." He stretched, almost reaching her creviced beam. "I guess it depends upon the husband, to know if the harlot improved her circumstances."

Another series of thuds raged even though the rain slowed. The sounds could've been the King's army marching in a parade. Madeline rubbed the lump on her crown. "Such a change in fortune, I'm sure she was delighted."

He dimpled. "I'm sure the striking harlot delighted her husband." Lord Devonshire stooped and touched her wound. "The bandages are holding." He sighed as if he hadn't been breathing. "You speak your mind with great authority for a bookworm."

"My lord, this bookworm puts great stock in the Bible."

Justain sat, propping along the cavern wall. The continuous belting of the storm sounded too familiar, like the routing of an enemy encampment. The fiends had to have given up by now. "Your frankness is refreshing. I guess I'm not used to women speaking this boldly in my presence."

She closed her eyes for a second. "No more about your harem."

Justain chuckled again and cleaned his fingers on scraps of his vest. Steeped in bits of cloth, hiding in a mineshaft, tending to wounds. This wasn't how he pictured his interrogation would end. He gathered up the stained fabric and covered it with soil scuffed by his boot. Madeline didn't need to see any more of the rags.

At least this girl had fire and brains. Caroline would shriek from the dust, let alone the pain and loss Madeline endured. The marauders would've strung him up by now, with Caroline's yowling leading the way.

He glanced at the bullet. He and his patient would make it out of this mine alive.

The lass tilted her countenance away from him. She must be exhausted, but it was too soon to let her rest. She might never awaken.

"Let's talk for a while. Tell me a Hampshire secret, Miss St. James. Lady Madeline. Madeline?"

The glow of a lantern rimmed the mouth of the cave.

"Did someone check these two?" The shout came from outside.

Justain scooped up the unresponsive girl and fled deeper into the mineshaft. Justain lunged behind a turn in the cavern's throat and pressed into a musty corner.

The unconscious woman lay bundled in his jacket, tucked in his arms. A lone set of hard steps, boot treads, echoed from the entrance. If only Justain had more time. Mason's flask? What if he missed a piece of cloth?

Footsteps approached his hiding spot.

How could he save the girl now, let alone himself? Justain crouched lower, drawing deeper into the shadows. The fishy stench of cheap whale oil torches burned his nose. Light circles whipped along the walls.

Madeline still hadn't moved. Her cold cheek lay plastered against his bare chest. "No more deaths on my watch," Justain murmured into her curls, and lowered her to the ground. He slipped the blade from his jacket pocket.

The enemy drew close. The man's scarred hand whipped the lit torch inches from Justain's.

A hot ore scar. The bandits are miners? Justain heard striking miners in these parts found time for mischief, but this was too much.

Hefting his knife, Justain prepared to thrust it if the man inched closer.

"Over here!" grunted the other vermin.

The heavy footfalls retreated. Another lucky hand for the card player. Justain waited until only the calls of grasshoppers sounded. He dropped the weapon and slid down the cavern wall. "Madeline." He picked her up, setting her in his lap. Justain stroked her forehead. "All is well, lass. Stir."

He wove his fingers into her thick raven tresses. "Can you hear me?" The locks were satin, but this wasn't the time for indulgence. The girl could slip away, never awakening. Justain traced her cheek with his thumb. "Madeline."

A small patch of air skirted his shoulder.

"Lass, open your eyes."

Her damp bodice rose slowly, barely filling her lungs. He tugged at her hem to recheck the bandages. His knots held fast; she hadn't sprung a leak. "All for naught. Not today, lass." He slipped beneath her jacket and felt for the stays of her corset; undoing it would aid her breathing. He tugged the silk of her dress and loosened the toughened cotton loops, a world of hedonistic knowledge finally put to good use. "Come back to me."

Only the grasshoppers answered him. He laid her flat on her back and planted his palms upon her stomach to pump air. "Lady Madeline."

She coughed.

Justain took his cloak and propped up her neck.

Her eyelids fluttered open.

"Whisper that you can hear me, that you understand my words?"

She touched his face, tracing the crevice of his chin. "You well?" she mumbled.

"Yes, but I asked you not to sleep. Do the people of Hampshire keep their word?"

Her gaze flew to the opening as if someone stood behind him. "Kent? I heard his voice."

"The tincture can jumble things, Madeline."

She brushed his ear. Her fingers stroked his hair. "Dust."

"It's everywhere in a mine." Justain caught her hand as the buttery-soft skin swept across his collarbone. He moved it aside. No need to complicate his new role as her protector. "How can you sleep and deprive me of conversation?"

Her pale face held much pain.

"What about a parable, Lady Madeline? Every steward of the Good Book can't miss an opportunity for witness." Justain put more space between them.

She nodded but closed her eyes again. He must've given her too much of the tincture mix.

"A parable for the prof…profl—" He punched at his ribs, to steady himself. This was no time for anxiety to take the reins. "A parable for a profligate. Seems a small sum for saving your life, twice."

Her jaw tensed. "A parable?" A shallow cough rattled within her throat. "Must be desperate for entertainment."

"Very desperate." He picked up Mason's silver flask and dusted it on his breeches. He was thankful it wasn't detected. "Let me get you some water." He crept to the entrance and captured rainwater.

He returned to the girl's side, putting the silver to her mouth. "Make the tale something to keep my interest."

She sipped the water. "The courtesan and the prophet."

He spilt it across her cheek. "Sorry." Justain raised the container. "That's a parable?"

"I wouldn't invent that." An element of humour laced her choppy voice.

Amazing. The lass was special. He propped against the cavern wall, sitting close to her. "I'm ready to be entertained."

"Prophet, Hosea and wife, Gomer." She took great care forming her words. "Gomer went from high Ton, a distinguished family, to being sold as common demimonde."

"Vanilla milk," he interjected. "Mother had the cook put vanilla in my buttermilk to make it more palatable. It just made it vanilla buttermilk."

She turned her head toward the cavern's ceiling.

"You must do a better job with the descriptions." He reached for Madeline's hand and leaned back, half-closing his eyes. "Feed me an image, something to stoke my imagination, not vanilla milk."

"I'm not Scheherazade, though it's warm enough for an Arabian night." Her fingers relaxed in his palm, seeming to welcome his touch. "Gomer means complete. She must've been a flawless beauty. Her colouring was red, with hair like the heat of flames."

❧

The girl coughed again. Her throat must be parched from all her tales. Justain's timepiece lay in his satchel somewhere in his crashed carriage. He rubbed his sore shoulder. An hour must've passed. The vengeance of the laudanum tincture should've lessened. "No, more lass. I can't stomach five loaves and two fishes." No amount of imagery could make a mess of five thousand starving people sound lurid, especially when the pangs of hunger tapped on his gut. "The pain, Lady Madeline. Can you manage?"

"Tolerable." She gritted her teeth and vaulted her noble chin. "Go stretch your legs."

"You're not a very good liar."

"My lord, please. A moment of privacy."

"Yes, my lady. I'll take the first watch. You're a fighter like me." He patted her hand, then slipped to the mine's opening. Justain soaked his forearms in a puddle and removed all evidence of Madeline's injury. Hours ago, he'd awaited an informant. Now he was in a mineshaft, playing nursemaid.

While he'd love to blame his doe-eyed patient for his dilemma, he couldn't. She'd attracted his attention as much as she had the thieves. "Tilford's highwaymen, striking miners?" Did they kill his Mason? The pain in his gut. His friend couldn't have survived. "A deceased passenger, a duke's daughter, and the Severn Gorge. Blast it." He pivoted, hoping he hadn't disturbed Madeline.

Her bare toes seemed unmoved. The bend in the mineshaft hid the rest of her. Perhaps she'd give him license for frustration. Madeline seemed to possess great understanding.

The rain began again. He dropped low to gain a better view of his new battlefield. The endless sheets obscured everything but a wavering glow in the distance. The bandits were still out there, wielding lanterns like a ravenous mob. Why won't they give up?

Bandit or not, with the fickle weather, he couldn't carry his charge out of the mine. Justain slapped his face with water. His stiff posture reflected in the puddle. He could've been in Burgos, Spain reporting on his foe's movements. He missed those days. Lord Wellesley barking out commands. Serving him were Justain's finest days. He drew no shame then, just praise. And Mason, who acted at times more like a father, that man was proud of him.

Justain rubbed his shoulder and wished to feel the braids of his epaulets. Right and wrong, who lived and who died, were easy to determine in a military uniform.

No more romancing the past. He stood and dusted the knees of his buckskins. With their dedication to finding hides for ransom, the bandits should be in the army.

He sighed. At least, he'd been of service to the Duke of Hampshire. There was no more doubting who she was. Fear of death transformed the biggest liars into paragons of honesty. Even the fiend, Barrow had confessed to his crimes when death held him in its sight. Barrow!

Justain's heart beat a thousand times. What if this bloodshed wasn't thievery but revenge? His anger burned. He clenched his fist as he recalled Tom Barrow shaking this hand, agreeing to farm Delveaux land in Dorset. The meeting gave no indications of the man's dark heart. Justain had no idea of the abuses, the man's determination to tarnish the Delveaux family.

He wiped his forehead. Justain should've shot the man between the eyes, but he'd hesitated when the fiend shielded himself with a child. Now the blackguard was free, and Richard was dead.

Barrow wanted Justain's blood, too. What if his henchmen had lured Justain to Tilford with false clues and planned to murder him there?

Justain stuck his hands in the downpour. He cupped rainwater and dumped it over his head. His arrogance brought injury to his family. Now the girl's wounds, the deaths of Mason and Mrs. Wilkins, all weighed on his shoulders, all his fault. He shook his head. Once he delivered Madeline to her aunt, he'd repay these Tilford thieves and find Barrow.

A noise arose over his shoulder. His patient trembled. The temperature seemed to drop with each new gust.

"Mrs. Wilkins!" Madeline tried to lift off the ground. Her arms whipped through the air.

"Please stop." Justain ran back, dropped to his knees, and captured her fingers. Those lovely jade eyes opened, and she held his gaze with dilated pupils. Her lip quivered as if she swallowed her tears.

"The rain won't last forever. Then I'll take you to safety." He placed her cold hand onto the ground. Lace took forever to dry, even from a simple afternoon shower. This poor maid hadn't taken a chance stroll with a suitor, but took a bullet and fell off a cliff.

Justain needed to set a fire, but if the smoke drafted towards the entrance, they'd be discovered.

Her body shook with tremors. She could be losing her battle to shock.

He scrounged up a pile of driftwood and timbers scattered about the cave and stacked the sticks to form a loose tent as he did with his regiment. He lit a blaze and hoped locating it close to the wall would let it draft deeper into the cavern.

"No, we'll be found." The girl shivered.

He shook his head. "I won't let you succumb."

Her cheeks coloured as she stared at him. Madeline pushed his jacket from her head. "Take this and warm yourself. I shan't be any more trouble."

"We'll survive this." He retrieved his coat and pulled it onto his arms.

Justain carried her close to the fire. He sank in the corner. "We'll share." The fire and his body heat should keep Madeline alive.

The kitten seemed shocked but hadn't the strength to protest. Exhausted, Justain closed his eyes. He needed to rest before the next disaster struck.

❧

Madeline tugged her arms about her. She was both cold and hot. Her leg felt like a huge stone. For one solitary second, she snuggled against the secure chest and welcomed the strong arms surrounding her. Then awareness filtered into her skull, and she tried to slip away.

"Settle down, jittery miss." The earl straightened his neck against the cave wall.

"I can't stay like this." Her palms slipped from the lining of his jacket to the hard sinews of his ribcage. She snapped her wrists away.

"You can't help flirting with me." He sealed his lids as if succumbing to the weight of the day. He looked tired with shadows on his countenance. "You're safe, Madeline."

"Safe?" She pushed at his shoulder.

"Whatever tormented you in the past, I won't hurt you." Though the earl teased her seconds earlier, his voice now possessed a sombre tone. "You could tell me what upset you. Hampshire run out of silk fans?" He smirked at her. The small grin was almost boyish. He leaned his head closer. "Was the duke's daughter kissed without permission?"

Her mind flashed to the horrid maze on the grounds of Avington Manor. Her elbow had wrenched from its socket as she fought Mr. Kent. She nearly suffocated from the odour of the evil man's tobacco snuff.

Madeline shuddered and threw her arm about the earl's neck.

"There, there." Lord Devonshire tightened his hold. "I'll protect you with my life."

"I can't believe Mrs. Wilkins's gone." Madeline choked down a sob.

Lord Devonshire moved a hand and caressed the curve of her back.

Her beloved companion should've stayed safe in Hampshire. If she hadn't flaunted the money as a measure of her independence, Mrs. Wilkins would be alive. Madeline couldn't contain her storm of emotions anymore. Tears soaked her cheeks. Her face drenched as her soul wrung with remorse.

"Silent tears come from practice. I know." The earl stroked her hair and whispered. "All will be well again."

She didn't want to become maudlin on Lord Devonshire, but a deluge stung her eyes. Madeline stiffened and wiped her face. Everyone she ever depended upon went away. She couldn't draw strength from the earl. He'd disappoint her, too. She pressed her fingers together and sought true peace. "Thank You, Abba Father, for Your provisions. Your servant has returned to You. Please grant her a shawl for the clouds. Mrs. Wilkins is given to drafts."

The earl said nothing but repeated his hypnotic massage along her spine. His hands spoke their own language, caressing her, convincing her he understood. Madeline submitted, savouring the light sandalwood fragrance of his jacket. She drifted to sleep, listening to the drumming of the rain and the crackle of the flames.

Dawn spilled into the cavern's entrance. The dying fire still bore some light. Justain shook his head to clear it of fog. Between his awful memories of reliving Richard's death and the creaking sounds of the mine, he stayed on full alert.

His eyes warmed to the rays of sunlight. It should be time to arise and get the girl to safety.

Muffled sounds of boots drifted into the shaft. "O'er here!" Shouts arose, ringing down the walls.

Justain kicked dirt onto the embers. He needed surprise to overwhelm the brigands.

"Smell. Smoke." The surly grunt accompanied the sound of a pistol's hammer cocking.

Boots advanced, scraping the mine floor, coming closer. The noise stopped in front of him.

Justain breathed gunpowder. A weapon pointed at his skull.

4

Justain had faced death before, but he always did it on his terms. Five distinct sets of footsteps crowded the mineshaft. Outnumbered, no weapon, and an injured woman splayed in his arms; what good would come from jumping the lead assailant if the others gunned him down? Dead, he couldn't protect Madeline. Maybe he could buy their freedom. He raised his head to face the fiends.

The gun lowered. "My lord, are you injured?"

"Winton?" It was Jonathan Winton, his loyal steward. Winton and four other men now stared his charge.

"I thought you said the earl was alone, Mr. Winton." A short, wiry man put down his rifle.

"At least this one has a pulse." A tall, crude man slapped his buddy's back and pointed at Madeline's bare toes.

Justain tilted his head toward the entrance as he caught Jonathan's gaze. "Winton, I need you to—"

"Yes, sir." His steward turned to the other men. "Go retrieve some blankets."

The laughing baboons left the cavern.

Justain placed the girl on the ground. He grabbed Winton's extended arm and pulled to his feet. "How'd you find me?"

"Your shirt, your cravat?" Jonathan shook his

head.

"All sacrificed for the girl's injuries." Justain righted his jacket and began fastening buttons. There was no way to look respectable.

"Yes, my lord. When you failed to arrive in Manchester, I started tracing your steps. I figured you stopped somewhere between Manchester and Tilford. We found the loose horse team west of the Severn Gorge."

One snickering fellow returned with blankets. Winton took the folds of grey and blocked the man from advancing. "Finish up outside. Lord Devonshire and his party will be leaving shortly."

"As you wish, sirs." He garnered a last leer before retreating.

Jonathan handed Justain the wool. "Was it another clue?"

"Yes, but it came to naught." Justain stooped to drape the blanket about Madeline. She moaned. He started to pick her up but gripped the rocks for balance. His muscles felt as if he'd been beat senseless by Gentleman Jackson on Bond Street.

"Sir, take a moment. You're not steady." His steward's freckled face held a frown. "I found Mason. He lay thirty minutes from Tilford. He'd taken a bullet to the chest."

"Blast it!" Justain wanted to punch something.

Jonathan dropped his head in respect.

What could Justain say to measure the life of his faithful advocate, his guardian counsellor? He sighed. "He took great care of my horses."

Jonathan nodded, perhaps acknowledging the unspoken.

"My favourite horse, Athena was meant as a joke,

a filly, instead of a stallion, but Mason took her and made her the finest horseflesh in Devon. He wouldn't let me be shamed."

"Sir, I should've been with you."

"What and get you killed, too? Your mother would have my head." Justain patted his steward's shoulder. "Let's get Lady Madeline to safety."

Jonathan's brow wrinkled. "Was a rendezvous part of the plan or last minute adjustment?"

Justain picked her up into his arms. "This is the daughter of the Duke of Hampshire. She was there, in distress, and I was assisting her to an aunt in Cheshire when the attack occurred."

Jonathan pinched his mouth. "Duke of Hampshire?" He straightened as if he wanted to salute. "How bad is she hurt?"

"Miss St. James took a bullet to the leg during the attack. I've patched her up, but with nothing more than horse tincture and a thin knife. I did my best."

Jonathan moved in front of him. "Sir, did you meet with the informant?"

"No. The only thing I saw close to a red neck cloth was her chaperone's scarf."

"Red, sir?"

"Yes, that was to be the signal."

"We found a man strung up in the woods behind Tilford. A red cloth was stuffed in his mouth. You could've been ambushed at Tilford. You've escaped death twice. Barrow will have you dead, and he'd throw you down the Severn Gorge to do it." Jonathan checked his bullets for his rifle.

"Bandits attacked us. Not Barrow." Justain stepped around his steward. He wasn't ready to admit responsibility.

Madeline moaned again.

He touched her forehead. It burned with fever. "Jonathan, did you bring a doctor?"

"No, the doctor had an emergency back at Much Wenlock. He awaits us there."

"Dr. White, Mama's old doctor, mentioned something about breaking a temperature with warmth." He hefted Madeline higher in his arms. The girl went from the weight of a foal to sacks laden with wheat. His muscles were sore. He stopped at the mouth of the cave to adjust his eyes to the bright light of the sun.

Jonathan sprinted ahead and intercepted the workers. "Men, hurry. Finished filling the wagon?" His voice sounded filled with frustrations. The hires must be shirking their duties.

"The earl must be sayin' goodbye to his piece, special. You'd think he had his fill." A round of hoots followed the ugly comment.

Justain waited, wanting to hear Jonathan's defence. Surely, his man would proclaim his honour.

"The young woman is refined gentry and shouldn't be spoken of in that manner." His steward's tone lacked firmness, hardly a ringing endorsement.

"Refined." The sentiment bubbled with whispers.

Didn't Jonathan know his words would ignite gossip? His steward cleared his throat. "Let's be ready to leave. The lady needs medical attention."

"It'd be for her own good if she died, then the scandal wouldn't do her in." One of the rescuers sneered, and all tongues silenced.

Incensed, Justain trudged forward and placed Madeline into a carriage. He scowled at the men.

Jonathan extended a hand, but Justain avoided

him climbing inside. The man had done enough today. "What of her companion?"

"The body was collected and placed in the wagon. Nothing else was salvageable: ruined in mud or broken by the impact of the crash. Only your satchel and this straw bonnet were preserved." Jonathan stuffed the hat back into Justain's treasured bag.

Justain nodded his approval. His gut ached as if it filled with rocks. Another scandal.

Winton's carriage stopped at the Gaskell Arms in Much Wenlock, the closest town to the Gorge. Justain didn't hesitate. He bolted from the shifty vehicle with the silent woman tucked in his arms and marched straight into the lodgings. Modest and clean, the whitewashed inn welcomed him.

Madeline's eyes opened. She stared at Justain as if she didn't know him. She screamed as if he skinned her like a rabbit for its pelt.

"Get Dr. Gemmel." A thin wiry man with a pencil moustache leapt in front of Justain. "Give her to me. I'm Smythe, the local constable."

"Smythe," a portly fellow said as he came from an open stateroom, "have the woman brought upstairs for me to examine her. Mrs. Blakeney prepared a room."

Justain stepped around the constable and headed up the carpeted steps.

A large woman stood at the top of the stairs. "The room is the first on the right. Poor creature. Is this handsome gentleman who saved her?"

"Perhaps." Smythe was on Justain's heels.

If eye rolling were a crime, Justain would be

imprisoned. "Doctor, you must attend to her now." Justain called to the rotund man. Then he gazed into the older woman's round face. "This door?"

Mrs. Blakeney nodded.

Justain marched to a dainty, pine-framed bed. He laid Madeline on the mattress.

"Let Gemmel and I have 'er now, sir." Mrs. Blakeney positioned herself between him and the unconscious lass. The friendly woman fingered his bare chest underneath his jacket. "I should see about your injuries."

"Later. Everyone but Mrs. Blakeney out of this room," Dr. Gemmel said. "I need to examine the lady." He opened his black bag and unpacked his tube stethoscope.

Justain hesitated. "No leeches, Doctor." The image of those heinous jars on his mother's bed table flashed in his mind. "She's bled enough."

"Lord Devonshire, Constable, please leave. I'll take care of her now." The doctor continued unpacking his equipment.

Smythe pulled Justain from the room. "There's nothing more you can do."

Mrs. Blakeney's black eyes winked at Justain as she closed the door.

Smythe dragged a chair from down the hall. "When she revives, I'm sure this will all be resolved. Let's hope Dr. Gemmel can get her patched up. Where are her parents?"

"I'll send word." Justain resigned himself to the chair. He let his thoughts blaze as he studied the grain of the door. "This is an old inn."

"'Bout two hundred years." Smythe straightened his olive waistcoat and started toward the stairs. "It's usually quiet, not like raucous Tilford."

"What are you insinuating, Constable?"

"Nothing, sir, but if Gemmel's not able to help the young lady—"

"Miss St. James will recover and tell you the truth of the mineshaft." The words flowed with such power that Smythe's face lost its condescension.

Thirty minutes later the hinges on the door creaked, as the rigid wood swung open. A grim-faced Gemmel stepped across the threshold. Justain squared his shoulders and braced for news of the girl's death.

5

Madeline died.

The evidence weighed on the grim doctor's face. He didn't need to say the words. Another innocent death stained Justain's fingers. He pulled at his collar. The coarse Nankeen fabric of the shirt itched and bound to his skin. During the wait his steward loaned him the trifle, perhaps as punishment.

"Lord Devonshire." Dr. Gemmel's hands smelled of sweet liniment, prep for the grave.

Justain smoothed every muscle in his face and peered upward.

"You saved the young woman's life by removing the bullet and controlling the bleeding." The man patted his large stomach. "But, between the blood loss and infection—"

"She passed. Say it. I've killed her."

His jowls hardened, his mouth thinning to a spot. "No, the young woman still clings to life."

She lives? Death lost a victory? Justain almost smiled.

"But she hasn't regained full consciousness," the doctor continued. "Do you have any idea what she means by coins? She mumbled that once or twice. "

"Must be referring to the thief she chased." Justain cleared his throat. "Is there anything I can do?"

"The next few hours are critical." The doctor

mopped his wide brow. "Can you get her parents here?"

"No, they're in Hampshire. It's at least three days hard ride or a week or two by carriage."

"Then let's wait. It'll be easier if they know the status of their daughter's health before they make the journey." Dr. Gemmel clasped his hands together with a resounding slap. "I must find a way to break the fever."

❧

Another day passed. Madeline hadn't awakened yet, but at least she wasn't delirious anymore. One more outburst and Justain was sure they'd hang him. He slouched in his chair outside Madeline's room

Jonathan Winton rushed the steps.

A smile almost bloomed within Justain, thankful it wasn't the flirtatious innkeeper, Mrs. Blakeney. She was far too eager to attend to his wounded shoulder.

"Sir, I'm ready to return to Devon. I'll bring back help," his steward said.

Justain leaned back further. The chair tilted against the wall. "Gather a few of my tenants, people I trust to tear up the countryside looking for my attackers. And send these dispatches to Dr. White and Reverend Delveaux."

The steward took the offered parchments and placed them in his satchel. "Shall I wait for you to finish the other notes?"

Justain's chair slammed forward. "What others, Mr. Winton?"

Jonathan's copper gaze turned to the threadbare carpet. "The ones to her father or the aunt in

Cheshire?" His steward never missed a detail or the absence of one.

"I'll inform them when the girl is better. We must keep this quiet until Miss St. James is able to vouch for my character. I won't have the Ton accusing me of despicable behaviour or an angry duke dictating my next course of action."

Jonathan shoulders sagged, but he nodded his agreement. "My lord, is there anything else you require?"

"No." Justain waved him away.

The young man started down the stairs.

"Wait, Winton." Justain stood and moved a step in his direction. "You are my conscience sometimes. I'll send an express post to her father tomorrow. Stay safe as you travel. There's been enough bloodshed."

"All shall be done as you've requested. For what it's worth, I know you to be a man of honour." Jonathan smiled. "I'll have a trunk of clothes sent here as well. Starched cravats are one of your few pleasures." He left Justain outside Madeline's door.

Mrs. Blakeney approached from the other end of the hall. He adjusted his collar again. "Ma'am, is Miss St. James any better?"

"Her fever's broken, but the poor girl hasn't revived." The large woman stretched over his head to dust a carving before moving further down the hall. "You should know. The bruising on her arm has begun to recede."

Justain rubbed his neck. "The lass suffered horribly down that hill."

"You wouldn't have done anything untoward." Mrs. Blakeney sighed at him. "You've kind eyes, and you take good care watching over her, paying all her expenses."

"Ma'am, I don't suppose that I could see her?"

The woman shook her head. "Only a relative should see the lady in this state." She trudged down the stairs.

"This is ridiculous." Mrs. Blakeney tied his innocence to his looks and fortune. Justain needed to go find a horse and flee, but a soldier doesn't desert, no matter how tempting. The mere possibility of Barrow's involvement kept his guard high. He wouldn't let Madeline fall into the clutches of the devil that killed Richard.

Constable Smythe arrived at the top of the landing. His clunky heels dug into the carpet, thumping the wood beneath. "Lord Devonshire, the service for Mr. Mason and Mrs. Wilkins is ready to begin."

The reminder of death extinguished Justain's ire. "Thank you." He'd represent both houses, the Delveauxes and the St. Jameses for the proceedings. "Lead the way, Smythe."

Hearing the local vicar mumble mystical words of forgiveness and a happy hereafter would be the perfect way to end this miserable day.

❧

The poor light of the room obscured the surroundings. Madeline rubbed sleep from her eyes and tried to focus. A brown dresser towered near the foot of her bed. It wasn't her white dresser. No spot of gilded trim. Where was she?

A pretty girl with dark braids napped in the corner. Who was she, one of Aunt's maids?

Madeline glanced to the window. A straight-shift curtain hung in its proper mount, but it wasn't Aunt Tiffany's residence. No, Aunt dressed a window with great embellishments.

Madeline turned her head to the ceiling. The smell of ointment wafted to her nose. A horrid mustard wrap banded her chest. She resettled her blanket to contain the smells and moved her stiff neck to the right.

A man leaned over her and grabbed her wrist.

Madeline slapped at him. "Help!"

6

Madeline cried out again as the beast's fingers clamped her mouth. She forwent useless screams and bit him. She'd have to protect herself with no more Mrs. Wilkins to shield her. The bald man lunged and grabbed her shoulder. She willed her fatigued limbs to obey but fought with paper strength.

With ease, the tart-smelling monster overpowered her and pinned Madeline's arms against the mattress. Her caged spirit awakened. Madeline wriggled, freed a hand, and slapped the beast's face. "He'll have your head. The duke—"

The door to the room crashed open. It was Lord Devonshire. Had he come to save her again?

"Miss St. James! Doctor, what the devil is going on in here?" The earl flung the animal away from the bed. "Doctor Gemmel, start explaining!"

"She's gone mad. I tried to calm her down before she injured herself." He tried to break away, but Lord Devonshire's powerful arms held him at a distance.

"Keep him away from me." Madeline turned her head as tears flooded her cheeks. She tried to move but found her leg too stiff to bend. "Keep them all away from me."

The earl blocked the man from returning, and marched to the footboard. He opened his large palms in a defenceless manner. "Miss St. James, I won't let anyone hurt you. You do recognize me?"

Madeline nodded.

"Gemmel, go get Dr. White. The maid will wait with me. Then, don't show here again."

The man slunk away.

The earl approached the empty chair. He stayed behind it. "Do you remember what happened? You remember that I didn't hurt you."

"No need to try to sway the patient." A stout woman with coal-black eyes entered the room. "You'd never harm a lady." She winked at the earl.

"Please tell her the truth." Lord Devonshire's chin held more than a day's worth of shadow. His proud shoulders hunched as if in agony.

Madeline coughed. Her mouth felt dry.

An older gentleman entered the room. "Gemmel said she's crazed."

She clutched tight to her blankets. Too many people stood in this tiny room.

"Should we strap her to the bed, 'til she's calm?" the woman asked. Evil must reside behind those dark eyes, just like Step-mother's.

"No, Mrs. Blakeney. Miss St. James awoke and is frightened by the pile of strangers." Lord Devonshire waited until he caught Madeline's gaze. He held it as if in a trance and sauntered around the bedpost, almost on his tiptoes. He began to recite, "The *Lord is my Shepherd, I shall not want. He…He.* I need help finishing it. Is there a Good Book-bookworm who can help me?"

"Is he makin' fun of such things?" Mrs. Blakeney asked before the old man motioned her to be silent.

"Look at me, Miss St. James. Your opportunity for ministry is over here." The earl was close now. His voice, serene and true, lay etched in her mind, guiding her through another treacherous strait. "Help me show them you have your wits about you, lass. He leadeth."

"He leadeth me beside the still waters. He restoreth my soul," she rejoined and released the covers. Madeline pointed to a goblet by the bed. "Please."

Lord Devonshire smiled even as he exhaled.

He'd fretted about her?

The earl poured water from a clay pitcher into a crystal cut glass. The oddity of clay and glass; Providence gave her, a young woman disappointed by men, a man as a friend.

"Maid, help Miss St. James sit," Lord Devonshire adjusted his thin cravat.

The silent girl stacked pillows and helped her to rise. The servant resettled the blankets and returned to her corner. If she'd worn a lighter shade of green, she'd disappear into the walls.

The earl placed the goblet to Madeline's lips. She drank as if it been years since her last. Maybe, it had been.

He refilled the cup and put it in her hands. His fingers slipped across hers, angling and supporting. His sandalwood fragrance fell upon her nose.

"Is the glass steady? Good." He released it. "Miss St. James, let me introduce you to Dr. Samuel White. He's my family's doctor from Devonshire. He'll make you better." The earl motioned for the man to come forward.

"I'd like to help you, my dear." The doctor's snowy hair reminded her of her father's.

Thank goodness, her father wasn't standing before her. She didn't have to return yet.

"May I help you?" the older man asked.

Madeline nodded. "Can you send word to my

aunt, Lady Cecil Glaston of Cheshire?"

"Of course. I'll need everyone out of the room but the maid. You too, Mrs. Blakeney."

Madeline tightened her grip on the stem of the glass.

"Don't be anxious, my dear," the doctor said. "Lord Devonshire will remain outside your door. That's where he's been for the past fortnight, awaiting your improvement."

"Fourteen days," Madeline repeated. Now, she felt nauseous.

"Come, Mrs. Blakeney. We'll be outside." Lord Devonshire led the woman away.

"Let's change the dressing on your leg, young lady. I'll need you to tell me if there's any sensation in it. Do you feel my thumb on your toe?"

Madeline's breathing faltered. "No, sir. I do not."

7

The light glowed brighter and brighter.

A heart shaped face hovered above Madeline. "Sweetheart." A long wispy lock of dark hair fell forward as the ghost whispered.

Mama had come to her.

"There's much I have to tell you, Mama." Her own voice sounded like a homeless kitten, yelping in the woods.

The ruby lips hovered above. "Wake up, dear. I've come to see about you."

She touched Mama's face and wiped a droplet from her silver eyes. Silver eyes?

Madeline propped up on the pillow. She mopped her own tears, for Mama's emerald eyes could only be seen in paintings or waning dreams. "Aunt?"

"Yes, child. They tell me you haven't had your wits for days." The dear woman draped in dark blue lounged at her bedside. Aunt Tiffany, Lady Cecil Glaston, had come.

She cradled Madeline's hand as she had many years ago, lightly tracing lines upon each finger. Then it gave comfort, helping Madeline grieve Mama's passing.

"You look like my dear sister. Angelique was beautiful and taken too soon." Aunt wiped her face. "I've missed you. Child, you must stop crying. It'll make me start up again."

Madeline rubbed away her own tears. "I'll try."

"I owe you an apology. After the duke stained Angelique's memory by marrying a harpy, I swore never to darken Avington Manor's marble floors again." She drew her lips into a sulk. "I didn't think the goat would refuse to send you to me."

"The one time Father agrees, this happens." Madeline pointed to her heavily bandaged leg. "And my poor Mrs. Wilkins."

Someone pounded on the door. Aunt snapped up and smoothed her imperial gown, looking every bit the grand patroness of Cheshire. "Come in," she said. Her voice sounded so poised.

Lord Devonshire appeared at the threshold. Serenity and strength rested upon his proud shoulders as he bowed to Aunt Tiffany. The earl slipped to her bedside and kissed Madeline's palm. "You smell less like liniment today, more like strawberries. Must be getting better."

She treasured his humour and tried to counter. "The apothecary makes the best perfumes. This one is ode to fever."

Lord Devonshire chuckled, and he turned a serious expression to Aunt Tiffany. "Lady Glaston, will you be dining with me this evening? We've much to discuss. I must satisfy the duke's demands of me."

Aunt squinted her eyes as she examined him. "You sound as if you are readying to leave, young man."

"On the contrary, Lady Glaston. I'm readying for the hunt. My men will be here tomorrow. I'll find the men responsible for injuring our fair Mad…Miss St. James."

Aunt smiled, but those lips didn't express approval. "Yes, we will dine at sunset, my lord."

The earl bowed, winked at Madeline, and left the room.

"So many rumours have come to me." She marched to the door and locked it. Then she approached and pushed up Madeline's sleeves. "Madeline, tell me the whole of it. Start with how you got strange marks, and is the earl who you are so cozy with responsible? Have you disgraced yourself?"

"Mr. Kent attacked me in the garden at Avington, the night before I was to leave to see you. He hurt me, not Lord Devonshire."

"That lousy nephew of your step-mother dare put his hands upon you? I'll have my man servant shoot him. No, your father has already done the deed."

Madeline shook her head. "He hasn't. Father doesn't know. He'd never let me leave Avington if he knew. You can't tell Father. Please say nothing of it."

The woman's face flushed purple. "I'll shoot him."

Madeline clutched at her heart. She felt faint. "Please keep my confidence, Aunt."

"I make no promises." Aunt softened her tone. "Now tell me about the earl. What happened?"

"Lord Devonshire saved my life," she said in proud tones. "He's very gentlemanly."

Aunt drew a hand to her mouth to cover a smile.

"I wish he hadn't. I'd be with Mama and Mrs. Wilkins, not waiting to see what else will be taken from me."

Aunt Tiffany took her in her arms. She blew kisses on her forehead and mussed her curls. "I'll make everything right for you."

Justain waited in the private stateroom of the Gaskell Inn. A mousy woman, Lady Glaston's companion told him Glaston would be late, but an hour late? Justain's stomach bore a low rumble. What could be amiss now?

Another one of the informant's notes arrived today. He ripped the red-inked parchment to shreds. Nothing could make him desert his obligations here.

Maybe Lady Glaston would take her niece to Cheshire tomorrow. Then he'd be free again to hunt Barrow. Perhaps he shouldn't have burnt the paper.

What was keeping Glaston? Justain retied his cravat, but the cotton trifle thinned in his fingers and made him look like a country baron, not a peer to Lady Glaston. From what he remembered, the old man always decried the showy opulence of the House of Glaston, but his father secretly coveted it.

That desire for fine things would be the only thing Justain willingly admitted he shared with the man. He fluffed the cravat as much as possible.

The door pushed open.

He stood as Lady Glaston entered.

The woman wore a cranberry walking gown. Military gold fobs ran from the collar to the floor. Justain didn't know whether to sit or salute.

"Sorry to keep you waiting. I had a late tea with Dr. White. The dear man likes to run on. Please be seated, Lord Devonshire."

She kept standing as he flopped into his chair. "I should thank you for saving my niece's life." Her pert nose pushed higher in the air. "But I won't. It's customary for a gentleman to protect someone in his care. Instead, I want to know why you hid her away in this quaint little inn." Her tone sharpened. "Didn't have enough romancing her in the Severn Gorge?"

Justain stared at the cold grey eyes. What did Madeline tell her?

She gripped the back of a chair. The jewels upon her fingers knocked against the pine. "What other conclusion can I deduce? You knew who she was and where she was going. Yet, I'm notified by an innkeeper more than two weeks after the date of my niece being shot."

He balled his fists under the table. "I sent word to her father. I've been following his instructions," Justain retorted.

Her gaze narrowed upon him. "Did you tell him you compromised Madeline?"

He didn't believe his ears.

Her lips flattened to a thin line. "No, you didn't. The duke would be here to gut you with his hunting knife, if he knew what you did."

"I've done everything in my power to protect Miss St. James." Justain pounded the table. "No one knew if she'd ever awaken. I had my family doctor expedited from Devon to see to her care."

She lifted her chin. "You'd rather her die among strangers."

Justain shook his head. He wanted to turn over the table. "What you are accusing me of, Madam, is unconscionable."

She tightened her grip on the wood. The faceted sapphires of her rings glimmered. "You compromised my niece with your private stay in the Gorge, and you sought to hide her from her family. I demand satisfaction. What will you do to make this right?"

"She'd been badly hurt. Marauders were hunting us. If we'd left the mineshaft to maintain your sensibilities, we'd be dead. Is that what you want?"

The matron's beautiful face twisted, filled with venom. "Death seems to follow you, Devonshire."

"What?" Justain leaned back in his chair.

"Between the bloodbath in Dorset and the Peninsula war, maybe you like death." Her sarcastic tone was deafening. "Is it safe for people to be around you? Have you learned to be more careful since you got your brother killed?"

She might as well have kicked him in his stomach. He hadn't expected the dressing down. "I cannot change the past."

"Right now Cheshire is all ablaze about a nobleman being caught red-handed in the Gorge. I even laughed at the story at a garden party last week."

Malicious gossip. Someone's life reduced to dust.

"It will only be a matter of time," she continued, "when the story possesses names. It won't be funny hearing my niece disgraced, run down by the Ton."

Justain squared his shoulders. "You have a solution. Say it, Madam."

"Marry my niece!" Lady Glaston commanded.

"That's your game?" He chuckled. "Did Madeline put you up to this?"

"You know marriage is the only solution." She released the chair. "That's why you've been secretive."

"Why sentence Miss St. James to a dangerous existence?" He folded his arms. "As you attest, my life's not stable."

"Well, you'll have to settle down and protect her." Lady Glaston marched to his side of the table. "And that queer inheritance on the males will be satisfied with your sudden marriage."

He looked up at the woman in surprise. Lady Glaston should play cards. She'd be a master.

"Yes, I'm familiar with the business. My Cecil and his brother, the Duke of Lancashire, delighted in the odd ritual."

Justain rubbed his neck. "And if I refuse?"

"I'll make sure that your name is in tatters. No one in polite society will want anything to do with you. Your family will be held as a blight upon the land. I will—"

He waved his hand. "You've made your point."

"That ring you now bear comes with responsibilities. Madeline is beautiful. She's fond of you. She'll be a dutiful wife. She'll help you navigate the straits of your title. When she's better, take her to Gretna Green and elope."

"If I do this I won't slink away to Gretna Green as if I've something to hide. It'll be with her father's approval. I'll write him right away."

"Then you agree?" The heart-shaped face—so like Madeline's—glowed with victory.

"It's up to the Duke of Hampshire." He arose. Anger boiled in his veins. "Enjoy your dinner, Lady Glaston. My appetite's gone."

He left without a bow and shoved the door open. He caught it from slamming behind him, wouldn't give her that victory, too.

8

Justain thrust her door open.

"Lord Devonshire, what has occurred? You look pale." Miss St. James sat up in her bed.

He gritted his teeth. "Maid, please step outside. I'd like to have a moment alone with Miss St. James."

The servant looked at the vixen for permission.

"It's all right. Please, wait outside."

The moppet curtsied and left the room.

"Now, sir, tell me what's amiss." Miss St. James's dark hair had been coiffed into ringlet curls and brushed until it shined. A pale green robe draped her long neck and shapely form.

He approached the bed. "What makes you think something's the matter, Miss—"

"Madeline. You don't have lightness in your step. Why so formal?" Her eyes grew wide. "You have bad news?" Her voice took a breathless tone. "Or have you found Mason and Mrs. Wilkins's killer? Please, tell."

"No." It would calm the angst in his gut if that were true. His gaze descended upon her, slipping across her nightgown.

Fading bruises covered her arm. The spacing, finger-sized splotches looked as if she'd been manhandled. He balled his fist behind his back. Some blackguard had forced himself upon her. The poor lass.

Her lips pressed into a line. "Lord Devonshire?

You don't look well."

Would Lady Glaston force a marriage, if she thought Justain capable of such a despicable act? The aunt couldn't believe it wasn't his doing. Justain rubbed his tight jaw. Perhaps the woman tried to pass off tampered goods. Great, a by-blow. And the bastard child would become his heir.

"I've not seen you sleeveless before." He stepped closer.

"Aunt says that I've nothing to be ashamed of." She bit her lip, seeming to wince at her own words. She cleared her throat. "The air will help the bruises go away."

"I see why someone thought…The marks are mere shadows but odd injuries for the accident." His temper seethed, but from indignation. Romance was one thing, but no one had a right to force himself upon a woman. Soothing his battered ego wouldn't be at Madeline's expense. "You should rest. Good evening, Miss…Madeline."

"Wait." She pulled the sheet up over her arm. "Anyone who's seen your bravery would never accuse you of a cowardly act." There was fight in her voice.

"How do you know what I'm capable of? You hardly know me."

"I know enough." Madeline softened her tone. "You've renewed my hope in men. You're not all intemperate and odious." She motioned him to sit. "Something's upset you."

He dropped on to the edge of the mattress.

"Whew." She put a hand to her forehead to steady herself. "Are you thinking of Mason? Missing his counsel?"

"Forgive me." He searched her perfect jade eyes.

She held his gaze for a second then looked down. Her manner was demure, innocent. Manhandled, yes, but not tainted, not carnally abused.

Justain was a man of the world, and his gut guided him. He sighed with relief. If he must wed her, at least her virtue remained true. "I should be more careful."

"Not going to answer me." Her pert chin lifted. A quiet strength, a subtle dignity set in her countenance. "At least you don't treat me like broken china."

"Well, people don't want to upset you."

"You mean they don't want me to start babbling again."

"I don't make you nervous." He lifted an errant strand of hair from her face and tucked it behind her ear. One stroke, then another, he caressed her lobe. Her breath caught. Her strawberry lips looked soft, almost parting in invitation.

"Why? Should I be?" she whispered.

Justain laughed. "If you had more common sense, you would be. Goodnight, Madeline." He kissed her hand then eased to his feet.

"When I'm better and return with Aunt to Cheshire, will you keep our acquaintance? I'm fond of letters."

"If it's permitted." He smiled at her. She wasn't party to the Lady Glaston's extortion. Another testament to Madeline's good character. "I'm fond of writing."

Her gaze intensified as if she wanted to read his mind. "My lord, do you trust anyone enough to share your burdens?"

"Frankly, no. Good evening." He crossed over her threshold and headed straight for his brandy.

ᘐ

Lord Devonshire seemed strange, stranger than usual. Madeline pulled the soft muslin sheet up to her cheek. It wouldn't be realistic to hear from him once they parted ways.

Perhaps, it was best. Pain brewed behind those sky-blue eyes. Father bore similar shadows upon his face. The duke trusted no one and let no one, not even Step-mother, ease his yoke. It would be the same being the earl's friend, witnessing his troubles and not being allowed to help.

The door to her room burst open. Aunt Tiffany marched inside. Her cheeks were cherry red, almost a match to her long walking gown. "The earl came to see you?"

"Yes."

"Let me explain." She paced from the threshold to the window. The buttons lining her long skirt clanked together like cymbals. She stopped and pivoted. "What did he tell you?"

"He came to see about me, as he always does." Madeline fluffed her pillows. "What was he supposed to say?"

Aunt Tiffany released a blast of air as if she were a fireplace bellow. She walked to the window again and adjusted the curtains. Her colouring returned to normal. "It seems he fancies you."

"He's kind to me, Aunt. That is all."

"I believe he will ask for your hand in marriage." The words floated in the air. It was pure madness. "Will you accept?"

Madeline shuffled her blankets, tugging them

about her stiff leg.

"How will you answer when the earl proposes?" As a veteran of love, Aunt had married and buried two husbands. She hunted for a third. The woman knew a man in love, but she had to be wrong in this case. It couldn't be possible.

Aunt stopped fidgeting with the window dressing. She charged the bed in high strings. "Aren't you in love with Lord Devonshire?" Her silver eyes slimmed to a piercing dot, singular in accusation.

Madeline released the scalloped edges of the woven coverlet. "I'm fond of him, but my heart doesn't burst when I see him."

Aunt picked up the delicate comb from the bed table. She played with Madeline's curls. "Who told you love was like that?"

"You did, with every poem you ever read to me. In the books you sent for my birthday. Let's forget this and venture to Italy. You will love Donatello's bronze of Judith. Can you not relate to a cast of a vibrant widow?" Perspiration drizzled Madeline's forehead, moistened her palms. Didn't Aunt know what it meant to retain her freedom?

"You're babbling, dear. Sometimes love is quiet, a warm feeling of contentment. You light up when Lord Devonshire walks in the room."

Madeline's head tugged to the right as Aunt parted a section of hair. "He amuses me, and sometimes he makes me want to box his ears. That's not love."

"You must accept him when he offers." Her voice sounded deadly serious.

"Aunt, I haven't had a season. I'm not ready to be engaged."

The woman flustered, turning one shade lighter than her dress, then uncovered Madeline's arm. "These bruises won't let you have a season."

She yanked at the sheet to hide the marks.

"Your father will request for you to be sent home to Avington as soon as you're able. The only season you'll have is to the dregs your step-mother will scrape up."

"Go home?" Madeline slumped against the headboard. She couldn't return to Avington.

Aunt grimaced. "You'll have to go back to that gilded prison without any protection."

"Kent will be waiting there. Don't let me go back." Terror pressed against Madeline's lungs.

"And if he petitions the duke for your hand, what do think your father will say? You never told him about how the beast hurt you. Your father thinks Step-mother's nephew is a fine young man with a fortune in mineral mining. The duke with his connections could arrange a barony or something to make the match more acceptable."

Would Father make her marry Mr. Kent? To be made to endure his sweaty hands. *No!* Madeline forced air into her nostrils. Hot tears trickled down her face.

"Marry Lord Devonshire. He'll protect you. I'm convinced of that now. He's trying to rebuild his family's fortune and reputation. A diligent pedigreed wife is what he needs. Dr. White says the earl's estate, Trenchard Park, is in want of a woman's care. It has the peace you seek."

"Lord Devonshire's confused. It's not possible. He hasn't known me long enough."

"Your father lost his soul to Angelique the night he met her at Almack's. And you know that love lasts beyond the grave."

Madeline shook her head. She didn't possess Mama's beauty or grace. "The earl must feel obligated because of my injuries. Dr. White has probably told him that my leg will be slow to heal."

Aunt squinted and hissed like a vent for the fireplace. "White hasn't discussed this with me."

"Or with me. Everyone moves about as if I'm crazed or oblivious, but it's my leg. I won't be a punishment to Lord Devonshire. I won't allow him to marry an invalid. I'll add no more burdens to his proud shoulders."

"It's his choice. And you'll never be a burden. You're too independent." Aunt took a ruby pin from her dark locks. She reached under the covers and jabbed at Madeline's toe.

The first poke felt of pressure. A second to her heel made her whimper.

"See? You'll walk again." Aunt settled the bed sheets. "The daughter of the Duke of Hampshire is to be admired. You've the connections the earl needs to be successful. You mustn't deny him his choice for happiness."

"I don't know. Aunt Tiffany, how would it work?"

"You'll learn to love the handsome devil. It won't be hard. You need to trust the warm feeling of friendship. It will grow. He'll be patient with you and protect and treasure you. The earl's the kind of gentleman I would've tried to find for you. Promise me you'll think about it."

"I'm tired, Aunt. Let me rest."

Aunt kissed her forehead and left the room.

Madeline settled on to her pillows, again. Did Lord Devonshire love her? Would a man who trusted no one, ever lend his heart?

ቖ

The pounding upon the door refused to quit. It felt as if Athena kicked in Justain's skull. He tried to block out the racket with the bedcovers, but the blasted noise continued. An empty brandy bottle clung to his stomach. The golden liquor romanced him last night, and now Justain's head suffered the lover's revenge.

"Devonshire. Are you alone in there?"

The voice sounded familiar. Justain pulled to his feet and slunk to the door. "A moment." He forced his eyes to focus on the lock. He wrenched it open, then tumbled backwards onto the floor.

"Wellington has arrived." A smiling face leaned over him. "You look worse for wear."

"Devlin? Goodness man, did you grow another foot? Weren't you tall enough?"

The indigo eyes of the reverend filled with humour. "You know it's bad form to drink alone." The six-feet-three-inch mountain dropped a sack and kicked the door closed.

"Who'd lift a glass with my worthless hide?" Justain closed his eyes and drew comfort from the cold floorboards.

His unsympathetic cousin tugged him to his feet, separating him from his icy respite. He helped Justain lay back onto the bed. "This is hardly the manner for the famed rake of the Gorge to act."

At this, Justain opened his eyes. "Devlin, would I lose any appeal to Heaven if I cursed at you?" He brought a hand to his aching head. "What brings you here anyway?"

The reverend folded his arms. "I've been in Lancashire ministering. I'd hoped to rendezvous with you, when my bishop forwarded me your letter."

"Let's continue this in a few hours? I'm sure to be better company a year from now."

"I'll retrieve a pot of coffee. It'll help return your sobriety. Then tell me all about your latest scandal."

"Don't you have some widow to save, some sinner to beat into repentance until evening?"

"No, I'm here to deal with this one called Devonshire." He left and pulled the door closed with a thud. Mean man.

❧

The strong aroma of steaming coffee wafted to Justain's nose.

"The earl's not feeling too well this morning, sir? If ya need help to strip 'im and put 'im in a bath, I'd be obliged." The torrid and frightening tones could belong to no one other than the flirtatious Mrs. Blakeney.

She pushed past Devlin to enter the room.

Justain closed his eyes tighter, feigning sleep.

"No, ma'am," Devlin answered. "I'll manage my cousin. Please leave us."

Mrs. Blakeney's scent, a mix of wood polish and dishwater, floated over him. Devlin needed to hurry and get the woman to flee before Justain returned last night's dinner.

"Ya sure? The Delveaux stock is solidly built."

The lady should know she flirted with an apostle. A lecture on Acts could start at any moment.

"I'll send for you, if we need assistance." Devlin's

stern tone attempted to shoo away the innkeeper.

Justain peeked. Devlin's kind but bone rattling condemnation should never be missed, especially if directed at someone other than Justain.

The reverend opened the door. His lips thinned producing his signature "repentance" look. "My dear, we won't need your special attention." Foolishness stood no chance.

"Yes, sir." The sounds of the woman's slippers almost running out of the room brought a smile to Justain's face, but it hurt to contract those muscles.

Liquid poured into a container, burping against the sidewalls. "A nice cup of coffee will bring you to your senses."

"Too late for that," Justain mumbled. He propped up against the bed frame and took the offered mug.

Devlin threw off his stark grey mantle, tossing it across the footboard. The object floated and folded neatly over the wood. The man did everything right and in order.

Justain took a long slurp. The hot liquid hit the bottom of his stomach, stoking rebellion. He might lose his battle yet. He siphoned a deep breath from the stale air to avoid getting sick and showing more weakness to his cousin.

"Are you going to tell me why you're celebrating?" Devlin asked as he steadied the cup.

"I'm to be engaged."

"You proposed to Miss Lavis? She said yes?" The unflappable man seemed aghast. He ran his fingers through his salt and pepper hair. "You'd sacrifice your happiness and propose to the golden-haired creature. Must you try to prove your worth to Devon by winning her admiration?"

"And don't forget the inheritance. Every earl must keep the properties in Dorset and not endanger Trenchard. Can't sacrifice the beauty of our home, but—"

"Any other woman would be happy to be the mistress of Trenchard, but not fair Caroline. She won't make you happy. She won't even try."

"You and Richard know I'm a glutton for punishment."

Devlin sighed. "You still speak of Richard as if he's rounding the corner."

Justain shed an uneasy chuckle. "Perhaps, I see him in my dreams."

Devlin's indigo orbs seemed to lance the veil between them. "You didn't kill Richard. He made his own choices. You need to free yourself of that burden."

Justain sank onto his thick blanket.

"Richard's gone," Devlin continued. "You can't live in his shadows. Don't let guilt destroy you."

"But, Devlin, isn't guilt the workings of life, particularly for you religious folk?"

"God gives freedom, but what Earl of Devon has ever known freedom?" The reverend refilled his own cup. "Between the inheritance and a lust for power and wealth, when have any known freedom?"

"You left out conquest. A man's got to do something with his nights."

"Be serious, Justain. Renounce the inheritance. Your holdings in Spain will eventually restore the loss of Dorset's income. Trenchard's still gutted from the fire. Rebuild her somewhere else."

"Mama's pride, Trenchard Park, will be finished. Only the west wing is left for renewal." Justain sat up to level his gaze to his cousin's. "I won't let Richard die in vain. Won't give his widow one more thing to hold over my head."

Devlin took a sip. "Richard abandoned her the moment the ceremony ended. He married the sickly girl to satisfy the inheritance."

"Shocked the devil when she got all healthy on him."

The reverend shook his head. "Richard ruined her life with empty promises."

"And now she adds to my guilt." Justain sighed.

Devlin put his mug down. "You still love Miss Lavis?"

"You don't understand." He squinted at the reverend's folded arms. He seemed troubled, never more human. "Devlin, my head is fogged, but did you not want me to marry or not marry Caroline?"

9

Justain shook his head. No one possessed a more charitable spirit than Gregory Devlin Delveaux. With a steady temperament, the strength of an ox, and the loyalty of the best foot soldier, he could've been the most productive landowner in the country. Instead, Devlin chose to press about in ministerial robes, testifying of baffling grace. "Caroline Lavis, will never love you," he said. "She love—"

"She loved Richard as did every girl in Devon." Justain put a hand to his head. The cold metal of his ring cooled his hot temple.

Devlin shook his head. "I'm glad you've forgiven her all the times she cut you with her words, made you the butt of every joke."

"The old man would leap from his grave at the chance for you to be Devonshire. You never stuttered, never tripped over your own feet."

Devlin cleared his throat. "The earldom demands a sacrifice, a marriage. And Caroline craves to wed a title. It's a perfect match." He reached for the cream pitcher. His knuckles seemed to tighten about the delicate bone handle.

Justain leaned forward. "What is it, man? Are you unglued over Caroline?"

"Marriage." Devlin moved to the fireplace and ran a poker along the inside of the box. He stabbed a piece of burnt black cloth from the logs and waved the thing at Justain.

"When my steward retrieved more suitable clothing from Devon, I felt compelled to put that plain jacket out of its misery. But please continue with your sermon."

"Marriage should be a pairing of equally yoked individuals." Devlin dumped the fabric back into the fireplace and vented the logs. Sparks floated about the dark stone. "You've adored Caroline since the day you took the blame for her breaking that Wedgewood vase in your father's library."

"The old man beat me unmercifully for that." Justain patted his ribcage. "All wounds heal. Will you continue to condemn Caroline for childhood indiscretions? Weren't we all chums before I left for the fight in Spain? Then when Mother fell poorly, and they summoned me from the campaign in Burgos, the two of you couldn't be in the same room without quarrelling."

"She's as beautiful as a summer's storm, but she'll never honour you or any man who loves her." Devlin took another jab then returned to his chair. "Richard was ill, too. I think Uncle wanted you close if things took a worse turn."

"No, the old man hoped to kill me with his own hands and deprive Napoleon. Then you'd be the earl."

"Justain, why is it that you forgive Caroline and no one else, not even yourself?" Devlin leaned back and put his feet up on the mattress.

"I should start somewhere. That's what your religion teaches, right, Reverend?" Justain relished parroting his cousin's sentiments.

"Forgiveness is available for those who repent, for

those who acknowledge a need to be forgiven. That's hardly Caroline." The man shook his head and fiddled his rumpled cravat, typical of Devlin's carefree fashion.

If Justain's head didn't throb, he'd lean over and fix it. "I'm always in your debt." He rubbed at his side again and scratched the scars beneath. "You even stopped the old man once."

"I loved your father. He took me in when my beloved parents died. Made me feel like his son."

"No, he didn't hate you." Justain lowered his voice. "I'm sorry, Devlin. It hurt you badly when Aunt Jess and Uncle Carleton died of consumption. You are my brother. Now you're my only living brother."

"I'll never understand Uncle's demons or why he took them out on you."

"Clumsiness or the inces-incessant stutter." Justain slapped his fist upon the mattress.

"Stop it, Devonshire. Deep down, your father would be proud. You'll restore the family fortunes."

"I gave the old man hundreds of reasons to be disappointed. And Richard, he'd've…" No need to antagonize his headache by reflecting on the past. "I'm glad you've come."

"I am my brother's keeper." Devlin's countenance lit with a smile. He relaxed his shoulders. "You offered for Miss Lavis. We're stuck with her becoming your mate. You've my congratulations. When's the blessed date?"

Justain took a nip at his cooling mug. "I'm stuck, but not with Caroline."

A twinkle glowed in Devlin's eyes. "You've taken pity upon one of the lovesick girls of Devon, one of the poor rabbits you ruthlessly hunted in courtship. Which one did you make an offer?"

The reverend unfastened his cuffs, pocketing the old man's treasured gold fobs. "Which one, Justain? I've consoled more than one disappointed father whose daughter had been charmed into believing herself in love with you. I still see the last man, all red-faced sitting in my rectory expecting me to coerce you into proposing." Devlin shook his head. "Then, who, Justain?"

"The famed rake of the Gorge must marry his mistress."

Devlin laughed.

"Reverend, it's funny that I'm being accused of compromising a duke's daughter?"

"You're serious." Devlin began to chuckle harder. "The girl was near death. No one seriously thinks you abused her."

"Lady Glaston demands I marry Miss St. James. If Richard were alive, he'd join you in a hearty laugh."

"That was Richard. A quick laugh. A quick death. He never wanted to linger in pain like your mother. He got his wish." The indigo eyes looked as if they withheld a secret. Devlin lowered his gaze and adjusted his bootlaces. "So you're going to propose?"

"As soon as I hear from her father."

Devlin shook his head then stretched and kicked one of the empty bottles under the bed. "I thought you swore to me not to indulge in excess."

"I never agreed to abstain, Reverend. I let you run on. I don't break promises."

Devlin sipped some more coffee. "Get out of this barrel of despair. And let's celebrate the impending good news."

Justain placed his head on the bedrail. "That would be a barrel of brandy. Despair doesn't quench the thirst."

ঌ৵

The ceiling Madeline had memorized seemed far away. At least, the floorboards provided a firm platform for her back. She stretched out, waiting for her strength to return.

Feet tapped and pattered from the room. The maid must be running to retrieve Aunt and the doctor. Madeline didn't know who'd fuss harder at her failed attempt to walk. Aunt or Dr. White.

Madeline grunted and tried to sit but was too weak.

Dr. White entered the room. His unpolished boot tips and rumpled pant hems hovered in front of her. "What are you doing, Miss St. James?"

"I wanted to test my leg, sir."

"Didn't I tell you to rest? But you decided to fall and injure yourself." He bent down and offered his hand.

She gripped it. "I've lain about too much. I need to know that my leg can hold my weight."

"My word. Maddie, are you all right?" Aunt Tiffany whirled in as the doctor helped Madeline to sit. Draped in deep blue with gold ribbons on her sleeves, Aunt embodied strength. To have her flare and confidence would be the greatest gift.

"Lady Glaston, your niece won't listen. She'd prefer to strain her recovery."

Madeline shook her head. "I have to know if my leg will heal. If I'm on a good path, maybe I can regain some say in my care or even where I am to recuperate."

"It will heal with time. I tell you this every morning. Lady Glaston, is she always this stubborn?"

"Yes," Aunt Tiffany and Madeline recited in unity.

The doctor scooped up her shoulders and pulled Madeline to her feet. "You're not ready to be trying to walk." He helped her sit on the mattress.

Aunt Tiffany folded her arms. "You need to listen to him, Madeline."

"Aunt, you wouldn't be trapped in bed for weeks."

"Depends upon the reason." She winked at the man.

Dr. White blushed.

Aunt stepped forward and pushed at Madeline's shoulders to make her lie down. "You need to adhere to the doctor's orders."

"I was able to put weight on it." She beamed at the woman. "I took two steps—"

"Before the pain became unbearable. I'll have a crutch made for you, but recovery will be slow. Lady Glaston, talk some sense into this girl, before she's fitted with a permanent limp." The doctor pivoted and left the room.

"I admire your spirit, Madeline, but you have to listen."

"I'm tired of listening to others. I keep expecting Father to walk through that door and haul me back to Hampshire. Or that Kent found me. Or…" She bit her lip.

"Or that the earl will walk through that door and propose." Aunt Tiffany patted her hand. "You're frightened that he'll make an offer." She turned Madeline's cheek. "You've decided how to answer him?"

10

Aunt leaned over the bed. Her balmy palm cradled Madeline's chin.

How could she make this independent woman understand? "You're strong and powerful. You embody freedom. I wish to be like you."

"I became who I am by marrying and marrying well. The late Mr. Canton made me a wealthy widow, a ripe prize for Lord Glaston. That dear boy needed my money to set him right."

Sour disappointment filled Madeline's stomach. "You didn't love them? They were both practical marriages?" How wretched. Aunt Tiffany, a calculating matchmaker?

"I loved them both dearly. Cecil Glaston took a piece of my heart with him to the grave, but I know that if my circumstances hadn't been advantageous, it would've been difficult for us to be together. Madeline, leaving won't change anything. You'll still be fearful of what comes through the door."

"Marrying the earl will solve my problems? I don't love him. When he grows to hate me because I cannot return his affections, what will save me?"

"You're not your step-mother. You'll never be like her. Honour his feelings. Treasure his friendship. Be his encourager when all else fails. Sacrifice your pride to heal his wounds." She smoothed Madeline's curls, drawing a ringlet around her fingers.

"I've no peace on this, Aunt."

The woman marched over to one of her hatboxes and pulled out a book. The cover was tattered, the pages yellowed. She searched the text for a verse. "Read this for peace."

Madeline took the Bible from her aunt's hands. *"Nevertheless let everyone in particular love his wife even as himself; and the wife see that she reverences her husband."* She read the marked passage aloud. "I don't understand."

"If the earl wins your love, it is the greatest gift to any husband. But all he's due is reverence. Just as a woman's heart craves love, a man's ego must feed upon respect."

Madeline studied the text, looking for a clause of escape.

"Where's your faith, Maddie? The Lord will never give you more than you can bear. He's orchestrated events to provide you with an honourable man, someone who'll protect and cherish you."

"I have faith. I just don't claim to know His will for me."

Aunt fluffed her pillow and kissed her on the forehead. "Do you reverence Lord Devonshire and respect the man that he is?"

Madeline thought about her brave friend. "I do."

Aunt smiled. "Keep repeating that sentiment, all the way to the minister."

The cool of the early dawn nipped at Justain's fingers. He didn't care, for his blood ran hot. He thundered through Tilford's stable door. The place was a maze of stenches—the perfume of horses ready for the day, the gnats of the muck, and the anxiety of a dying highwayman.

Donald Masterson, one of his trusted groomsmen, applied pressure to the bandit's chest wound. "We kept him alive. We know, my lord, that you wanted to see Mason's killer yourself."

"Ya. I shot the driver. And this is what I get for it," the bandit said through blue lips.

Winton drew close to Justain. "Sir, this man was shot in the leg the night of the attack."

"Mason or I got him."

Winton seemed to wait, as if anticipating Justain to gloat. It wasn't the time to celebrate. "Sir, the fiends camped near Tilford."

"How come we didn't find him sooner?" Justain stowed his flintlock beneath his cloak.

Constable Smythe stomped forward. "These ore men are a tight lipped group. No telling what story they told the locals. With all the strikes, it's too easy to gain sympathy."

Justain didn't want to talk to the useless Smythe. He walked around the fellow, pounding the short distance to the dying man. "Who finished you off?"

"Ye think there's hon'r among thieves?" A cough and gurgle left blue lips. "They thought I'd slow 'em down." The man was almost the same shade of ash as the grey residue of Tilford.

"They dumped him in this stable. The bandits probably have a twenty-minute head start." Masterson's normally cheery face was solemn, the red of his cheeks drained away in the sombre morn. This wasn't the knights and warrior games they played as children.

"Twenty minutes you say." Smythe pulled a deputy aside and barked out orders.

Justain crouched low. "Is the devil of Dorset behind this? Did Barrow shoot you?"

"It was…" The assailant sputtered a violent cough. "It was the devil all right."

"Confirm to me Barrow's hand in this." Justain slapped the criminal's jaw trying to shake the truth free.

"Followed evil for revenge." He closed his eyes.

Justain shook the man. "Where is Barrow?"

The bandit didn't respond. His cold hand held no pulse.

Justain released him and pulled Masterson away.

"Who's Barrow?" The constable stepped from the shadows coming close to Justain. "My lord?" Smythe's usually smug voice was soft and filled with questions.

Justain arose and faced Smythe. "The attack wasn't random. Tilford was an act of revenge on my person for a slavery ring I ended in Dorset. Tom Barrow, their leader has vowed to torment me. His men are known for carrying flintlocks with pearl black handles." He pivoted to his steward and groom. "Winton, Masterson; let the constable clean this up. Go back to the Gaskell Inn and get a few hours of sleep."

Justain left the stables. The full weight of his responsibilities stacked on his shoulders.

Madeline took a second bite of the buttered cross bun. The doctor had allowed her to have solid food. She didn't realise how strong a craving one could have for bread. The crust melted on her tongue.

Mrs. Blakeney pranced about winking at Aunt Tiffany. Dressed in tartan skirts, the large woman fluttered about as if there were a man present.

Aunt brushed Madeline's hair, pulling and pinning until it had enough shine to replace candlelight. Aunt, too, acted strange and stuffed Madeline into a peach robe. The itchy collar made from two layers of lace kept flipping up on her chin.

A hard knock rippled down the door.

"Come in," Mrs. Blakeney responded in a soft, almost girlish voice.

Madeline became queasy. A lump formed in her throat.

Lord Devonshire entered and charged to the foot of the bed. His cinnamon coat draped tan breeches. His elegant face lacked the teasing tones she longed to see.

He bowed, then addressed Aunt Tiffany. "Dr. White assures me that Miss St. James is well enough to answer a question." He fondled his starched cravat as he addressed the women.

"My niece is doing well today." Her tone was civil. Aunt moved from the headboard. Her heavy rose walking dress swished as if a breeze floated through the window. "We'll be outside for a moment."

Mrs. Blakeney groused as Aunt towed her from the room. They left the door wide open.

Lord Devonshire seemed distracted by the show, but like a marionette on strings bent on one knee. "Miss St. James, Providence has brought you into my life." He opened a velvet box exposing a perfect ruby ring. "Will you do me the privilege, the honour, of marrying me?"

No harps. No feeling of sentiment. If he loved her

as Aunt said, Madeline saw no evidence of it. "I need no gifts."

"It's a family tradition to bestow this jewel to the future countess of Devon."

Kent had connived and tried to trick her, but this man bore a ring to seek her hand.

She shook her head. "I'm grateful, but—"

Sounds erupted from the hall, a mixture of moans and the garbled cry of "headstrong girl!"

"Miss St. James, may I?" The earl took her hand and slipped the jewel on her finger. The ruby sat within a simplistic weave of gold braid. "Its weight is a measure of the protection I offer."

It was a perfect fit, as if it were made for Madeline.

He knitted his brows together. "You don't like it? I know some like a more ornate setting, but it's been passed down amongst the generations of Delveauxes."

"No, it's beautiful. If I could have any ring, I'd choose this one, but it's our circumstance that's gifting this to me." Madeline tried to give it back, but he closed her hand about it.

Lord Devonshire's forehead became riddled with lines. "Our situation is unique, but our responsibilities must be served." He scanned her face as if words were etched on her cheek. "You think I'm not fit to have your hand?"

"Don't put words in my mouth, my lord."

The man swallowed; a raspy noise fled his throat. "You won't have me?

Madeline licked her lips. "I don't think we are rightly matched." The ruby felt heavier, perhaps laden with a sense of obligation.

"Maybe, I didn't hear you." Lord Devonshire tugged on his cinnamon-coloured lapel. "You're refusing my offer?"

She should be indebted to his heart. He saved her life twice. Shouldn't that be enough to say yes to him? Madeline closed her hand tight about the ring. "Is this God's will for our lives?"

The earl feathered his fingers over his full lips. "This is—"

Aunt coughed long and hard. It sounded as if she'd fallen flat in the hall.

"Sir, you should go see if things are well with my aunt." Madeline waved him to the door.

He took her hand and splayed her palm. The ruby sparkled. "I'm not concerned with the antics outside this whitewashed bedchamber, and I lack the wisdom to discern Providence's will. But, Miss St. James, I know that I must do this, must make you my countess."

All of her hopes of finding her own peace, of claiming a cup of independence ended on the rocks of the Severn Gorge.

The bed swayed, and she refocused upon the earl's countenance.

Lord Devonshire sat upon the edge, and imprisoned her hand in a crush of warmth. "I'm rushing you?" He swirled circles upon her lacy sleeve with his thumbs. It reminded her of his manner in the carriage. He kissed her wrist, lingering as if smelling a rose. "No more liniment."

She shook her head and tried to remember how to breathe. Must be the doctor's potions making her dizzy.

"And my family ring looks well upon you." His handsome face bore a fresh shave. Sandalwood anointed his skin. His eyes seemed determined, fixed upon securing an answer. "I'm not an errand boy to be waved off. If you're in love with another, tell me."

"There's no one else."

"Not even a Mr. Kent."

"No!" Madeline shrieked. She stifled her arms from trembling. "I'm not in love with anyone."

His eyes regained their glow, twinkling with some newly found humour. "Then why cannot I have all your love? *I cannot breathe one other sigh, to move…Nor can I entreat one other tear to fall…Sweetest love, I—"*

She placed her fingers on the earl's mouth to silence his mangling of Donne's poetry. "You choose the responsibility of a lame wife?"

He looked to the open window. Perhaps he'd escape through the billowy curtains.

Madeline wanted to, but the stiffness in her leg prevented it.

"But you're not. It takes time to heal, particularly from field surgery." Lord Devonshire adjusted his crisp white cravat as if it choked.

"I've no complaints of your actions. You saved my life."

He reached over and seized the heinous wooden crutch leaning against the pine headboard. "One of Dr. White's contraptions. Have you tested this?"

"I've stood with the evil thing."

"You're being silly." The earl put the implement down. "Time will make you strong again. These inconveniences will go away."

Madeline applied a shaky palm to his chin. "You've done so much to protect me. Too much. Lady Glaston won't tell you because she wants me settled, but I might never walk under my own power. I may be a slave to a staff forever. You don't want that burden."

Lord Devonshire gazed at Madeline as if he memorized her face for a canvas. He pulled near. His warm breath cascaded her neck as his lean nose nuzzled her jaw. "Strawberries. Always smell of the luscious fruit, and my hunger for you will not die." He retook her hand and spread it against his silky waistcoat close to his heart. "I'm well aware of your condition, and I know my responsibilities." He traced the outline of her legs, tucking the linen sheets about her. "I will enjoy carrying you to the ends of the Earth, and if you have to use a staff, there'll be no lovelier, no more graceful countess for Devonshire."

Such tender words. A tear escaped her eye.

The earl leaned in and kissed the droplet away. He lingered softly brushing his lips against the hollow of her cheek. "Marry me, Madeline. I shan't have no as an answer. My lands in Devon and the green pastures of my holdings in Ireland or Spain—"

"Your wealth is immaterial."

"But they will give you the peace you seek. You'll have the time to recover, free from fear. I'll hide you from the nightmares. The ones that plagued you when you were ill."

A chill raced her spine. He could protect her. The man had proven that. "Are you sure I'll make you happy?"

He gathered her in his arms. "Let me tend to you."

The noble beating of his heart sounded in her ear. Could anyone ever defeat these strong arms? Not possible. All she had to do was say yes.

His mouth descended upon her forehead. "Sweet girl, take the humble protection of my name."

Was he her knight, the man meant to treasure her? Madeline sniffed his scent. "Sandalwood."

"I always make sure I'm clean shaven before I seduce a lady in her bedchamber."

"What?" Her pulse raced.

Lord Devonshire chuckled. His deep voice rippled through her. "Trust that I will always provide for you."

Maybe they'd build a lasting future. The smell of his skin banished the last vestiges of fear. "I accept Providence's hand. You do me an honour."

The earl lifted her chin. He leaned down. His mouth floated above hers. "Tell me you'll marry me."

"Sir, I'll marry you."

Shouts erupted from the hall.

Madeline grimaced. "I'm sorry."

Aunt Tiffany and Mrs. Blakeney bounced back into the room.

Lord Devonshire released her. He bowed and left the room in haste.

Mrs. Blakeney shut the door.

Aunt Tiffany ambled to her side and inspected the ruby.

"Your mind should be eased." Madeline fell back upon her pillows. "I'd hoped travelling to Cheshire would be an adventure of a lifetime. Now everything is spinning out of control."

"No, everything is being made right, child."

❧

Madeline awoke in a bright white room. Her head lay on a taffeta pillow trimmed in cream tassels. Gauzy sheers draped her bedposts. Aunt's strained face pressed against the material.

"Wake up, Madeline," she said. "We must get you ready."

Were they in Leicestershire? "Aunt, we've been freed from the Gaskell Inn?"

"Yes, and it's an improvement." Aunt Tiffany moved to her bedside. "Dr. White said you'd sleep through the ride. He was right."

The doors to the bedroom opened. "Lady Glaston, I'm here to prepare my mistress for the service." The young lady bore calm grey eyes, deep like the colour of her skirts.

"Who are you?" Madeline stretched and filled her lungs with the cool air.

The maid traipsed to the footboard. "The name is Anne. Anne Regent. I shall be attending you."

"Your future husband procured her." Aunt rolled her silver eyes. "He refused to allow me to get one for you." Aunt Tiffany swished to the closet. "He didn't want a spy in his household." She unwrapped a parcel.

"If you don't mind me saying, the master's very guarded when it comes to Trenchard. I've been on many interviews to be hired on." The maid was young and clearly didn't know it wasn't her place to respond. She continued, "If I wasn't cousin to one of his mates, I'd never have been considered."

Aunt glowered at the outspoken miss. "Anne, what is this famed Trenchard like?"

"Well, it had been dormant for several years. The fire took a lot out of it. The master, even before he became the earl, began restoring it. Now he's got workman round the clock painting and fixing. It'll be ready in a few months."

"Wonderful." Aunt grimaced. Her lips pressed into a frown. "I'm sending you to a burnt out barn."

"Aunt, please." Madeline shook her head. The woman could be harsh.

"No, it's idyllic with meadows and orchards. The great house used to hold grand parties," Anne said, and she started to twirl and hum a lively tune. "My lord is determined that it return to its former splendour. The future countess will love it."

"Miss Regent, the way you express your opinion, I take it you are new to attending a lady." Aunt didn't wait for the maid to answer and ordered, "Help Madeline sit up. It's time to get her ready."

The girl approached and sank in an off-balanced curtsy.

Madeline looked upon Miss Regent with sympathy. No force could stop Aunt in the middle of one her causes.

Miss Regent took Madeline's outstretched arm and towed her to the edge of the bed.

"Good, now go tell my manservant Gunter to have a milk bath readied for my niece."

"Yes, madam." With one more tilted curtsy, the maid fled the room.

"Milk will even out your complexion." Aunt took a cream-coloured bundle out of the closet and laid it out over the coverlet next to Madeline. The fabric of the dress felt smooth and cold. This was happening. She'd be married in this gown, frosted in satin lace like the bliss icing of a wedding dessert.

"Here." Aunt Tiffany presented Madeline a velvet-covered box.

"You shouldn't have. You've done too much."

Aunt frowned again. "I didn't. It's a present from the earl. He wishes for his intended to wear it tonight. Open it." The woman who loved surprises didn't seem to bubble. She seemed set on a tepid boil.

The case bore signs of age, a matted nap and a

faint odour of soot. No doubt, Lord Devonshire kept it near a hearth. The hinge whined as Madeline opened the lid. A strand of twelve pearls lay inside. "They're beautiful."

Aunt shook her head. "They were crafted well, but six are dipped."

Madeline stared at the woman. "What? You peeked?"

"Of course I did." Aunt held up the necklace. It sparkled in the candlelight. "I'm not sure if your mother or step-mother took the time to teach you how to value jewels." She rolled three alabaster coloured beads between her fingers. "These aren't real. The earl's father was a spendthrift. Probably sold off the real ones."

Madeline took the pearls and returned the delicate strand back into the box. "Why does it matter if they are real or not?"

"You need to know your worth. The earl should value you enough to bring you the rarest jewels and not painted glass."

"If it's from his heart I'll treasure it."

Aunt enjoyed the finer things, but wasn't materialistic.

Madeline's stomach felt queasy. "Are you hiding something? What are you trying to tell me?"

Aunt pulled a chair close. Her long emerald skirt swallowed the arms and rakes of the seat. "Love must be tended to, nurtured. Not pacified with cheap baubles. No matter how this union was created, you'll be the Countess of Devonshire."

She closed her eyes for a moment. Lord Devonshire and Madeline had been through so much. They both lost people dear to them. They'd bonded, and she possessed his love. Their future would be bright. She patted her aunt's hand. "Why so dire?"

"The remorse." Aunt Tiffany shook her head. A renegade grey lock swept out of formation to shade her forehead. "Many will want to treat you as if this marriage held baggage. As if somehow you don't deserve to be happy."

Madeline lowered her gaze. "The rumours will die down. Let's not talk about that and focus upon this evening." She smoothed her thumbs over the material again tracing the sheer neckline of the gown. "It's lovely, but isn't it immodest."

"You'll be covered from head to toe, but the illusion of a choice flower or ripe pear needs to be maintained." She stood and began pinning up Madeline's hair. "Got to give the old boy encouragement to get through the ceremony."

She sought Aunt's silver eyes. "Why does he need that? He's in love with me, right?"

Aunt cheeks brightened, and she kissed Madeline's forehead. "Why else would the earl propose? I'll go see what's keeping your milk bath."

11

The soft aroma of white camellias emanated from garlands draping the mantel. Brilliant candlelight reflected off the gold bee pattern on the walls, giving the room a romantic feel. Madeline reclined on a white bench in the middle of the parlour. Aunt had her wretched crutch painted ivory to blend into the setting. It lay against the back of the chair announcing "crippled wife."

She closed her eyes for a moment. The earl's love would cherish her. He didn't care about her infirmities.

Madeline twisted the earl's pearl necklace around her pinkie. Having it hung on her neck made her more comfortable with the dress. The gown covered everything like Aunt said, but it didn't possess Madeline's style. The cream gown fit tight, and it strangled her about the bosom. Shimmering pearl buttons adorned the sleeves. Aunt had them added as a finishing touch to match the earl's gift.

She loved her shimmering gloves. They were long and fairy-like with shiny stitches. She waved her palm in the air. The Delveaux family ring with its large ruby contrasted well with the off-white fabric. Lord Devonshire would touch her hand during the ceremony. A nervous tingle raced her spine. She slipped her thumbs along the pearl necklace.

The painted door swung open, and a man in his

early twenties with reddish-brown hair entered the room. "My lord wanted you to have these," he presented yellow and white acacias.

Madeline hesitated to touch the flowers. This marriage was really happening.

"They're for the ceremony, ma'am," he said.

She took the small bouquet. "Thank you."

"The name is Winton, ma'am. Jonathan Winton. I'm the earl's steward."

"Pleased…I'm pleased to meet you." She wished her voice hadn't squeaked.

Mr. Winton bowed. "Be at ease, Miss St. James. My lord is a good man."

She looked at the door. "Where is the earl?"

"He's with Reverend Delveaux."

Madeline traced the delicate petals. "The earl's brother?"

"No, ma'am." Mr. Winton wiped his forehead. He looked disturbed. "The earl's brother is deceased. Reverend Delveaux is his cousin. They are waiting for the vicar of Leicestershire. Excuse me." Mr. Winton bowed and left the room.

Waiting with a reverend for the vicar…Justain didn't seem to have a reverence for God, but he did endure all those biblical tales she told in the mineshaft. Madeline sniffed her flowers, savouring this moment of peace.

The world slowed to a crawl when the crimson door opened again. The vicar in his green and white robe swept to the fireplace in front of Madeline. Behind him were Mr. Winton, Lord Devonshire, and a man with striking blue eyes. It had to be his cousin.

The earl sat next to Madeline on the bench while the reverend strolled to his left. Lord Devonshire placed an open palm in her direction and motioned with his gaze.

She complied and rested her hand in his.

"Dearly belov'd," the vicar began beneath his white whiskers. "We are gather'd together here in the sight of God…"

Madeline quieted her knees beneath her skirts. Perhaps, she should've taken some of Dr. White's medicine to calm her anxiety.

She glanced at Justain. The earl's cravat was immaculate as was his azure jacket and ivory waistcoat. He was very handsome.

"Young lady! Young lady do you consent?" the vicar asked.

Aunt looked as if she were about to faint.

"Wilt thou have this man to thy wedd'd husband, to live together after God's ordinance in the holy estate of matr'mony?" His thick Welsh accent grated her eardrum.

The earl gave her hand a little squeeze.

"Yes," Madeline replied and wove her fingers between his.

The vicar continued, "Wilt thou obey him, and serve him, love, honour, and keep him in sickness and in health; and, forsaking all others, keep thee only unto him, so long as ye both shall live?

"I will."

The vicar took Madeline's other hand and placed it in Lord Devonshire's.

She took a deep breath as the earl began to repeat the minister's mumbled words. "I, Justain Meriton Devonshire, take thee, Madeline Angelique St. James, to my wedded wife, to have and to hold from this day forward…" His voice was strong and clear as if he addressed parliament. "And thereto I plight thee my troth."

She held the earl's gaze and hoped he could read her mind. He must see her solemn promise to trust him and to learn to love him.

Lord Devonshire looked away as the vicar gave him more instructions. The earl repeated, "I thee wed, with my body I thee worship, and with all my worldly goods I thee endow." The way he pronounced each syllable with a crisp pitch convinced her. He loved her. God must make her worthy of his heart.

Before the minister could finish, the earl's cousin interrupted. "There's a special exchange that occurs for all the earls of Devon whose nuptials fall before their twenty-eighth birthday." Reverend Delveaux took the onyx ring from Lord Devonshire's right hand and replaced it with a gold signet bearing combined stones of onyx and ruby within the crest. "The family lands are again unified within the house of Delveaux. May the blessings of God be upon the earl and his bride." Lord Devonshire seemed more animated, rolling the ring about his finger.

A veil tore from Madeline's eyes. It wasn't reverence, but land. A wave of discontentment ripped through her. Yet, he may still love her.

The vicar took charge again. "And they shall remain in perfect love and peace togeth'r, and live accordin' to thy laws, through Jesus Christ our Lord. Amen."

The old man separated their hands, mumbled something then took Madeline's hand and gave it to the earl. "Those whom God hath joined together let no man put asund'r." He lifted their linked fingers, "I pronounce that they be man and wife together, in the

Name of the Fath'r, and of the Son, and of the Holy Ghost. Amen!"

The deed was done. The dark cadence of the minister announced a litany of blessing about the procreation of children, about living together in honesty and fidelity under God.

The earl gripped her shoulders. His eyes widened as he drew her close. Defiance swam in those sky-blue pools. His intent was clear, to mark her to all the witnesses as his property like his lands. Madeline shut her eyelids and waited for Lord Devonshire's kiss.

12

The earl's full lips brushed hers. The warm sensation lasted for a second, then disappeared. He released her and bounced to his feet then moved near the vicar.

Madeline drew a hand to her cold face. The kiss wasn't harsh but the lightning and harps she'd imagined from a first kiss didn't materialize. He didn't love her. The realization felt like falling and hitting the ground. It hurt to breathe.

Aunt Tiffany brought her a piece of fruitcake. "Here, my dear," Aunt said as she lifted a forked morsel into the air. Smothered in white bliss icing, the confection seemed rich.

She couldn't eat. Tears threatened. Thinking she had the earl's love made Madeline feel safe. She only possessed his name.

Aunt brushed Madeline's cheek as if the woman knew Madeline struggled with disappointment. "I must leave you now, but cleave to our talks. You are the Countess of Devonshire."

"Lady Glaston, let me help you to your carriage. I had it readied for you, bags and all." Justain's voice sounded cold as if he held bitterness against Aunt Tiffany.

Madeline put the cake down and grasped the woman's wrist. "When will I see you again?"

Aunt turned to Lord Devonshire then back to her. "When you invite me to Devon, I'll come. Write me. Let me know how you're getting on." Aunt Tiffany kissed her forehead. "Goodbye, Lady Devonshire." She sailed to Justain and gave him a hug.

He looked startled, tweaking his thick cravat.

"Take good care of my niece. Come along, Gunter," she called to her loyal servant. Like the whirlwind which brought the woman back into her life, Aunt Tiffany left the room, fastened to the earl's arm.

The door banged shut.

Madeline gazed at Reverend Delveaux. He bit his lip, no doubt holding in his amusement. It wasn't funny to be misled.

"Welcome, sister." His voice boomed. The tall form came forward.

She willed her palm to rise. *Hand, don't shake. Show no twinges of fear.*

He kissed her wrist, then stepped away. "My formal name is Gregory, but everyone calls me Devlin."

"Thank you, Reverend Delveaux. You're Lord—you're Justain's cousin?" She referred to her husband by his given name to at least sound like an equal.

The man smiled and ran his fingers through his salted sable hair. "Yes, though I'd like to think we're as close as brothers." He possessed broad shoulders like Justain and seemed to exude an air of strength.

In spite of things, she was the new Lady Devonshire. Justain was her husband. Madeline cleared her throat. "Please sit. Let's become acquainted."

"I'll stand," the reverend said. The man's long

frame easily made him six three or four, even taller than her husband. "You've vowed to love and honour Justain. Are you going to live up to that commitment?" he asked in cool tones as if he inquired about the weather.

Her cheeks now boiled. Was it possible to combust like a log in the fireplace? "I'm not sure I understand, sir."

"My cousin is a good man."

"So I've been told." Madeline picked a petal from her bouquet and cast it in the air.

With an oval face, very like the earl's, the reverend continued, "He deserves the support and care of a good woman."

Support and care? Had she not been mourning the loss of the same sentiment? Something inside her awoke. Meekness brought nothing but agony and a marriage formed in deceit. "What concern is this of yours, Reverend Delveaux?"

"Call me Devlin." He pulled out a pocket watch and adjusted the fob. "I feel a sense of obligation to Justain and now to you. I know the choices you both made aren't easy. If I can intercede, I will."

Madeline sat erect and smoothed the lace of her skirt. Did everyone but her know this was a marriage of convenience?

Devlin stooped. His dark trousers now blended into the carpet. He levelled his gaze to hers. "When God brings two individuals together, sometimes there are trials, but He'd never put you on the same path if you weren't meant to walk together."

He seemed sincere, but what did she know of any man's character? "Does Justain intend to walk with me since he married me to secure property?"

"Actually, an inheritance, but I'm sure that you, sister, had your reasons for marrying."

"Devlin, did you force him to announce that our wedding satisfied some sort of condition? And why declare it during the ceremony? Couldn't you leave me any illusions about this marriage?"

He shook his head. "My cousin cannot be forced to do anything. He can be reasoned with, if the arguments are sound and rational."

She blinked. "I do not have irrational arguments."

"I'm not trying to insult you. I'm trying to give you insight to the man you've married. Justain is as stubborn as a rock in the ox's path, but there's no one more loyal to his friends."

"I'll keep that in mind." She yanked the ring off and set it aside on the bench. She tugged off her perfect gloves. Madeline wanted to cast everything away.

Devlin lowered his gaze to the thick navy carpet. "You're a woman of faith? Justain says that you are."

"I am." Though His will for her life grew darker every minute. How would Justain treat her since he had no love to offer? She rubbed her forehead.

He picked up the ring and suspended it in the air. "Please?"

Madeline let him put it back onto her finger.

"Cling to your faith, young woman. Justain doesn't see how blessed he is. Perhaps, you'll open his eyes."

❧

Justain tried to hand Lady Glaston into her carriage, but she stopped him. "Take care of my niece. She's a remarkable young lady."

"It's a little late to be concerned about her welfare. You foisted her onto me." He did little to conceal his contempt. "Show no remorse, Lady Glaston."

She touched his arm. "Be mad at me. Hate me. Not Madeline."

He gazed into the pale eyes. "I know that she's as much caught in this web as I am."

The woman stopped him from straightening his cravat. "You're forever adjusting this thing." Lady Glaston fluffed it. "In life, we do things that we may not always like, but it's necessary for our stations."

He drew her hands away. "If that helps you sleep."

The grand dame stepped into her cream-coloured coach. She leaned out the door. "When you stop nursing your pride, you'll see that this is best. Make Madeline happy, and I'll be in your debt. I'm good to those I owe."

"God speed to Cheshire, Lady Glaston." Justain shut the door and waited for the caravan to leave. A lively public house lay next door. He'd held out there with his steward until the ceremony. Winton made sure he didn't get intoxicated. No need to make his wedding any more of a spectacle.

Justain trudged back into the inn. He planted his foot on the first tread of the stairs leading to his wedding party. A swell of laughter floated through the open window. "Brandy, we'll visit again tonight." The light from the wall lanterns reflected upon his band. The ruby and onyx stones glowed. Richard last wore this band, and the old man before him. In spite of everything, Justain fulfilled the inheritance. This time he wasn't the scourge of the family.

Only one more thing to do. Take control of his life.

Justain balled his fist. He was the head of the Delveaux family. The newest Delveaux needed to submit to his authority. He started up the stairs taking the treads by twos.

Justain pushed open the door to the parlour. His cousin offered scriptures to his wife and the maid. Neither girl looked receptive. Madeline rubbed her neck as if distressed.

"My dear," Justain said, "have you given Devlin a tongue lashing so soon? Wait for a proper visit to chastise him."

"Thank you for your well-wishes, Devlin." Madeline's jade eyes seemed dourer. She was already steeped in regrets. Perfect.

"Well, I'll take my leave." Devlin gathered his thick cape and eased it about his shoulders. "I'm heading back up north for a missionary tour; I'll be visiting Lancashire and then Scotland."

"Travel safely, old boy." Justain adjusted his cravat.

"It seems a dangerous route to go north," Madeline said. She held out her hand to Devlin. She didn't shrink when he kissed it.

Justain tapped the minister's arm. "My cousin knows how to avoid danger. He doesn't gamble like me."

Devlin shook his head. "Madeline, you're a welcome addition to the family. I look forward to getting to know you." He tweaked Justain's elbow and left the room.

"Anne, I'll send for you when I need you. I wish to speak to my husband in private." Madeline's usually soft tone sounded sharp. Maybe the kitten possessed claws?

Miss Regent curtsied and traipsed away.

A good fit of anger could do his dirty work. "Did I take too long downstairs?" Justain asked.

"No." She pulled a loose tendril of ebony behind her ear. "I was just wondering about the inheritance. Why you hadn't mentioned it before?"

"Madeline, you'll find you've married into a number of peculiar traditions."

She looped her fingers about great-great grandmother's necklace. "I understand tradition, but you could've told me."

He chuckled. "We had to wed, and I thought the inheritance would complicate the issue."

Madeline lowered her gaze. "Had to wed, not wanted to?"

He pivoted from her and snuffed a candle on the mantel. "Honestly, it's none of your concern." He turned back to watch her seethe. "My affairs are mine, alone."

She didn't explode, just shook her head. She smoothed her countenance. "I'm ready to start this marriage. How do we begin?"

"Begin what? I think it's a little late for formal introductions." Justain folded his arms. He wanted a tantrum. A spoiled maid lived in every girl of privilege, no matter how demure she seemed.

Madeline took a deep breath and released it. "Lord Devonshire, Justain, I want to know how to be a proper wife to you."

He wiped his mouth. "We're strangers."

"We're not strangers." She kept her voice low though her grip on her bouquet tightened.

"Yes, a few stories have made us old friends." He took a noisy intake of air. "You're very young."

Madeline wrapped her gloves about the stems of her flowers. "But the passion of your proposal has confused me. The inheritance must be extensive for such a performance."

"You're a lovely lady, Madeline." He moved behind her. "It's easy to drink of beauty and want to recite you poetry." He drew his thumb down her satin sleeve. A scared little girl would emerge with prompting.

She didn't jump or swat his hand away. Instead, Madeline sat erect and pulled his palm to her cheek. "I will be a good wife to you."

Her skin felt so soft. He moved away. "You're not serious." Justain flopped onto the bench next to her. "Dr. White's medicines sometimes have adverse effects upon people. Let me send for Miss Regent."

"I know my own mind." Her face flushed, glowing with determination. The poor misguided creature. "How do I prove my intentions?"

What was Madeline looking to gain?

He shook his head. "You need to rest. Miss Regent will ready you for bed. We'll get an early start tomorrow."

"I'm not tired." She cleared her throat. "As a daughter of the peerage, I understand the dignity of your title. I will be an excellent partner to your station." The matronly arch of her tones. The lift of her chin. She was serious.

"This is ridiculous. Madam wife, you shall retire to bed and forget this crazy notion."

"You won't order me like a disobedient youth. I'm your wife."

"But I can, Madeline. That's why you wear my ring."

"We"—she softened her voice—"we need to be on common ground to make this marriage work."

He chuckled. "Who said we'd make this marriage work?"

13

Madeline sat still. Her ears burned. "I'm not sure I understand."

Justain smirked. "We've come to this marriage to survive scandal. We've done that. Now let's rebuild our separate lives, taking stock of our sacrifice. Over time, we'll become acquainted." He sounded as if he'd read lines from a play, but with no feeling or vigour. Their marriage, their vows to God meant nothing to him.

Her heart pounded so hard the ribbons of her dress could burst open. "Separate lives?"

He combed his sable hair with his fingers. "Well, divorce, even it were possible, is no option for a Delveaux."

"It's not one for a St. James either." Her spirit rose. "Why would you marry me if we're to live separate lives?"

Justain straightened his ivory waistcoat. "I guess I loved your eyes and ebony hair."

The comment might as well have been a slap. Her face stung from the strain of keeping her countenance smooth. Aunt told her to remain unruffled, no matter what.

He stretched his long legs as if bored. "I'm a realist. We're not in love. Well, I'm not in love." His tone dripped in smug clips as if he'd won her heart.

"This is a marriage in name only. I've no wifely expectations of you, and rest assured, I won't assert my husbandly rights…tonight."

Perhaps it was her nerves, but she started to laugh.

Justain craned his neck toward her. "Are you well?"

"Quite fine, my lord. Do you play chess?"

He furrowed his brow. "I beg your pardon."

She smiled at his confusion. "When I play chess with my father, he'll often distract me with a sacrificial pawn when he's really on the hunt for my queen piece. He does what he must to win."

Justain's sky-blue eyes narrowed. "No, I don't play chess."

"What are the terms of this ruse, sir?" She shifted, knocking her abandoned bouquet to the ground.

Moving from the bench, he picked up the buttery flowers and placed the bundle onto the mantel. When he pivoted back, his handsome face held no smile. "In Innesfrey, there's a lovely cottage. I'll provide you with servants and all the books you could possibly want. We'll visit several times a year and develop a friendship."

Her shaking fingers twisted about the pearls. "Where's Innesfrey?"

"It's in Ireland; you'll love reading poetry on the green hills. There it won't be awkward. We can learn one another without wagging servants' tongues or the Devon Ton to interfere."

"You're banishing me to Ireland. Your pawn isn't subtle." Madeline bit her cheeks. "I suppose if I bear you no trouble, you'll lavish me with other expensive gifts." She pulled the strand from her neck. "You can stop your laughter, if you think I'm fooled by paste.

You must aim higher if you intend to bribe me."

Justain's face became ashen. "I meant no insult to the Duke of Hampshire's daughter. It's a tradition. The first Earl of Devonshire had little money." Justain took the necklace from her lap and held it in the air.

The light danced on the luster of the spheres.

"To honour his wife, who married him in spite of his lack of fortune, he had this crafted. She understood the symbolism of it. By their fourth anniversary, he'd replaced it with one of equal length but of real pearls. Now, it's part of our wedding ritual symbolizing loyalty in adversity."

He put the necklace in his coat pocket. "I've one request of you, madam wife." His tone became harsh. "You must remember our respective families, and keep your actions above reproach. I won't tolerate humiliation or gossip."

She'd insulted him. Madeline didn't mean to do that. "Ireland's too far. I'll rarely see my father."

Justain studied her for a moment. "Well, it would be unorthodox, but I could ask the duke to allow you to remain in Hampshire. I'll adjust my travels to visit with you there."

She couldn't live at Hampshire. It was better to live alone than near Kent's rage. This chessboard was horrid. Her husband enslaved all her pieces, leaving barely a knave for defence. She gripped her elbows.

"You look overwrought. Take your medicine. I'll have your maid ready you for bed. Tomorrow, we'll head to your father's for a short visit and then off to Innesfrey. I trust you'll be up to the ride. Good evening." He bowed and paced to the door.

She couldn't let him leave. Not like this. "No, please wait!"

Justain stopped and pivoted to face her.

"I'm sorry. I've offended you." She licked her lips. "I should know that you'd never fool me, but how can you treat our vows so lightly? We pledged before God."

The taut muscles in his jaw seemed too relaxed. "Those are just words, Madeline."

"I pledged to love, honour, and trust you. I wouldn't have said those words if…if I didn't intend to live up to them." She raised her shaking hand to draw him from the door.

Justain's gaze seemed fixed on the ruby studding her hand.

She extended her arm. The Devonshire ring sparkled. "Dearest, don't leave."

He blinked and squinted as if to clear his eyes.

"One more moment of your time." She forced a smile.

Hesitation crossed Justain's face. His brows rose.

She patted the bench. "I can't chase after you."

Justain plodded back and sat.

Madeline placed a palm on his shoulder. "You've sheltered me, saved my life, and yet now you throw me away."

"I've not treated you ill. You're not making me into the old m—I'm not a villain."

"I wish to live up to my vows and take my place at your side." She curled her fingers about his azure lapel. "I'm your wife. Let me fulfill my duties."

He moved her hand. His thumb swirled against her palm before he let go. "This is some hysterical reaction. Madeline, I'm not locking you away in the Bedlam Asylum."

"To send me far away as a discarded item or to

return me home like a naughty child, Justain, commits me to lunacy."

He rubbed his forehead. "It wouldn't be like that. I'm trying to give us time to adjust to this arrangement, lady wife. Look at me. It's hard to say the words."

"That is why I should be near, to remind us of our new responsibilities."

"No one ever needs to remind me of responsibilities!" It took several minutes for Justain to reign in his emotion. He slumped against the bench; his shifting weight made it rock.

Devlin said rational arguments. How would she make this turbulent call in her spirit sound rational? Oh, heavens. She did want to be married to Justain.

He adjusted his cuff of his bright white shirt. "Have you had your say?"

Justain possessed such strong arms. He could defend her dream of a safe and loving home. "I'm not trying to be at odds with you." She straightened the precious ruby. He needed to share this dream. "I want to be faithful to my vows, Justain."

His eyebrows arched as she purred his given name. "Why?"

Madeline cleared her throat. "I won't break a promise to God," she said softly.

"You can do that from Hampshire or Innesfrey."

She shook her head. "No, I'll become another bad memory that you'll wish to forget."

"What of your own desires, Madeline Delveaux?" He leaned his head back. "Are they to be cast aside because of empty words?"

"I want peace. How can that exist if strife festers between us?" Madeline placed her hand on top of his. "I owe you my life. Even though you married me to secure an inheritance, I chose to join my life to yours."

His sky-blue gaze darted across her face. Did he understand?

"I don't see how this works. You're too young, and I'm too jaded."

"When I agreed to marry you, I vowed to esteem and keep you. I won't break my vows. I fear God too much. Leaving me in Innesfrey or abandoning me in Hampshire will embitter me. How do I honour you, if my spirit is heavy towards you?"

"Are you saying you can't be left alone for a season?" He leaned forward and tugged at his boot. The black leather had been buffed to a shine. "I travel often to manage the family properties. My travel is sometimes dangerous. It's no place for a wife."

"No, the earl's wife should be waiting at home in Devon." Madeline smiled at him. "I want to put my all into being a good wife to you, and your helpmate should be at Trenchard."

He slumped his shoulders as if she'd asked for all the King's gold. "But Trenchard is my respite."

"It shall be mine, too, and I'll help you make it a place to be treasured. Miss Regent says it's in need of repairs. I'm sure I'll be helpful."

"Miss Regent been running on?" Justain closed his eyes for a second. His teeth clenched. "And when my wife doesn't get her way, it'll be exposed to waterfalls of tears and tirades."

She pulled his hand to her face. "Do you see tears?"

He stroked her cheek then drew away. "If I set you up as mistress of Trenchard Park, people will think that we are—"

"If people think that you're happily married, is

that terrible? Justain, would it be a bad thing if they see a woman filled with gratitude for her valiant husband?"

A long space of silence packed the gap between them. She must be swaying him with her arguments. Emboldened, Madeline clasped his fingers allowing his ruby and onyx stone to touch her faceted ring. "You've saved my life and given me your name. Let me show you my gratitude, but I do have one other request."

He looked to the ceiling and then down to the fireplace. "And that would be?"

"One chance to prove that I could be a good wife to you and as a token of this commitment, we end our day with a prayer and a kiss…on my forehead."

At this, Justain became animated. His gaze fell upon her. Heat crept up her neck and down to the trim anointing her bosom.

Madeline's pulsed raced. She'd advanced her argument right back to those husbandly rights he'd forsaken. "It's a custom my mother and father enjoyed until her death. It symbolized their dedication to their marriage."

His hands tightened about her ring finger, and he drew it to his mouth. "I'm not exactly a praying man, but your line of reasoning is breathtaking. Dear wife, we've a long ride tomorrow." He kissed the tender flesh of her palm. "We should be off to bed."

"To bed, husband?" She stopped her arm from rising to cover her chest.

"Yes, to bed, with you at my side." His eyes glittered with danger.

The warmth spread to her cheeks. Consummation; she pledged not only her fidelity but also her body.

His face held a wide grin.

Madeline would have to bear him touching her to pass the test between a bride and wife.

Father, give me the will to submit. Aunt said to not be afraid. Madeline stroked his sable hair. "Let's be off to bed." The queen surrendered to the king.

Suspicions be gone. Did it matter why she wanted this marriage as long as this curvaceous creature requested he bed her? Grit and refined beauty, wasn't it a deadly combination for him. Justain could have her and still cart his troubles off to Innesfrey once they visited Hampshire.

"Well, my wife, we should consummate this marriage and install you as the mistress of Trenchard." Justain dragged his hand up her arm.

The heat of her skin warmed her satin sleeve.

Madeline lowered her lashes and whispered, "I want us to find a common path. I'm ready for any challenge we need to bear."

His anger at being forced to wed hadn't dampened his attraction to her. And her boldness drew him to her lips. He stood and pulled his bride to him.

She winced from the sudden action but reclaimed her thin smile.

Should he inquire if he'd hurt her? No, Justain didn't want a truthful answer. "You're taller than I remembered." He nipped her ear. "I didn't tell you how sweet you look. I'll have you out of this quickly."

Her face reddened. "I've pledged to God to be your wife. Tell me what I must pledge for you to accept me."

He held her against his breast, hoping to smother

any more words of oaths and God.

"To bed." With a quick motion, he swept her into his arms. The sweet smell of strawberries emanated from her hair. His fingertips itched to touch her.

Madeline's arm travelled down his side. That delicate hand could number every muscle on his body. He wouldn't mind. The tender digits landed in his pocket. She pulled the necklace out and cast it about her. "I'm ready."

The beads, the traditions, another unhappy Delveaux bride. Sanity reclaimed him. "You're not ready for this, Madeline. Trust me; you'll love Innesfrey. There I'll watch my child bride grow into an amazing woman."

"I'm no child." Madeline wound her arms about his neck. With a shaky grip, she drew closer.

"I won't think less of you if you abandon—"

Her soft fingers stroked his lobe. The sensation sparked like kindling wood. Madeline's lips were close to his nose. He should lift his head and kiss the vixen in his arms. Instead, he tasted the pulsing vein on her neck. "Milk?"

"A milk bath to prepare for the wedding." She kissed his cheek. "I'll be a good wife to you."

"Have you no pride?" He sampled the hollow of throat. "Are you so weak, you'll accept any token of affection, to consummate this marriage?"

"Do you know how much strength it takes to let you touch me and know it means nothing to you?" Her voice sounded raw. "Do you know how much strength it will take not to hate you when the deed is done?"

Justain stomped to the bedchamber and kicked open the door.

Warm candlelight greeted him and illuminated the

snowy-white furnishings. He carried his martyr to the vast canopied bedstead.

Madeline's hands clutched his lapels. Her heart beat like summer thunder, pounding louder as she drew closer.

He pulled back the gauzy crown skirting the canopy and laid his bride on a silken, powder-blue coverlet.

14

Madeline's heart rose to her throat. What should she say now? She'd offered herself to Justain, demanding he claim her as his wife. The cold pearls tangled and drizzled to the side of her neck. She'd insulted him by returning it. Aunt was right. Respect mattered greatly to him.

Justain tugged a lock of hair from her cheek. The corners of his lips pressed into a tight line. "So, you're ready to consummate this marriage?"

Madeline stilled her limbs against the linen. "If this is what it takes to prove my loyalty, let's be done with it." She closed her eyes. Until tonight, Justain was gentle, always kind with his passion. She needed to trust that kind man wasn't a ruse. She forced arms upon his shoulders to welcome his embrace.

His fingers slipped across the length of her chin. The touch was feather soft. "Open your eyes, Madeline Delveaux. You may not have the sense to relent, but I do. I'll send your maid in to help ready you for bed."

She sat up, astonished. "But you don't."

The dark cloud on his face cleared. "I'm not interested in chasing you around the bed." Justain stormed to the open doorway. "I'll retire in another room."

She dropped to the mattress. Heavy footsteps approached the bed again.

He'd changed his mind?

Her heart stopped as she gazed up at her husband's blank expression. "Justain?"

He bent over the bed. His powerful arms dragged her to him. The candlelight danced in his eyes.

She didn't resist. "It'll be a few months before I'm fast on my feet and make good sport of the chase."

A tiny smile bloomed on his lean face. "I forgot your kiss, madam wife."

Aunt's words tumbled in her mind. Madeline pinched her lips and leaned into him.

He took his palm and wiped the strain from her countenance. "You'll grow up in Innesfrey. Don't fight me on this. You'll be safe there." He kissed her forehead and settled her amongst the ivory pillows. "And one day you'll want my touch, not suffer it."

An eternity passed as his foot treads fell away. The door banged shut. Quiet enveloped her room. She wrapped her arms about her and waited for the onslaught of tears to begin.

❧

Justain lost track. He sipped his fourth or fifth glass of brandy. People crowded the public house as if it were an assembly. Its burnished oak walls must hold many secrets. Hopefully, Justain's secluded table in the corner would contain his.

"Lord Delveaux?" The accented voice giggled. It was a sweet Spanish gait. "Or shall I say my Lord Devonshire."

"Emillae," he called to the voice, "my dove, my favourite duenna."

A dark-haired lass clad in purple silk stood at his

table. "It is contessa, remember? Had my lovely companion been half as bold she'd have my title. Sometimes the meek inherit nothing."

He looked up into the dark brown eyes. "What brings you here?"

"You." She batted long lashes at him. "There's only one J.M. Delveaux."

"But surely, you haven't married again." He pushed a lock of hair from his eyes. "You enjoy your freedom too well."

"My cousin Margarite has wed." Emillae's shawl fell open exposing a daringly low neckline.

He set down his glass. "Cousin? I thought I knew everything about you."

"I kept her away from you, you naughty boy, but I see by the ring on your finger that congratulations are in order." The Contessa Salvador smiled as she gazed at the shiny band on his finger. "You finally got that Caroline to run away with you, even before your twenty-eighth birthday."

When did he tell Emillae about the queer tradition? Well, the vixen could always get anything out of him. Lucky for him, she didn't side with Bonaparte. The contessa was ten years his senior, but no one would've guessed it from her warm smile and robust figure. "I didn't get Miss Lavis to love…to marry me."

She tapped her fan. "Well, you're more diabolical than I remember. You compromised her into accepting you. When you set your heart on something, you'll do nothing but succeed."

"I deserve no such praise, my dear lady." Justain patted a chair, inviting Emillae to sit with him.

"Oh, Justain, darling. Please indulge me. Tell me

what's wrong. You know my greatest passion is to manipulate the lives of mere mortals." She fondled his arm. "And you're one of my favourite mortals. I still remember the gangly young officer following behind Wellesley. Your intriguing eyes wouldn't let you blend into the background."

"Yes, Emillae." He looked at the wanton creature. "You helped me see life from a new perspective."

"You didn't seem to complain as I plied you with the finery of Spain, awakening all of your sensual appetites."

Justain smiled. Emillae was a world tour, an adventure for any young man, even one at war. "You stopped writing…must have grown bored, leaving me to miss these wonderful dark tresses."

"I'm not good with letters, Justain. And I require my suitors to spend more time with me than foxing around the countryside."

"It's called war, Emillae." He took another slow sip of brandy. "But you've been the beneficiary of my interest through the years. I believe I'm much more attentive without the threat of gunfire."

Emillae pulled her chair close, as if to hold an intimate conversation. "I should be mad at you, Justain."

"What have I done? It's been two years since I last saw you, my dear Contessa."

"Your little 'secret admirer' campaign almost ruined things for me with Lord Branford."

"Branford lacks my colour. He'd never send you one perfect hyacinth each day for a month. Those purple blooms are hard to come by."

"He also would never leave me." Emillae signalled for a servant. "May I have a pot of tea?"

"Chamomile and cream for the lady, my good sir." Justain returned his gaze to his glass.

"You remembered, but you were always good at details. My favourite flower. My favourite poem, *A Farewell to False Love*."

He sat up. "Who doesn't admire Sir Raleigh's lyrics?"

"Justain, only you would seduce my mind. Far more interesting than any trinket."

"You taught me well. When you chose to forgo meeting Branford in London to meet your unknown admirer, that was a great victory for me, Emillae."

"I'll never forget your attention to detail. The cottage laced with my sweets and adorned with playful pink hyacinths. I should've known something was amiss with the perfume of distrustful lavender. You'd mixed it with the hyacinth. Your knowledge of flowers is impeccable."

"Well, you can't farm potatoes every day." The old man taught him one useful thing.

She clanged her spoon. "I should still be angry."

He smiled. "Yes, I believe you were, and then you weren't."

Emillae sipped her tea. "Well, you silenced my protest with kisses." She fluttered almond-shaped eyes.

Justain turned back to his glass. As time passed, the victory seemed more tarnished. He only seduced her to assuage his hurt pride. Didn't Madeline sacrifice her pride to prove something to him? He shouldn't put Madeline in that position.

With a shake of his head, he returned his gazed to the contessa. "My behaviour to you was abominable. I'm sorry, Emillae, if I hurt you."

The woman shifted in her seat. Her rouged cheeks

darkened to the colour of the walls. "Why should I be angry when I've done the same thing time and time again? Though no one likes to know they're nothing more than a campaign."

"I'm on a different path now." Justain forwent looking into her wistful eyes and returned to his liquid absolution. "I didn't marry Caroline. I convinced the daughter of the Duke of Hampshire to follow her heart and elope." Justain kept his secret. He wouldn't give Emillae a reason to gloat. "We married this evening."

"She's a lucky woman. I always thought once you broke with that, how do you say, Gideon complex, hiding in the winepress instead of seeing your natural power, you'd be unstoppable."

"I know I've not been in this club long enough to hear you referencing the Bible." He now admired his bride's surprise with his same admission.

"I recently campaigned for a retired vicar in Sussex. Not as successful as I'd want, but a few concepts stuck." Emillae saucily tossed her head. Her jet-black curls bounced from the effort. "Since you're down here, I assume the wedding night is not well."

"You needn't be concerned. It's been a long day." Justain turned up his glass and concentrated on tasting the last droplets.

"Well, she's in the most skilled hands. I'm sure you will overcome her reservations." Emillae touched his hands. "Such firm palms, Delveaux. I mean my Lord Devonshire. What new skills do they possess?"

"You're incorrigible, my delightful vixen." His shimmering band clinked against his glass.

"If you're in the mood to swap tales of woe, Justain, I'm staying close by. Pray let's finish this conversation in private. I assure you there's much to tell." Emillae's eyes heated with forbidden promise.

15

The vixen leaned into Justain. She unpinned a curl and slipped it between her fingers. “Shall I lead the way?”

He remembered the feel of those silken threads, the smell of jasmine that spiced the base of her neck. Temptation must have a pocket scope and the ability to spot a weakened man.

“I believe, Justain, I have a bottle of your desired brandy.”

He tapped his wedding band upon the glass again. “No. I’ll be returning to my wife.”

She straightened his linen cravat. “Are you done with your vices, me and brandy?”

He moved her fingers from his Adam’s apple.

“No one’ll know, my Lord Devonshire.” Her alluring accent. She puffed the invitation between cherry lips.

Justain would know. He’d be no better than the old man cavorting while his bride was underfoot. Justain paused then said in earnest, “I’m sorry. I hope I haven’t started a new competition between us.”

“All’s fair, Justain.” She patted his hand and stood to her feet. Emillae leaned over his chair. Her scent tickled his nose. “No changing your mind?”

Where was Jonathan when he needed him? Couldn’t the man find a reason to bounce in and interrupt? Justain pushed back in his chair away from the forbidden fruit.

Emillae giggled as she smoothed her dress. "For what it's worth, I'm glad you abandoned your childhood zest for Caroline Lavis. There's no woman, not even Miss Lavis, who lives up to the vision you painted."

He rose and nodded to the contessa. "Goodnight, Emillae." Justain wouldn't discuss Caroline with her or anyone. No one would understand his feelings. Now, there was no reason ever to voice them again.

He returned to his bedchamber and hoped for cleansing sleep.

Justain closed his eyes. He'd received two propositions. Sleep needed to render him unconscious before he leapt up and accepted one.

❧

Madeline kept moving the polished silverware, shifting her teacup on the mat of white linen in front of her. Her gaze flew over the dish of fresh marmalade and tray of hot cross buns to the white bench and mantel, the site she'd given away what little freedom she possessed. Her appetite wouldn't revive. She didn't want to go to Hampshire or Innesfrey. Why not Florence, where men built beauty that lasted for centuries.

Anne waved another spoonful of Dr. White's strange herbal medicine.

Madeline refused to take more and motioned for the girl to move and not spill it on Madeline's plum skirts. With a clear head, a plan, something would stir. Maybe she could convince him to take a wedding trip to Florence, see Giambologna's *Abducted Women* or Michelangelo's *David*.

"The master's sleeping late? Must've made a night of it, Lady Devonshire." Anne's cheeky grin possessed no guile, just simple girlish joy.

"You can go to my bedchamber and pack. I believe Lord Devonshire will want to leave as soon as breakfast is over." She'd let the poor creature believe "the happy couple" were of one accord. Aunt always said a woman built or tore down her house. Madeline decided to build. "You're dismissed. I'll attend to the earl."

"You're not going to hop with that crutch and serve toast?"

She smiled. "No, I'm not hopping, but I hope to learn how to balance better. Please now, Anne."

"Yes, ma'am." Anne made a sloppy curtsy and left the parlour.

Reading would calm Madeline's nerves. She sat back in her linen-shrouded chair and thumbed a collection of poems then closed the book. "What do I say—"

The door opened, and Justain stepped forward. "Good morning." The strained chords in his voice cut through the air.

His poor eyes were red and held a slight puffiness. She wanted to put a warm towel on them. "You haven't slept well?"

"I suppose I didn't." He moved to the walnut sideboard. He looked immaculate in a jet-black jacket and a bottle-green waistcoat.

"Is it difficult to sleep in many different beds?" she asked.

"Pardon me?" Justain rotated, his smile thinned to

a tight line.

"With you travelling often from Trenchard, it must be difficult to adjust. I think that without Dr. White's potions it would be difficult for me."

"Yes." Justain poured a cup of coffee. The chocolate aroma wafted from his steaming mug. He slogged to the table. "Is that my book?"

"Every good bookworm seizes the opportunity to indulge. I had Miss Regent request this of Mr. Winton, the sonnets you read to me at Much Wenlock." She patted the cover. "I didn't think you'd mind."

"Beginning to exercise your dominion." His eyes narrowed. "Giving orders to the staff." His tone was harsh.

Madeline swallowed some tea. Anne should pack her things straight for Innesfrey. "Is there nothing, I can say to make things…less awkward?"

"Keep the book." Justain sipped his coffee.

"Let's head to a neutral place. Maybe a trip to Italy. You will love the sculpted works of the masters, meticulous marble and bronze."

His brows pushed together. "You want to see marble?"

"I'm not asking this right." Her speech would work so much better on Aunt Tiffany. Madeline knew what to say to entice that woman, but Justain was a mystery. "I'm partial to the works of Michelangelo, and a learned man like you will love them, too."

"We're off to Hampshire. Your father's expecting us."

"Father knows?" Gall rose in her throat. She gripped her fingers about the table leg.

His brows rose. "I had his permission to wed you."

"I didn't think you'd be able to tell him with the elopement." Her cheeks froze as the blood drain away. "Does he know the circumstances?"

"Yes." He cocked his head to the side and smirked. "Madeline, are you well?"

The gold bees on the wall started swirling. "Justain, he approves?"

"He does. Do I need to get your talkative maid?"

She took a deep breath and shook her head.

"Your father isn't well. He'll be glad to see to you."

Madeline didn't know what to react to first. Father knew. Father approved. Father was ill.

"He's never sick." She pushed the china teacup away. Her cheeks throbbed. "If this is a joke for taking your book, it's in poor form."

"I wouldn't be that callous."

Every desire to stay calm abandoned her. "When were you going to tell me?"

"I waited until I knew you were strong enough to handle the news." The monotone sound of his voice grated every fibre of her being. An argument should have passion.

"I am strong." Madeline pushed herself up with the crutch. The quick action scuttled the book onto the floor, separating its linen spine. "Why would you hide this from me? After what we've been through…always tell me the truth."

Justain picked up the book then moved to steady her. "Why are you questioning my decisions?"

She tightened her grip on her crutch. "When will anyone understand I have a voice?"

He brushed lint from his dark jacket. "Madam, for the most part that voice has been steeped in hysterics. I myself prefer it muted."

His words stung, but Madeline returned his gaze. "There should be no secrets between us."

"I take no orders. I give them." The hardness in the earl's words left no room for misunderstanding. He controlled her destiny.

"Father's as strong as an ox."

"The duke says he's quite ill."

Tears drizzled down her face. "You're lying. He can't die, too." She punched at his shoulder. "When will Death leave me?"

Justain wrapped his arms about her and pressed her against his chest. "No one said he was dying."

The crutch slipped from her hand and hit the floor hard. She leaned into Justain with shaking limbs.

"Are you frightened of me, Madeline?"

"No, I've seen your character." She lowered her head. Death scared her.

His finger traced her chin. "I've pledged to shield you from harm. I always keep my promises."

Shield her? Her heart pounded against his. A dark vision of their mineshaft crossed her thoughts. Justain's tender words rang in her ears. Of course, he had no other motive than protecting her. "It's difficult to trust. I've been disappointed often. Forgive me. I wasn't thinking."

"Sometimes reacting without thinking isn't horrid." Justain's low voice washed against her forehead.

Madeline focused on the pearl buttons of his waistcoat. Something happened when he held her, when his hand touched her face. He tipped her head. Madeline held her breath, swimming in the reflection of his sky-blue eyes.

Justain inched closer to her mouth.

Her nose edged his strong jaw. She closed her eyes. "Please, let me prove that I can be a good helpmate."

The pressure of Justain's hands changed. Instead of holding her, he lowered her to the chair. The moment disappeared. The curiosity that heated Justain's eyes fled. The blue was cold and distant again. He handed Madeline the pieces of his book. "We should get ready to leave. I'll send your maid in for the final preparations." Justain bowed and bolted from the room.

Madeline glanced at the opened door. He'd erected that wall again. She was sure on the other side lay her dreams of home and family. She dropped her head on the table. Prayers for her father rose in her heart.

Justain paced from the inn toward the livery stable. Leicestershire bustled. He sidestepped a carriage rumbling down the cobblestone lane. Angry voices drifted from an open shop where patrons dickered over imported silks. He balled his fist within his coat pocket. Could he just kiss his bride without her asking for more than he could give?

He clipped past a bakery. The smell of fresh bread didn't brighten his mood. It might as well have been the pungent smoke pouring from the distant bell-casting factory. This wasn't a good morning. Justain's head rang, and he fought rebellion in his stomach.

He sighed and turned into the whitewashed stable. It buzzed with groomsmen readying travellers and braying horses: a golden palomino, a mottled roan, and a dozen other colours, but nothing finer than his onyx Arabian.

A little tyke with a barrel hoop came tearing out of a pen. The boy lost control of the metal band as he tumbled and made a hole in his breeches. The toy came to rest on Justain's boot.

The little boy's cheeks brightened to scarlet. He gazed down at the ground and shoved a hand into his torn pocket. Justain stooped low and picked up the hoop. "Here you go, little man. Be more careful."

The little boy smiled a toothy grin and took the offered toy. He tipped his smudged cap then ran off. If only everything was as simple as a child's game.

Jonathan Winton coughed.

Justain stood erect. *Now he arrives*. Where was the man when Justain had to contend with the seductress Emillae?

His steward smiled at him. "When we return to Devon, the orphans will need some instruction on how to keep the hoop upright. From what I remember, you did it well."

Justain grimaced at him. Their friendship extended more than fifteen years, almost to the day the old man hired Winton's mother as his tutor. Jonathan always knew how to catch him doing something ridiculous. Good thing the man could keep a secret.

His steward cleared his throat. "My lord, everything's in order." Jonathan went back into Athena's stall and fastened a bridle on the black beauty. Athena's satin ears poked through the leather crownpiece as Jonathan fitted everything tight. "We can leave in an hour, unless you prefer to take Athena for a ride?"

"No, Jonathan." A good ride on horseflesh always helped Justain analyze his problems but never with a thick head. "I need you to make arrangements to send Miss Regent back to Devon."

Winton's nose wrinkled. "Your wife will need assistance during our travel?"

"I'll rely upon the staff at the inns to service her. Miss Regent has been filling my bride's head with the grandeur of Trenchard Park. My wife should be happy with Innesfrey."

The steward led Athena to their carriage. He signalled to the groomsmen to begin harnessing the horse team. They tugged and tied the long rods of the carriage into place and banded the wide overgirth straps around each horse.

Jonathan paced backed to Justain. "Your countess won't return with us to Devon? I take it that she's uncomfortable with her new marital state."

"No. She wants to become the mistress of Trenchard."

The steward opened Justain's leather pouch and arranged correspondences. "That sounds like a good thing." He handed the bag to Justain. "All's in order, my lord."

Justain slung it about his shoulder. "It doesn't make any sense for her to want to be the mistress of a place she's never seen. No more of this today." He rubbed his eyes.

"Sir, we've at least two weeks to traverse by carriage. Wouldn't it be more pleasant if you were in a more charitable mood?" The red-haired man possessed little temper, though he surely had Irish rebellion in his blood. He had thrown rock-solid punches in all their youthful routs. Yet, since Justain had elevated him as his steward, the young man argued with him only on dire occasions.

Did Justain look that bad now? "Why, Winton, are you trying to soften me?"

"For your own welfare. But never mind, sir. I'll make arrangements for Miss Regent right now."

His steward left the livery, and Justain headed back toward the inn. He kicked a loose stone in his path. It skipped across the lane toward a man and woman. They were arm and arm running toward the vicarage. Just shy of the ornate pine door, the fellow stopped and stole a kiss from the lass. Another eloping couple.

Madeline fit his arms well. And when she said she knew his character, his chest swelled. Maybe when his head cleared, Justain would find a way to ease the tension with his bride.

❧

Madeline leaned back in the stateroom chair utterly amazed. She'd never seen hair that colour before. Parts of the servant's locks were deeper than henna. Parts were highlighted dark pink, darker than Madeline's skirt. Other sections matched the thin rug covering the coaching inn's floor. How could the woman find the time to dye her hair to this strange hue when it was obvious her full time duty was to flirt with husbands?

Worse than the woman's forwardness, her smoothing of Justain's lapel, her bending immodestly to retrieve his napkin, was Justain's response. His dour mood evaporated.

"My lord, would you have more cheese?" The

woman asked as she leaned over him again blocking the view of the evening feast.

Justain's gaze settled on Madeline for a second, before he whispered something to the servant.

The servant laughed. Her hand grazed his jacket again.

He chuckled as if he were still wet behind the ears. He lapped up the empty praise and two helpings of bread.

Madeline glanced at her empty plate before gazing at him again. At least, they were out of the miserable carriage. Two days of travel in their dark cage, strange inns, and barely a word spoken between them. Granted, Dr. White's medicine caused her to nod off almost as soon as they were underway, but this was ridiculous.

"My lord, may I be of additional service?" the fiery redhead asked him. She stretched almost atop him waving a tray of apples.

"No, I'm fine." Justain seemed to take his time answering. He needn't stare. The maid's tight fitting tunic left little to the imagination.

Is this why he wanted her banished? So he could cavort as if he was unwed? In public, they were man and wife. He needed to remember that.

"My dear, will you please refill my glass?" she asked the servant in cool tones, only a hair more condescending than she intended.

The woman traipsed to Madeline's side of the table, her hips rocking the whole way.

What was the polite way to remind the chesty scarlet woman it was bad form to make advances to a man with his wife less than ten paces away?

Madeline forced a smile. "My husband, what else

will you have? I'm sure this lovely maid will find something to satisfy you."

He chuckled. "I believe the food will suffice."

"Will you require further assistance? I hate to detain our server from her other quests." Madeline's voice remained vibrant. She kept her expression pleasant and steady, despite the brazen woman's return to Justain's side. Step-mother would make a scene. Madeline refused to, though now she had more sympathy for Lady Dana.

The maid placed one of the sandwiches on his earthenware plate.

Justain waved her off.

She wiggled to the door. "Is everything to your liking? Nothing more you need?"

Before he took a bite, Justain lifted the bread to unveil its contents. "Slices of roasted mutton with a drizzled mustard stripe. You must send it back."

The girl lost her smirk. "I'll get the cook. He's right outside." She swayed to the door and returned with a portly man clad in a sand-coloured coat.

"Good man, I believe this sandwich is made improperly." Justain didn't look distressed. A touch of devilment loomed in his eyes.

"I'm sorry, sir. What's the matter?" The cook looked down, perhaps searching for a hole to jump through. "We use the finest cuts of meats."

"I'm sure you do, but that's not what I am talking about. Look for yourself." Justain handed his plate to the anxious man. "Next time, bring the spicy mustard in some container." He handed the cook two shillings and a few pence. "This is for dinner."

"Good, sir. I'll see ye get a dish of spicy mustard." The cook and the servant retreated, closing the heavy stateroom door.

Justain helped himself to the spread again, beginning with the dish of roasted chicken.

"You enjoy adding your own condiments and are a passionate eater."

"You sound as if you are making a list." Justain continued his mission of eating, cutting a slice of mince pie.

Madeline set down her glass. "I think it's good for a wife, even one in name only, to know what pleases her husband."

"My countess looks serious, but how do we know this is not some passing fancy, like the reward of a new or stolen book?"

"My fervour for books has been with me a lifetime. I've just met you." Madeline wet her finger and added figures on a napkin.

He laughed a hearty belt. "Now what are you drawing over there?"

"You paid a few shillings for a feast. I have to get my math right. Since you'll deprive me of servants in Innesfrey."

He cleared his mouth. "You'll have servants enough."

She leaned forward. "Why send away Miss Regent?"

"I only need to be concerned about one woman on this trip." He bit his lip.

Madeline's heart lurched. "We're still in danger?"

He forked some chicken. "Eat, Madeline. Let's try to have a pleasant meal."

"How is this pleasant?" Madeline pushed her tin plate aside. "You go out of your way to pretend I'm not here. Do you hate me? Why do you treat me ill?"

Justain's face went blank. He lifted from his chair; it creaked from the quick shifting of weight. He marched toward her.

Madeline gazed at the door and wished he hadn't chased away the staff.

"You're not going to cry?"

"No." She didn't hide the anger in her voice. "This loathsome marriage isn't my fault."

The noise of his boots stopped. He now stood next to her, handsome in his navy coat and buff breeches. He raised his arm; the buttons of his sleeve jingled. She'd pushed him too far. Madeline should be frightened, but she squared her shoulders. Justain would never hurt her.

"Madam." Justain plopped down next to her. "You're right. I've not been charitable. And it's unsettling to find you've married a difficult man."

Justain agreed with her? He'd changed the landscape again.

"We cannot continue like this," he said. "I propose a truce. Let's forget about Innesfrey and Trenchard. Let us focus on friendship."

She felt a small twinge of relief, but she couldn't let her guard down. Too many secrets hid behind those sky-blue eyes. "I don't understand."

"Our lives are now bound together. Even with my initial plans, I intended to visit you at Innesfrey and find common ground." He seemed sincere, his hands thoughtfully folded on the table.

"I welcome the forging of a bridge."

"How can I not try to befriend a woman who becomes jealous from an overly-kind servant?"

Must he label the turbulence in her spirit? Madeline brushed back a drooping curl. "Why would I not be jealous? She made you smile."

A slow grin illuminated his countenance. "Well, now you have." He drew an apple from a platter.

Madeline sipped her water. As confusing as his moods, Justain didn't have a dull bone in his body. A sense of energy filled the air when he was about even if she wanted to box his ears.

"This has been a long day for you. It's at least a two-hour ride to our destination for the evening." Justain sunk his teeth into the fruit. Juice dripped his lip.

Without thinking she reached with her napkin and wiped his chin.

A smile laced with dimples bloomed on his face. "At the Queen's Inn, you'll be properly attended." Justain revisited his task of eating.

Madeline's appetite returned. Maybe her marriage wasn't hopeless.

Justain took a final bite of his apple. He was a dunderhead. He had a beautiful woman to dazzle, and yet he chose to sulk. Madeline smiled at him over her glass. Her lovely jade eyes glowed. This time would be much more rewarding, enjoying her company than being at odds.

He helped his bride to her feet. "Lean into me for balance."

Madeline winced and threw her arms about his neck.

His hands surrounded her tiny waist as if it were an automatic response. He stopped gazing into her perfect eyes and spun Madeline's dark emerald coat about her shoulders. "Lady Glaston does know how to highlight your best attributes." He flipped the hood onto her head and tied a thick bow under her chin.

"Miss Regent said I looked like a duchess in it."

"Your title is countess." Justain lifted her with great care and carried his bride out of the inn and into the carriage. He tapped the roof, and the coach lunged forward.

Justain leaned back onto the thinly padded seats. He considered their meal a success, but the tension he thought he'd eased seemed to return, wrinkled upon Madeline's forehead. The girl looked disturbed. Was this shift unsettling to her? Had he been that much a brute?

The carriage hit another bump, and she almost toppled to the floor. "We're going off the main road." Madeline's voice was tiny; he had to strain to hear.

Justain folded his arms. "This is a safer way."

The overgrowth of brush scratched the walls. She covered her ears in a frantic manner. "The trees are close. It's like a maze."

He stretched out in the black cabin. "Pretend we're going on a secluded journey."

"Secluded?"

They hit a gullet that rocked the cabin. Madeline crashed to the floor. She wrapped her sleeves about her head as if trying to curl into a green ball.

Justain knelt beside her. "Are you hurt?" He held his hands out to help her back to the seat.

She scanned from side to side, as if looking for a place to hide.

"There's nowhere to run in a carriage." He put a palm on her shoulder, and Madeline recoiled. "What is this?"

She didn't respond. Tremors ran along her arms.

"Don't be afraid. I'll keep you from harm. Let me lift you off the floor." He attempted to pull her into his embrace.

Madeline stiffened her posture and drew her face from him.

"You're terrified." Justain stroked her neck making a light path. "Come back to me, Madeline. It's Justain."

"I don't want to ache anymore." She pulled away again and pressed against the stitching of the seat bolster.

"Your leg is pained?" He caressed her back trying to coax Madeline from the corner.

She didn't move.

"I won't let anyone hurt you." He dropped flat to the floor and drew Madeline onto his lap. He tightened his hold to stop her from shaking.

"No harm?" She touched his face.

"None, my sweet girl. We're far from the gorge." Justain tilted her head against his chest.

She stopped resisting and dug her way beneath his jacket. Her tears were thick, wetting his cravat.

It took a while for her silent waterworks to cease, her breathing to even. Justain moved his shoulder trying to renew circulation. He didn't realise how much pain she still bore. Between her injuries, the loss of her maid, the hellish attack, and boorish husband, it must be great.

"I'm sorry, Justain. I've rumpled your neck cloth."

"You don't have to be brave all the time." He brushed a lock of hair from her face.

"Father says to never show weakness." She tried to smooth his crumpled cravat, but her fingers trembled too much. "He says it's a trap for others to ensnare you."

"No, it's what you do with the acknowledgement, whether it becomes a millstone or a badge of honour. I used mine to set goals, to make sure that everyone feels the value of my success." He lifted her and eased onto the seat. "But this is not about weakness, Madeline. You were afraid. Tell me why."

She turned up her face. "I remember being thrown to the ground."

Justain steadied her in his lap. "You're thinking of Mrs. Wilkins and that terrible drop down the Gorge?"

Her nose wrinkled. "Have you discovered…who attacked us, who killed my friend and your driver?"

Justain's gut was his best guide. Right now, it hummed, divining that Madeline was afraid of something greater than Severn Gorge.

She cleared her throat. "It'll ease my mind to know who killed them. You know who's behind it?"

"I was told it was ordered by the devil."

She punched his stomach. "Must you joke?"

He clasped his bride's fingers. "Must you be violent, my lady."

"Tell me the truth. I'm in command of myself now."

He tugged at another satin lock of her hair. "I travel a great deal to manage the Delveauxes' properties. To Spain and Ireland, as well as Dorset. I've made careful investments for the past six years. My brother Richard became preoccupied, and he had me manage the family lands, too."

Madeline toyed with the frill of his cravat, but she hadn't relaxed. She still shivered.

"Without actively attending the properties, I'd

allow my family's resources to be wasted." He fought the edge growing in his voice. He thought of Dorset.

Her palm touched his jaw. "Tell me what you suspect. I need to hear the truth."

The carriage again hit a rocky patch, sending her forehead squarely into his shoulder, the shoulder he'd injured at Tilford. He bit back the pain.

She massaged her head. Her raven curls dropped about her face. "A name. Let's be united in purpose." Her voice was soft, a lullaby.

He shifted his gaze to the window. "I don't want you to be alarmed."

"Too late for that." She chortled a tense offering.

He sought the cat's-eye jade, looking deeply into their depths. "You're not like other women. You won't let me off the hook with flattery or bribes."

"Baubles are misunderstood, Justain, but truth…It's the gift I want from you."

"If I avoid that questioning look of yours, we'll never develop a friendship."

The docile creature lowered her head. "All I ever want from you is the truth."

He raised her chin. "I could quote you more poetry?"

Her face radiated, no. "There's a picture of you in my head. It's of a valiant knight girded in truth. Your weapons of righteousness, your sword and shield, are raised for battle."

"A knight?" His fingers tangled in a silken strand. He couldn't help himself. "That's a tall order to live up to."

"Let me have something in this world to count upon." Misguided lovely creature. She believed in him.

"You win." He tucked her head beneath his chin

and prepared to share the agony of his soul.

16

The softness of her ebony curls tickled Justain's chin. Madeline smelled of strawberries, sweet like the best fruited tarts. She tightened her desperate grip about his chest. Could she tell he wanted to escape the truth as much as she wanted to hear it?

Madeline rotated to peer at him, ending the caress of his jaw. He tucked her back under his chin. He refused to watch the light in those jade eyes dim as he told her how he killed Richard. "About six months ago, Winton and I were reviewing Delveaux land in Dorset. One of the tenants, Mr. Barrow, established a gristmill on the parcel I leased him. Every time we came, he seemed to be visited by younger cousins or nephews."

"Something was amiss?" Madeline smoothed a button on his waistcoat as if to calm his tension. Maybe her own.

He cleared his throat. "Barrow always paid his rent on time. The farming and mill seemed productive, though Jonathan and I never saw any animals, at least, no animals to work the grinders or pull the carts." He stilled her fingers. "And the children were in poor condition."

"He abused the children?"

"The blackguard used them to work the equipment, whipping and beating…the scars on one boy's back." Justain turned to the window. Gall turned in his stomach.

"Did you stop him?" She gripped his fingers.

"Mr. Winton and I rode back with a constable and a few of my best groomsmen. When we confronted Barrow, a battle ensued." Justain closed his eyes to lock those images in his mind. Madeline didn't need to know about the vicious bloodletting that day. "Somehow he pinned me. No way to aim, duck, and seek cover. Winton shot down from the ridge. When Barrow returned the fire, I was able to get to a more defendable position."

"What next?" She sounded breathless. Did she see the battle in his mind?

"My gun misfired. I saw him smile, take aim. Then a shout from the bushes, 'Shoot at bigger game!' And he did just that. He pivoted and pulled the trigger." Justain dropped his head against the seatback. "I'd heard that voice all my life."

"Did Mr. Winton befall injury?"

"No. Richard, my older brother. I'm not sure where he came from. Perhaps, he knew I was in danger. He and Devlin claimed to have bells going off in their heads whenever I was in trouble. But Richard had become so reckless. He didn't carry a gun."

"Older brother? But you're the earl? Oh, Justain, I'm—"

He drew a finger to her lips. No sympathy would remove the images of Richard flailing on the ground, his turquoise coat oozed red. "Barrow and his men scooped up two of the score of children and made us stand down until they fled. I should've shot. Should've had my men shoot. They killed the boys a mile up the road."

"Poor lads." She wrapped her arms about his neck. "At least, you said goodbye, helped Richard make peace."

"He could barely speak. He shook his head from side to side and mouthed 'avenge.' I promised him I would. Richard looked at me, sort of half smiled and closed his eyes. It wasn't fair. He died, and Barrow escaped. I failed my brother; I should've at least pulled the trigger. Richard won't rest until I do."

"Justain, you didn't want to risk shooting a child."

"Yes, but Barrow's still free. Many were injured or killed, and the Ton thinks I overreacted and drew Richard into my mess." Justain wanted to punch at the shadowed walls of the carriage, but Madeline held him too tight to move.

He inhaled a long breath of her fragrance. "Not a day goes by I don't second guess my actions. Was there a better way? Why Richard? Why not me?"

She raised her head. "It wasn't your fault. Don't condemn yourself."

"Some people thought that it was none of my business. The Ton wants nothing but white glove affairs. This had too many black marks: dead men and children, a deceased earl, too many innocent victims."

Madeline shook her head. "But you're a hero, a grand knight for the orphans you saved."

He pulled her back to his chest. Justain didn't want to look into her face. "A hero doesn't rent to evil for the income or create a haven that sanctions cruelty. A hero doesn't get his brother killed."

"You didn't kill Richard."

He released a heavy breath. "He shouldn't have been there. And I shouldn't have had to say good-bye, not until we were both old and grey."

"I know my Mrs. Wilkins is at rest. She had great hope in God, but I'm selfish. I want more time with her. If I had known that day would be our last, I would've told her again how much I loved her."

"Well, regret is the lover of my soul." He attempted to chuckle, but the notes were bitter. "You think a few words make everything better? A prayer to a distant God makes a difference?"

"I do." Madeline reached for the tender spot behind his ear.

He sank his head forward, pulling nearer to her delicate fingertips. It eased the strain in his back.

Her soft lips skirted his cheek. "Death has no announced schedule."

❧

His proud voice sounded humbled. He hunched his warrior shoulders. Justain's handsome face twisted in brokenness. He'd never been this unguarded, this open. Beneath his armour beat a wounded heart. Madeline wanted to tell him she understood, but Justain didn't believe in words. She pulled him close and kissed his lips.

He tightened his embrace. His mouth applied a dazzling array of pressure upon hers. He traced her smile, lingering as if searching for the opening hinge. He continued tasting her lips. His nurturing sent quivers down her spine. Then he relented.

Justain turned to the window. His hold slackened. The wall between them formed again.

She toyed with the buttons on his cream waistcoat. "What happened to the children you rescued?"

"I set up an orphanage to house the younger ones.

Those who were of age, I sent to boarding schools."

"And Barrow is still free. He should rot in prison." She put her palm over his tight fist.

He threw his head back on the seat. "I'd been too caught up in building my fortune. I'd paid off the old man's gambling debts two years earlier. I could've been more selective in my tenants."

"Barrow's the murderer. Not you." Madeline tugged on his lapel to regain his attention. "You saved many children that day. The little ones must enjoy when you come to visit them. Do you read them poetry?"

Justain adjusted his cravat. "I haven't had a chance yet because of my travels, but they're well cared for, with the best tutors."

"Oh…well, I'm sure that your time is consumed with the management of your holdings." Didn't have time for them? If Justain sent her to Innesfrey, he probably wouldn't have time for her either. She'd be alone again.

She lowered her chin and dwelled on Barrow, not the sudden ache in her stomach. "Barrow is behind Tilford?"

"The Devil of Dorset planned Tilford. I won't be surprised again." The outline of a gun bulged from his coat pocket. Did he intended to kill the man who sent them crashing into the Severn Gorge? Did Justain know death offered no chance to repent?

"Let me ease your spirits." His voice sounded pleasant, but his nostrils flared. "I recall you told me three parables. It's my turn to entertain you."

"Make it something humourous." She smoothed his lapel. "Take my mind far from Tilford."

He gazed at her for a long silent moment. "Picture

this, Madeline. The old man, my father, had the house decorated with red and white roses, my mother's favourite flowers."

"The flowers of unity. How romantic." She closed her eyes.

"Yes. The roses were everywhere, along the banister, in the library and parlours. I believe he gutted every Dutch farm. Father gave me one special task, to deliver a diamond necklace to her as she enjoyed breakfast."

The dim cabin jostled. The wheels must've hit a rough patch, but Justain held her fast. Madeline relaxed in his arms. "He loved your mother."

"It seemed that way at the time." Wham! The carriage rocked, but Justain kept her in place.

Safety. She hadn't felt this protected in a long time.

"Father dispatched me from the library, and I took the stairs two at a time." He cleared his throat. "I was five, and I followed instructions as well as any child. I stopped on the landing to look at the strand again. I leaned over the sill too far. As I swung that magical rhombus in the sunshine, the butler startled me, and I dropped the necklace out of the window."

"Oh, my." Madeline giggled. She loved his dreamy voice. "What did you do?"

"Ran to hide behind my mother's skirts until the necklace was found. She interceded for me, but I still couldn't sit for a week." He stretched and touched the low ceiling. "It's your turn now. Tell me about yourself, your life before we met."

She tapped his stomach. "You still owe me two stories, sir."

"Oh, come now, Madeline. One story; let me know more of you." His voice upon her ear felt like a tawny breeze, determined to persuade her into confession.

She kept her gaze on his buttons. "If you're going to be rid of me after Hampshire, does it matter?"

He lifted her chin. "By Hampshire, you may not think I'm worth two guineas. Let's wait until after Hampshire to decide our future."

"Well, I do know you to be a man of your word." She shook his hand to seal the deal. Justain possessed strong rough hands, perfect for building a future, their future.

Madeline sighed. "When I was six, I went to the seaside. Mother let me run barefoot in the water, much to poor Mrs. Wilkins's steady complaints. I remember devouring teacakes until I couldn't breathe. Laughter. I still hear Mother's laughter as she challenged me to collect seashells. I miss her."

"Did she give you your love for sculpture as well as the arts?"

She gazed at him, puzzled at his question.

A smile tugged at his lips. "Most young women ask for a wedding trip to Bath, not to traipse around old marble."

"Haven't you realised I'm not most women?" She lowered her head, again focusing on his buttons.

"'Tis true." He stroked her cheek.

"When she died, I hid myself away in Avington's hall of statues. It gave comfort to be around things that men made that didn't die. Sculpture lasts beyond the grave of the artisan." She sighed and marvelled at how easy it was to share a tiny piece of her life with Justain. "In a small way, they've made a difference by leaving something special behind."

He adjusted his tailcoat, enfolding her deeper within his arms. "When did your mother pass?"

"When I was twelve. I hope to have one small measure of her courage." She closed her eyes and leaned against his shoulder. "I wish to collect on the two stories you still owe."

"I do pay my debts, my dear. Let me tell you about horses."

❧

The chambermaid closed the heavy door of her room, leaving Madeline all alone upon another strange bed. She fluffed her thick pillows. When Justain carried her out of their carriage, the beauty of the Queens Inn mesmerized her. The high maroon brickwork made it seem warm and inviting, so unlike the cold grey of Avington Manor.

Regal hand-blocked fleurs-de-lis covered the sea foam coloured walls. The linens smelled of rosewater. She snuggled against the sheets and allowed the fragrance to soothe her stiff muscles. The hard fall onto the carriage floor hurt, but it hadn't reinjured her leg. She braved the pain, but shrank away from confessing all to Justain.

The bruises on her bare forearm, the marks inflicted by Kent, were gone. Madeline wanted to tell Justain about Mr. Kent, how the beast tricked her into the garden maze at Avington Manor, but she couldn't. What man wants a wife whose judgments were in question? She threw her hands over her head. She hadn't won Justain's trust.

Her fingers touched a carved bedpost. Acanthus leaves ran the length of it; a symbol of athletics framed the bed. Aunt Tiffany would be delighted, but the woman's wild talk had emboldened Madeline. She'd kissed Justain. For one brief moment, it felt as if he needed her arms about him. He had seemed to welcome her offering of understanding.

Justain promised to decide about their living arrangement after their visit to Hampshire. If they decided to separate, she wouldn't see much of him. The man hadn't found time to visit his orphans, and they were in Devon. Was it the thought of being alone or being without Justain that distressed her?

A solid knock sounded upon her door. "May I come in?" Justain's voice vibrated through the wood.

A shiver skirted her arm, and she sat up. "Yes, my lord."

A scratch of metal clicked in the lock, and he entered. A tiny gold thread woven in the piping of his burgundy brocade robe matched well with the formality of the wall pattern. "How is my wife this evening?"

The word wife flowed easier off his tongue. Was she becoming dear to him? *Oh, let it be so.* A tingle raced her spine. "Quite fine." She extended her hand to him. "Do you stay here often?"

He started toward her but cracked open the heavy paned window. "Staffordshire is wonderful. And the steamy fog makes for interesting nights." After crossing the floor, Justain kissed her hand and sat on the edge of bed. "Maybe even romantic nights. You've been waiting for me."

"Yes…for you to kiss me goodnight." That sounded insipid. She shouldn't be nervous around him.

A twinkle lit in his sky-blue eyes as he touched her cheek. "Will you be able to sleep?"

"The maid is to check on me."

He scooted closer, bunching up the cream-coloured coverlet. "What if I attend you?"

Madeline's cheeks flushed. "I'll relish the attention."

Justain smelled of sandalwood, his face freshly barbered. "What if I stay with you this evening?"

17

Madeline threw her arms about Justain's shoulders. "How did you know that these strange places make me uncomfortable? Of course, you would. My knight would." She shuddered.

"Knight, humph." He moved her hands back to the mattress and kissed her forehead. "I'll sit with you until you fall asleep." His eyes clouded as if another burden dropped upon his shoulders. Justain leapt up from the bed and tied tight his robe. "I'll read to you until you drowse." He pulled a chair close and picked up his tattered book of poems from the night table.

She smoothed the blanket. "You know what I want?"

His brows arched.

She studied those mysterious sky-blue orbs. "Tell me about Richard."

"He cheated at cards." Justain lowered his head and thumbed through a few pages.

How to make him gaze at her? Words would have to do. "Tell me about his other nature?"

Justain lifted his head. "What, his drunken one? He was a mean drunk."

She shook her head. "I don't want to hear about his weakness. Unless that's what changed him, made him so reckless."

"Pardon me?" He rubbed his neck.

She pushed up higher onto the pillows. "Did drink control him?"

"No more than it does anyone. Well, Richard did say it was for medicinal purposes. Everyone has pain, even a starchy miss."

"My father changed." She looked away to the window. If she squinted, Madeline could picture her father pacing, throwing a goblet at the low wall on the patio. Step-mother knew how to provoke him.

"You miss him, the duke?"

"Yes, very much." She turned, examined Justain's face, the tiny scar on his chin. "Was it a woman that changed him?"

"You want to know about Devonshire's, I mean Richard's womanizing?" Justain closed the book. "Those tales of conquest aren't fit for feminine ears."

"Then tell me a story that is fitting about Richard."

He rubbed the piping of his lapel. "We used to play knights of the realm. I was his armour bearer. Richard and I trailed the woods of Devonshire almost every day when we were children, looking for kingdoms to conquer. I remember him keeping me upright on Zeus, his chestnut Exmoor, whose coat was as thick as a beaver's. It took forever for my feet to grow into the stirrups."

Justain fussed with his thick sleeve. "That pony moved like the wind. I still remember the day I finally held the reins myself. Mason hung my saddle next to Richard's that evening." His voice radiated.

He must've loved his brother.

"The old man was so pleased." His voice soured. "My father gave me a filly to ride. My Athena."

"Somehow, you, coaxing a female about Devonshire seems fitting."

Justain chuckled. "Richard and I were inseparable. I was his faithful servant. There was freedom racing betwixt the tors, skirting the tree line, looking to vanquish the enemy." His hands tightened on the ends of his sash as if they were upon his horse. "The scent of lilacs and heather was strong; it hung in the breeze."

The intensity of his feelings for Richard and Devon seemed to match the apathy he held for his own father. She wanted to ask, but stayed with tidbits he offered. "You were close to Richard."

"One does begin to rely on someone heavily who's always there to mop up the broken pieces. We shared a passion for the outdoors. He'd miss all types of appointments to take another ride about Trenchard's grounds and the craggy vistas of the moors. Richard loved the change of seasons. For a few days in the fall, the great house is framed with orange-red leaves. The green hills are endless with colour."

Justain was ebullient. The love of his home etched in his smiling countenance. She wanted to think of Avington like that but couldn't. Her home hadn't seemed that wonderful for many years.

He pulled out a timepiece from his pocket. "It's getting late." He stood and stretched. His long arms almost hit the ceiling.

"You're at ease telling stories. If my father talked more, I'm sure his spirit wouldn't be burdened. He'd deal better with his pain." She bit her lip. She shouldn't have revealed that.

"Always making observations. I like your naiv—conclusions." His eyes were kind, though she could fill in the shortened word, *naivety*.

She patted the bed for Justain to sit next to her. "I don't suppose I could coax you into another tale, my good sir."

"Another time. I'll tell you about going hunting with Devlin and Richard."

"A minister with a gun?" Madeline yawned. "That's hard to picture."

"Oh, lass. He's the best Delveaux by far. He split a viper between the eyes at sixty paces." Justain put back the walnut chair and approached the bed.

His gaze fell upon her. It felt warm as if the sharing of confidences began a bond. She should be more honest with him. She sucked in a breath. "Justain."

A solid knock pounded along the door. "Lord Devonshire, a post has come for you." Mr. Winton's voice held an urgent tenor.

The lazy smile upon Justain's face disappeared. "I'll join you in a moment, Mr. Winton." Justain leaned over her and kissed her forehead. "I've more tales. The sordid details of a few of my scouting expeditions for Lord Wellesley, the Marquis, now Duke of Wellington. They'll curl your toes. But not tonight. My wife needs to sleep."

He straightened and marched out the door as if he were soldiering to battle. Something brewed.

She pulled her hands in prayer. "Abba Father, let the work You've begun in our lives continue to grow. Reveal to me the obstacles which burden our path." A sour taste swirled in her stomach as she lay against her pillows. Not all answers to her prayers coated the tongue.

18

Shadows from a flock of geese scampered overhead covering their picnic blanket. The calls of the birds filled the air, blocking all earth-bound noise. It didn't matter, for at this moment, Madeline couldn't speak.

Justain leaned in close. His fingers swept along her chin. He raised her head so their gazes tangled. His lips brushed hers for an instance, but he moved to her brow. "You'll be all right as I exercise?" His words vibrated her lobe, spread a tingle down her spine.

She nodded and waved him off. As he moved, she instantly missed the scent of him, the warmth his breath falling on her skin.

Justain leapt upon his beautiful onyx horse and raced the fertile grounds. With skies now clear, the lowered sun seemed only a few miles away. Hopefully, Justain and his steed wouldn't give chase. She rather liked having him underfoot even if his attentiveness was disconcerting.

She brushed crumbs off her muslin skirts and took care near her throbbing leg. It hurt from her ankle to her shin, but to walk under her own weight exceeded the pain. With her crutch in one hand and Justain's support, they'd taken a turn about the floral beds. Mint and sage scented the landscape. It was extraordinary.

She stretched out on the thick tartan blanket.

Justain whipped past. He jaunted close to the ever-faithful Mr. Winton, a few trees away. He had his steward watch over her as Justain jumped the hedges. The earnest man shuffled through letters and envelopes. He appeared relaxed though a rifle leaned next to his boot.

More mysterious papers.

She'd pressed Justain to disclose the nature of his posts, but he changed the subject to sculpture.

Why wouldn't he confide in her? And why did it hurt so much when he didn't? Something was clearly wrong with her thinking.

Madeline munched on a grape and sipped tart lemonade. Young Mr. Winton was an amiable man. His red hair and freckles should denote a temper, but he always appeared calm. His placid nature seemed to have a steadying influence over Justain. He was their timekeeper, marshalling the couple from stop to stop. It was wrong to be envious of Winton's ability to discuss anything with Justain, but yet she was. She stroked her forehead. When had she become so irrational?

Her gaze returned to the broad shoulders of her husband. He held his seat so firm, he could've been in regimentals. Justain and his mount moved as one, graceful and masculine. They flew across the field. Justain's long legs blended into the saddle, symbolizing their union.

They approached Madeline's right and jumped a low gate. The pleasure of it rippled across his face. The perfect statue appeared human, caught in bliss, different from the measured tones he showed her. She put a hand to her stomach. Now she envied a horse?

The unguarded man of the Queen's Inn was gone,

and this new manifestation seemed to take pleasure in stirring up restless discontent. The man found a reason to have his arms about her and kiss her forehead countless times a day. Aunt Tiffany touted the wonders of having a husband's favour. This didn't feel wonderful.

She rooted in the picnic basket for a napkin and found a folded piece of parchment with her name. It was written in Justain's hand. It was the third one in four days. The paper captured one of Donne's meditations:

No man is an island, entire of itself; every man is a piece of the continent, a part of the main. If a clod be washed away by the sea, Europe is the less, as well as if a promontory were, as well as if a manor of thy friend's or of thine own were.

Her heartbeat quickened. Was he admitting to needing her?

Justain leapt from his saddle and handed the horse off to Mr. Winton. "You can leave us now."

A knowing nod passed between the men as the steward left. Justain and Madeline were utterly alone in this garden paradise.

"You found my note." He paced toward her in his immaculate bottle-green tailcoat and knelt onto the blanket. "You are a patient angel." He bussed her forehead. It should bear some permanent mark by now.

Justain smirked and dove into the basket but kept his gaze toward his disappearing steward. Then he turned to her. His smile could rival the brightest celestial star. "You're glowing."

She rushed her hands to her cheeks. How could she not with her personal sun so near?

"I take it you enjoyed this lyric." His thumb brushed the silver buttons of her sleeve.

Slipping from her fingers, the parchment fluttered to the ground.

Justain claimed her wrist and pressed it to his lips. "You needn't be embarrassed. It's normal for a man to show affection as he courts a beauty."

"You're courting me?"

He lay against the blanket, dangling a bunch of grapes above his mouth. "I know you haven't had a season, but when a man is taken with a woman, he courts her in both words and deeds."

"I've seen the words," she replied. "Donne's are lovely. And your deeds like this picnic are nice. I'm glad we finished journeying early enough to enjoy these grounds."

He smiled at her with a wicked grin. "I've only begun."

Could her face melt from the heat of his promise? Molten energy existed beneath his smooth countenance. Madeline was sure of it, but how to release it? She picked up a fan and moved some air about her. "With Mr. Winton gone, how shall you protect us from the crickets and birds of the field?"

"I'm sure my brute strength should suffice." He lifted her with the ease of a feather and stashed her close to his hip.

"I see," she said, "but what of the bears that hide in the hedges?"

"The knife in my boot or the blunderbuss pistol in my coat pocket will solve all problems." Justain's tone became serious. He took a short pistol from his coat and placed it in the picnic basket. "I shall protect you."

Madeline straightened his cravat. Her fingers

shook.

He moved her hands. "That tickles."

She smiled at him. "Achilles's vulnerability?"

"Don't start something, Madeline. You don't know how I'll finish it." He traced a line down her ribcage that almost made her jump from his arms.

"What happens in this courtship?" She swatted more air with the peacock printed fan.

He held a purple orb for her to bite. "You'll come to admire me. Begin anticipating what will come next."

She shook her head, refusing the fruit, too enthralled to eat. "I already admire you."

He tossed the grape between his perfect teeth before propping up on an elbow. "Then come close to me."

She leaned into him. "As you command."

"Oh, no. I don't take unwanted liberties. Kiss me, Madeline."

She touched his face, copying what he'd done so many times.

He looped his fingers with hers. "Like you did in the carriage. That memory hasn't left me."

Something stirred within Madeline. She wanted to be held in Justain's arms. Maybe it was the key to him being unguarded. She kissed him.

❧

Her soft tongue grazed his cheek. Justain wasted no time in enfolding her in his embrace. He'd been tempting her this past week, finding ways to hold her hand during their isolated travels. He'd stroke her hair for no reason.

Madeline's lips slipped to his neck.

He groaned and lifted her head. "What is it that you want of me, Madeline? I'm your humble servant."

She smoothed the crush of her fuchsia gown. "Everything, but you'll only give this much." Madeline motioned with her fingers an inch.

He patted her hand down to the blanket. "You don't think that you'll win everything or that I'm not capable of giving more?"

"It's getting late. We should settle in for the evening." She started searching for her crutch.

He sat up and pushed the staff from her reach. "Answer my question."

"You hide me notes that speak of unveiled emotions. That's not you. You're restrained, even in the way you kiss me." Madeline set the dishes back into their basket. "I believe you'll always hide parts of yourself from me. You don't trust me enough."

"Trust?" He shook his head. "My sending you notes has nothing to do with trust."

"You're right." Madeline put a final plate away. "Your heart has too many defences. My knight bears too much armour."

"Well, a man needs to know when his attention is wanted. You should speak of your desires."

"Why, for you to kiss me on the forehead? Pat my head like a good girl." She tossed a mug into the basket. It clanged as it banged against the other dishes. "Sorry. I guess I hoped there was more to it. The poets make a kiss sound grand."

Excellent. Madeline felt frustrated. Justain untied the ribbons of her bonnet and tossed the hat to the blanket. "I've never thoroughly kissed you, Madeline."

The heart-shaped face studied him. She narrowed her eyes. "Thoroughly?"

His words must have puzzled her, but if he was to do this now it must be right. "May I?"

Madeline nodded her consent.

He flicked away the pins from her chignon to free the bundled tresses. Then, gripping her shoulders, he drew her back into his arms and nibbled the edge of her jaw. "The poets don't lie." His lips covered hers. Tasting and nipping, he found his reward, the moist temptation of her deepest kiss.

Trailing his fingers down her back to encourage her, he felt her tremble. Should he relent?

Her flailing hands settled on the space between his shoulders. She tightened her grip and pressed further into his embrace. Madeline sought his mouth with urgency, matching his intensity.

Justain pulled her to his chest as he sank against the heavy wool.

She touched his face and smoothed away wisps of her hair drizzling down his cheek, then reclaimed his lips.

His thoughts spun. Strawberry fragrance swirled around him. Justain hadn't expected Madeline to be this warm, this inviting. Who was being seduced?

This was too public a place to conceive a Delveaux heir, but would her exploring mood last if he moved them indoors? "Madeline, we should go in before it gets dark."

"Not yet." Her thumbs twisted in the tails of his cravat, yanking it asunder. She lingered about his Adam's apple before returning to his mouth.

The measured pacing of their romance erupted in flames. She was kindling wood, and her warmth blazed his skin.

He wrapped his arms about her tightly. "Shall *we*

retire for the evening?"

She abruptly pulled back. Her large eyes seemed filled with questions. No, she wasn't quite ready to surrender.

He released her, sat up, and closed the basket. "We have a long ride tomorrow. I suppose I should get you settled into your room?"

"Yes, I think that's best."

19

The carriage swayed about the bend in the path. They were getting closer to Hampshire. His opportunities to seduce Madeline were becoming fewer. Clearly, she was partial to him, but something kept her distant. Was there someone else? Or worse, did this duke's daughter think him unworthy? Had his courtship somehow proved him unworthy or ill-suited for her hand? He adjusted his cravat. Where were these insecurities arising?

Justain leaned closer, posting very close to Madeline's tender lips. "Did I mention how beautiful you look today?" The buttercream walking gown made her jade eyes resplendent.

"You did." She looked at the floor then held his gaze. "I think we should discuss my parents."

He studied the lift of her chin and her succulent pouting mouth. "You don't think I'll measure up to your parents' expectations?"

Her eyes opened wide. "Is that it? You didn't measure up? Did your first love not want to risk her heart for you?"

"What does—" He hadn't thought of Caroline in a while. Justain turned to look out the blasted window.

"I've a theory." She tugged on his sleeve. "I believe all men become difficult because of a woman. Particularly, if they've been spurned."

"What would you know of this? I've never met a more sheltered lass in all my days. Was it some wretched poet's sonnet that has led you to this? A marble etching? Some text out of Psalms, perhaps?"

She reached for his hand again. "I've seen it; a mild and gentle soul turned beastly from rejection. And my father, who never raised his voice, now bellows. His marriage to my step-mother has soured him. And by your reaction, I guess I'm right." Her soft fingers tried to weave between his.

Justain relaxed and allowed the comfort. "Well, I don't bellow and try hard not to be beastly. Let's abandon this talk. It's your turn to tell a tale, something scandalous, please."

She wound her fingers deeper into his palm. "Why wouldn't your first love think someone so brave and charitable worthy? Providence has made you worthy."

Why couldn't Madeline be a normal woman? He cleared his throat. "Must you bring God into this? You don't have to come up with another harlot tale. I'd settle for the one with the water and the wine."

"You haven't told me of your beliefs. You do have faith?"

"Did Devlin put you up to this?" He released a tight breath. "I believe in God and creation, but I don't have the close relationship I should. How do I put this? I've enjoyed my bachelorhood, and my pew has grown cold from a lack of worship attendance. I've other priorities." Justain pursed his lips. Was the wall between them religious? Is that why this slip of a girl judged him?

Everything made sense to Madeline. Some woman had abused Justain's heart, and he had no relationship with God to repair it. How could she help Justain feel God's acceptance? "Unclear priorities lead to confusion, but a sense of self-worth comes from Providence's love."

He pulled away and folded his arms. "Madeline, is Avington Manor a monastery? Do monks run about the lawns tolling the bells of the chapel."

"No. But the bells of St. Mary's do ring for births and wakes. How did you know?"

"I study architecture. I'm prepared to see the marble and gold." Justain rubbed the base of his neck. "My choices are my choices. It's too late to change now. Don't indict me until you've tasted the spoils of living."

"I may not have lived, as you would call it, but I have seen enough to know that spoils do not make a life complete. Knowing that Providence surrounds me with true care and compassion makes my life worthwhile even when things go horribly wrong." She stroked the length of his sleeve. "I don't want to invite your rancour, but as your helpmate, I need to let you know that you haven't fallen too far to receive grace."

He shook his head. A thick lock of sable fluttered down his crinkled forehead. "I've spent many years in the world, and I've not been a choirboy or a monk."

She stretched and brushed the hair back into place. "But even a harlot can be redeemed if there is faith."

Justain leaned back upon the seat and closed his eyes. "This harlot is going to take a short nap. Wake me when we reach Exeter."

So this was his way of dealing with things. This past week, Justain's romantic overtures had turned her bones to butter, and she'd melted in his arms more than once, but passion solved nothing. If they couldn't find a true foundation, she would end up alone and heartbroken. *Abba Father, what do I do now?*

❧

Noisy patrons surrounded them. Justain set his glass on the wobbly oak table.

Madeline focused on her pewter plate, not looking up at him at all.

He hadn't done anything wrong, but a well-placed apology would dispel the tension that now existed between them. The crowded, whitewashed inn wasn't romantic, but the rooms upstairs would do nicely. There had to be a way to salvage the evening.

He'd swept others off their feet. Why was this one difficult? Maybe he should give up and focus upon his visit with Madeline's father, the Duke of Hampshire. She seemed concerned about it. Was there something he didn't know?

She brushed a tendril of glorious raven hair back into place behind her tiny lobe.

Right now, it didn't matter that Madeline was the most understanding woman he'd ever met. Or that she genuinely cared for him. How could he fix the air between them?

His wife's graceful fingers wrapped about her teaspoon.

A wave of laughter rumbled to his left. The stateroom felt oppressive, packed to the brim with noisy travellers. He'd have to strain to hear Madeline. That is, if she said anything. Time to make amends. He sucked in a short breath. "I'm sorry if I was short with you in the carriage."

"No, it's I who should apologize. I'm pushy like my father." The heart-shaped countenance didn't appear to be surrendering to his way of thinking, but if it led to Madeline throwing her arms about his neck, he'd accept her paltry offering.

Justain cleared his throat. "You're handling the crutch well."

Her face lit with a smile. "I nearly fell three times. It was good that you were close by to steady me."

"I'm used to having you in my arms. You'll have to allow me time to accept your independence."

She laughed. Her eyes brightened.

He pushed his plate of beefsteaks out of the way. "I know I have a difficult nature. Mayhap, it takes a woman like you to change me."

"I don't want to change you. I like you very well as you are."

Sentiment. She was partial to it. A word or two of mush wouldn't kill him. "It's been a long time since anyone's actually cared enough to want to help me. I've grown up a second son, the one that's expendable."

"That's horrible." Madeline dabbed at his cravat with a napkin. "You've a spot of gravy." Her fingers trailed his throat, maybe by accident, maybe not.

His breathing quickened all the same. Justain moved her hands. If they weren't in public, he'd nibble his way to her pulse. "Had my father known how things would turn, I'm sure things would've been different. No harm done."

His dribbling of emotion seemed to work. She sighed at him but didn't have a pitying look about her.

Someone tapped his shoulder. Winton. He hadn't

heard him approach.

"My lord," Jonathan interrupted. His face was tight with exigency.

"Won't this keep until later?" Justain kept his countenance smooth, not wanting to alarm Madeline.

"This needs your attention immediately." His steward's voice shook. Whatever the news, Jonathan Winton, his rock of Gibraltar, had broken.

"What is it?" Justain braced for the evil.

Jonathan whispered in his ear.

20

For one second, Madeline feared the worst, that her father had passed or even Justain's beloved cousin had experienced an accident, but she didn't feel that in her spirit.

Justain pounded the table then stopped and eased his fist to his lap. Something dark had occurred. "Place guards there at all hours. I don't care how much the caregivers protest. This is too important."

"I've prepared this message for your signature." Mr. Winton pushed thick paper in front of Justain and motioned for a servant to bring warmed wax.

"Always thinking ahead, my friend." Justain tried to make his voice sound normal, but anger steamed from his flared nostrils. After signing it, he gave the paper to his steward.

"A page is ready to take this back to Dorset straight away." Mr. Winton turned to Madeline. "Good evening, ma'am."

"Good evening." Madeline's nerves tingled. She stilled her shaking fingers.

The steward bowed and made his way past the crowded tables.

"What's happened? Pray tell me. Please spare no details, Justain."

"Lower your voice, Madeline. Some matters of the estate. Nothing to concern you."

"My husband is vexed almost to the point of punching through the table, and I'm not to be alarmed."

He scanned from side to side as if their conversation drew onlookers. "You shouldn't be troubled. Let me escort you to your room."

"Justain, tell me."

"Please, let's not discuss this here." He adjusted his cravat. "Finish your tea."

She leaned closer. "Is that an order?

Justain didn't answer, seemed to stare through her. He yanked her from the seat and carried her through the swarm of people out of the stateroom. "Mr. Winton will retrieve your crutch."

Madeline clutched at his shoulder. She could bear it no longer. "Justain, I demand to know what has happened!" Heads whipped around. The din silenced for a second. The muscles in Justain's arms tensed beneath her fingers.

He marched faster, fleeing the stateroom and started up the steps. The treads shook with his pounding footsteps. "Demand! Demand, madam? I ask little of you but propriety."

A hall maid tried to get out of his path. Justain motioned for her to open the door to a bedroom. If the servant hadn't been there, he might've kicked it in.

Justain sat Madeline at the vanity and trudged back to the threshold.

"Please, Justain. I must know what new trouble has arisen."

He slammed the door shut. "Someone has set my orphanage ablaze. The caretakers put the fire out, but..." The look in his eyes hardened.

"But what?" Madeline shivered. Those poor

children witnessed flames.

"The smoke..." He turned to the window. "The smoke has claimed one boy."

Madeline choked up but refused to cry. She needed to show her husband that his mate was a capable partner. "God have mercy on his soul."

"God! What does G-God have to do with this? I failed in my mis-mission to protect them. I underestimated Bar-Barrow's influence." He bit his lip, slipped his balled fist into his jacket. "This is my fault. I'm grieved to the depths of my soul."

"How's this your fault? Did you order the blaze?" Madeline would defend Justain to the ends of the earth.

"Of course not, but unless I'm perfect in my actions, something goes wrong." He ran his fingers through his hair. "Please, I've told you what has happened. Now be silent on the matter."

As much as she wanted to respect his authority, she needed to reassure him, model God's love and understanding. "What else could you have done? From what I know of you, the place must be fastidious, run in the most disciplined manner."

"Obviously not. I should've had guards on duty at all times. At the first signs of trouble I set them on Trenchard a week ago. I didn't think Barrow would touch the children."

"You were making a home, not a prison. Some things are impossible to predict."

"No, Madeline, I should've known. When I try to reform my life, put things in order, something goes awry. I never get to choose. The old man drags me from the military just when I began to distinguish myself. Richard drags me into solving his debts to save the family. Now, I'm dragged into marriage to a sentimental missionary who'd rather sermonize than obey a simple instruction."

His words drove a spike into the pit of her stomach. She took a slow breath hoping to chill the fire brewing within her abdomen. "I thought we started to find a common path."

Justain leaned against the bedpost, then adjusted his cravat. The starched thing could be a truth detector. He'd been pretending?

Her dreams threatened to drizzle from her eyes. She drummed her forehead. "I'm so naive. You said you didn't take unwanted liberties."

"Oh, don't give me those sad pouts. You're a beautiful woman—"

"And you're biding your time." She squeezed air into her lungs to muffle a sniffle. He mustn't think she was both naive and weak.

"You know this marriage wasn't part of either of our plans, but I'm trying to enjoy this purgatory."

"I didn't know this was hard for you." Her pitch sounded frostbitten, similar to the duchess's. Her step-mother knew how to sound both as a victim and as if she'd stabbed someone at any moment. Madeline stilled her quaking knees. When would she learn? Whatever she cared for never lasted. Even the illusions disappeared. "Sorry to be a bother."

"I'm used to disappointments." His fingers splayed over his mouth as if in regret. He cleared his throat. "I'm able to do well at running the family estates, and a tenant that I allowed to farm uses the property for child slavery. I set up orphanages to care for the affected children, and I end up putting them at risk again. Something always goes wrong. I spend my life waiting for the next accident."

God wouldn't leave him in despair. And he'd never seek repentance if Madeline returned evil for evil. She rubbed her eye, obliterating a renegade tear. "You don't know what's in a man's heart. You had no way of knowing Barrow's true character. More so, you don't know whether he's behind this fire."

"I feel that he is. Right now, I'll agree with my gut. It's my only consistent measure. Are we done?"

Part of her wanted to comfort him. The other half wanted to throw objects at him. She flattened her palm on the freshly waxed vanity away from a heavy glass candlestick holder. "This world is dark without God's light, and unexpected things always happen. God has set you apart, but He'll never give you more than you're able to bear."

"That's no consolation. It doesn't explain why the victims suffered again. It doesn't explain why the child..." He shook his head. "You and Devlin with your Bible pounding. You should've married someone who shares your beliefs." He stormed out of the room. The oak threshold shook from his exodus.

Madeline looked at her wan reflection in the mirror. She should've thrown the holder.

~

Justain stomped across the landing. He shouldn't have slammed the door, but the blasted woman sat there, judging him, chatting him up about Providence. He fumbled for his key. His finger traced the bow of the metal.

The image of Madeline's proud chin lowering as she swallowed his bitter diatribe wouldn't leave his head. "I'm just like the old man." He blinked and pounded his skull. The lass attempted to help, and he repaid her kindness with his foul temper. Just like the old man. Was it possible to hate himself even more than normal?

Someone tapped his shoulder. Justain whirled around ready to strike.

"Sir?" Jonathan Winton stood near. "The letter has been dispatched. Are you all right, my lord?"

"Fine."

Jonathan held Madeline's crutch.

"My wife needs that." She'd want to regain her independence. Even faster after this night.

Jonathan walked past him and unlocked Justain's room. "I suppose you require your nightcap, but maybe not. You've stopped these past weeks…avoided."

Brandy would temporarily drown away the mess he'd made of his marriage. Justain sucked in a low breath. "Madeline wouldn't…We'll be at Hampshire tomorrow. I won't be indulgent. Her knight. I shouldn't be presented impaired."

Jonathan's copper eyes smiled. "No, it wouldn't be right."

"Go see about my wife. I wasn't generous with her."

"Get some rest." Jonathan slogged away.

Perhaps, his steward, his friend, could intercede.

❧

A sharp knock upon her door startled Madeline.

"Ma'am, may I enter?" It was Mr. Winton's voice.

She sat up and smoothed the tears from her face.

"Come in."

"The master asked me to deliver this to you." He stretched to put the crutch close to the vanity. "Lady Devonshire, may I speak?"

How odd to hear her title.

"Yes." She waved him closer.

The steward, clad in a simple black jacket, edged forward. "Don't let the master's dark moods upset you, ma'am." The round face and freckled cheeks seemed earnest.

Madeline took off her wedding band. It rattled along the vanity top. She wasn't about to discuss her marital situation with her husband's steward. "Was there anything else?"

The young man lowered his head. It seemed as if he studied the lacings of his boot. "My lord stopped drinking."

"I don't understand, Mr. Winton."

"He stopped because of you. I know the master well. Nothing but trying to please you, to be the person you see him as, has made the difference."

"Because of me?"

The young man came closer. "I thought you should know."

She handed him the collection of Donne's poems. The broken book spoke of dreams. She wouldn't be fooled into wanting them again. She wouldn't be fooled into wanting Justain again. "Is there anything more he told you to say?"

Mr. Winton rubbed his forehead. "My lord didn't send any message."

"Thank you, Mr. Winton. Please send up a maid to help me?"

"I will." He bowed and started to the door.

"Sir," she said, "wanting Lord Devonshire's best isn't enough."

"It's the beginning. It gives Providence something to work with. Good evening, ma'am." Mr. Winton closed the door behind him.

Madeline stared at the silvered mirror glass. Did the girl—no. Did the woman looking back have the strength to do God's handiwork?

21

Justain hated the silent treatment. Give him the threat of bullets, the sound of cannons, but not total isolation. He'd become accustomed to the winsome understanding in Madeline's voice. It was mean of her to deprive him of it.

She rested on the dark leather seats bundled in a bewitching fuchsia gown. The pelisse hugged her neck with violet frill. She looked like a flower. The woman should scream at him for yesterday's argument. He deserved it. Then this silence would be over. They'd get back to the comfortable path they'd been forging.

But Madeline uttered not a peep, not a jot.

He'd practiced an apology and searched for an opportunity, but Madeline didn't join him for breakfast. She barely murmured good morning when he came to fetch her for the journey. Justain fumbled with his cuff. A fresh entry in his ledger smudged the linen. Could things get worse? To be presented with spots on his clothes and blemishes to his character.

He attempted to stuff the book back into his satchel. It caught on something. Justain rooted in the bag and found the tattered collection of poems.

Madeline was done with it and him, too. She had to have given it to Mr. Winton last night. "We're getting close to Avington Manor."

She nodded.

He turned to the window. Fortified walls of stone and mortar hung overhead. How much rock had he dropped upon his marriage? Justain reached for her hand and pried it from her folded arms. "You're not wearing your ring?"

"I'll put it back on at Hampshire."

"Please put it back on now, Madeline."

She dug into her reticule and unpacked her band. After a quick tugging off of her butter-coloured glove, Madeline slid the ring onto her slim finger.

"Good." He rubbed his chin. "We're not going to meet your father without a civil word between us?"

She leaned against the seat. "Couples at cross purposes are the monastery's forte."

He adjusted his cravat. "We shouldn't quarrel in front of the duke. He mustn't think you're unhappy."

Madeline looked away. "Father's perceptive."

"Will you let me apologize?"

"For speaking the truth?" She shook her head. "Avington is large. We won't have to see much of each other. Then let's leave in a week."

"One fight and you give up. I'm disappointed. What of all that talk of us being on one accord? One disagreement throws your knight from his horse."

"Still a knight, just not my knight." She sat up straight and pushed an errant tendril under her floppy bonnet. Why didn't her grand aunt burn the thing? Yet, the hat had survived near trampling at Tilford, the Severn Gorge, and being crushed at a picnic. More things needed to be as resilient.

"The Duke and Duchess of Hampshire are a curious lot." Her sweet voice held an edge. "Sometimes they stand upon formality. Sometimes not. One never knows what will happen."

Justain wanted to reach for her hand but didn't think it wise. "Let me tell you another story to make amends."

If Madeline's eyes were daggers, she'd be a widow.

"I suppose you won't show me your hall of Hampshire sculptures."

Her lovely jade eyes clouded, and she looked away.

He balled up his leather evening gloves. "Pray let's start over."

She gazed at her dainty slippers. "Why? Are you afraid to disappoint my father?"

Now that strike hit close to home. "I like to pass tests. That's what my father impressed upon me." Justain swallowed a deep breath. "What will it take to restore your opinion?"

She stuck her chin in the air. "To get this visit over as soon as possible."

Justain peered through the window. "The leaves are starting to turn. I hope the good folks of this county take the time to admire the colours. The hillside's striated in three shades of red. This is stunning country, not the moors of Devon, but beautiful."

"Why are you tormenting me with a place I'll never see?" She released a heavy sigh. "The tree roots cling to different sections of the steep ridge adding to the variety. Watch the sunset." She pointed to the clouds. "Sometimes the sky tries to match the hues of autumn."

Perhaps as the sun came closer to earth, it'd thaw the frost between them. "Magnificent," he said. It was simply beautiful. "God's paintbrush, I think you called it."

"Father and I used to watch the sunset from his study. We're arriving late." Her voice softened, and she smoothed her skirt over her knees. "He'll be in bed."

"He's going to be fine." He covered her hands with his. Justain made his hold light to allow Madeline the opportunity to snatch her fingers away.

She didn't. "Father's rugged but overly dramatic. It's a cold or a ragged nerve." She eased to the window. "This was the first time he's been able to spare me to leave Avington."

"Pray, let us start over. I don't want to…Madeline."

She stared out the window.

"Madeline?"

"Yes." Her eyes blinked as if awakening from a daydream. Probably designing how the duke should torture him.

"I've called to you twice. Are you ignoring me?"

"It's not possible to ignore you." She sat up straight.

The carriage stopped. They'd arrived at the St. James's estate.

Justain popped on his top hat and jumped out of the carriage. He hoped to catch the last measure of sun to warm his cold feet. Madeline wasn't going to be charitable. Justain would be on his own to impress the duke.

It had been less than twenty-four hours since his foul eruption. It seemed like days. Not having Madeline's jade eyes smiling at him took a toll on Justain, more than he wanted to admit.

Three marble statues stood atop the opulent entrance overseeing their arrival. "The beasts don't seem happy."

A sense of foreboding pricked his gut. Meeting his father in-law, the grand Duke of Hampshire, made him nervous, not the fear he'd ruined something special. Justain turned the ring of his lineage to point to the darkening sky and declared to himself, "The Earl of Devon will win over his father-in-law and wife."

He yanked on his blasted leather gloves then reached back into the cabin. "Shall we, my dear?" Justain hefted Madeline from the seat. "It would've been good for your parents to see us arrive in my original Berlin. It would've made a good show."

"Father has three coaches, plus a barouche. Well, he had three. You weren't able to find our carriage while I convalesced at Much Wenlock?"

"No. I'm sure something as opulent as a chestnut coach will turn up. My people haven't stopped looking." He carried her up the wide stone stairs of the large white portico, the façade of the house. "I'm giving you notice, Lady Devonshire. I intend to restore your good opinion."

She pulled close to his ear. "Welcome to Avington Manor, the ancestral home of the St. James family." The words tingled against his lobe.

Changing a woman's mind should've been his profession. Justain would restore the peace of their garden picnic. The lush grounds and the sunsets of Avington Manor were meant for romance. Their romance.

A groomsman brought her stave as Justain lowered Madeline to the pristine marble floor. The cranberry veining of the tiles highlighted cream washed walls.

Powdered-haired servants in sapphire coats and

stockings descended upon them demanding their outerwear. Justain complied and seized the opportunity to remove Madeline's gloves. He held her warm palm against his.

He looked up to the ceiling.

Muses must've painted it. It bore an angelic theme. Golden trim and filigree abounded. It was magnificent, making Trenchard Park seem small. "This is quite a house, Madeline."

She nodded. Her cheeks held a tiny bloom of colour.

A smile blossomed in his spirit, and he laced his fingers with hers. She wasn't immune to him.

A fair-haired woman descended the carpeted stairs in a long, flouncing, black dress with shiny jewelled buttons.

As he waited to be announced, Madeline slogged forward. "Step-mother, how's Father?"

The stylish but austere figure didn't answer and continued winding down the rust padded treads. The woman's gold tresses were pulled back tightly in a chignon, the same style as Madeline's before her aunt's tweaks. The style wasn't becoming on her.

"Step-mother, is Father better?"

The woman stopped on the landing. "Wretched girl, he's sleeping. You'll be able to see him in the morning. I don't wish him disturbed right now."

"Duchess, we've ridden a long way." Justain caught Madeline's arm. "It will ease my wife's mind to see her father."

The lady stumbled as if shocked by his words. She straightened and redoubled her efforts to descend. "Wife? And who might you be?"

"I am the Earl of Devon, Madeline's husband."

Justain's gait was slow and deliberate, so the duchess could sense his nobility. He bowed as she came close. The woman inspected him with her nose upturned. Another overly important mama of the ton.

"You've married? Eloped without telling anyone?"

Justain blocked the duchess's advance toward Madeline. He wouldn't let the woman harass his wife, no matter who she was. "We wed with the duke's permission."

Suddenly, the duchess's facial expressions honeyed. A smile graced her face.

"Darling girl, I was taken aback by the news. Your father and his mysterious stationery…he told me of your accident."

"That's because I wanted you to be surprised." A haggard voice bellowed over the crowd. An old man supported by an older gentleman entered the fray.

"Father!" Madeline limped to the duke and hugged his neck.

Charles St. James, a tall, stout man with a full head of grey hair bundled Madeline in his embrace. "My Maddie is home."

"I've missed you, Father."

With his arms still about her, the duke pivoted to an idle servant. "Fetch me a seat!"

Two panicky groomsmen returned, bearing a gilded chair. They situated it in the middle of the hall. The servants must've studied the stone busts appointing the entrances to each hall, for they showed no emotion to this distasteful scene.

"Meriwether, help me sit." The duke's weak voice still caused everyone to jump to attention. At full strength, the man must be impervious.

"You should rest, dear. Make your valet take you

back to bed." Madeline's step-mother grimaced at the sick man. Her lips twisted in open disgust. No, she was worse than matrons of Devonshire. Those women twittered behind his mother's back, not out in the open. The duchess smoothed her puffy sleeves. "I'll greet Madeline and this ne'er-do-well."

"You won't be pawning off a St. James to one of your measly relations." The duke sneered at his wife in victory. "She has married the Earl of Dorset."

"Earl of Devon." Justain extended his hand to the man.

The duke hunched his shoulders and drew back with a smirk. "One backward county is as good as another."

Justain retrieved his ignored palm. He wanted to fan air about his neck to relieve the heat rising from his collar but lowered his arms to his sides.

"I've just been informed of Madeline's elopement. I suppose it makes no difference that I'm the last to know. I have missed the opportunity to be of counsel to her in this important decision."

"Yes, Lady Hampshire, I'll be the only one foolish enough to listen to you about marriage." He laughed and smiled at his daughter. "Don't we look the pair? You on a crutch, me as weak as a newborn kitten." He glanced at Justain. "Devonshire, you've kept her safe." His hazel eyes blazed with a fiery intensity. Wasn't he grateful?

"She's my wife. I'll always keep her safe." He secured Madeline's crutch then gripped her fingers.

"No one cares how improper it is to be greeting people in the hall." The duchess's nose and cheeks brightened to beet red. "What are the servants to think?"

"That's your remedy for everything." Lord St. James shivered. "It's time for my medicine, Meriwether."

The valet nodded to a hesitant maid lurking in the hall.

"Dana, embrace our new son-in-law. He wrote me of his besotted love for my Maddie. I couldn't refuse."

How should he react? Justain sought Madeline's gaze, hoping for a signal. She didn't notice him. She viewed the floor tiles as if she were hoping for a crack to open and swallow everyone whole. At this moment, he wished the same.

❧

Madeline pushed into the shadow of the duke. As her father continued his diatribe, she raised her gaze to the mahogany stairs and waited to see if anyone else would descend and join the chaos.

"You coward! Didn't dare to ask my opinion?" her step-mother wailed.

"Why? To wallow as the hog in the mud of your voice?" Father's baritone words sounded tired. He seemed weaker than she'd ever known.

Their backbiting could awaken the dead, but no one sank upon the carpeted stairway. Madeline started to exhale, but she caught sight of Justain.

His brow creased. His jaw drew tight, and he gripped his wrists behind his back. They looked raw, as if Justain wrenched them for restraint. Her anger at her husband dissipated.

"My duke, you will now go to bed. You'll never get well if you continue to be boorish." Step-mother's nostrils flared. "I will stop interceding for you and leave you distressed."

"No, your leaving wouldn't distress me." Father's eyes smiled. "I should obey now before she explodes, or worse, calls the vicar down on me. Come along, Meriwether." He shuffled from the foyer with the valet's support.

"Meriwether has probably readied Madeline's room. He knows everything the duke is up to." Step-mother adjusted her heavy bracelets. "Hobble and show your besotted freebooter where it is."

When Step-mother insinuated that Justain was a pirate, he winced before recovering his face of stone.

"Step-mother, please don't disrespect my husband."

Justain squared his shoulders and stepped forward. "In a few days, my wife's lady's maid, Anne, will be arriving. She'll need quarters. Also, we are travelling with my steward and a groom."

"Overrun my house with visitors…With Mr. Kent still up north and my son away, I suppose we'll feed the lot of you."

Madeline rubbed her ear. She had heard correctly. Mr. Kent wasn't here. She'd be able to sleep without fear.

"I may have some use for this Anne in the short run with Mrs. Wilkins no longer with us." Step-mother patted a dry eye. "Sorry for your loss, Madeline. I know you two were uncommonly close. I'll inform Meriwether."

"Thank you, ma'am." What was worse false sympathy or open mocking?

"I have to commend you, Madeline. Whoever would've thought a colourless girl could land something this interesting." She circled Justain. "I mean, he does not look penniless or easily tricked. I suppose he finds your fortune too great to miss. Goodnight." With the barb hurled, she whipped out of the room.

Justain's chiselled chin dropped. His hand checked his cravat as if he needed to make sure his face wasn't on the tile.

"My room is up the stairs and to the right, but I'll request a guestroom."

"Don't utter another word." He thrust Madeline into his arms.

She gripped his neck, and her stave crashed onto the floor.

Justain charged the burnt red path, marching to her bedchamber.

22

Justain burned. He rammed open the first door atop the stairs. His shoulder throbbed from the action, but the pain couldn't match his angst, his grief. He thundered into the bedchamber.

Madeline's quivering hand stroked his cheek. "Don't let them upset you. Don't let them win," she whispered.

"I was called a ne'er-do-well, a usurper who married to secure his position with his wife's fortune." He tried to soften his stance. It wasn't her fault, and at least she didn't participate in the dressing down.

Her cheeks simmered red. She must be mortified, too.

Justain plunged her bottom first onto a flowery chaise. He tried to forget his discomfiture and focused instead upon the white moldings and pink furnishings.

He trailed his finger along the filigreed trim hugging the threshold. "I was excited about visiting Avington Manor, to enjoy the grandeur and nobility of the Duke and Duchess of Hampshire. It's even foolish to remember the address I rehearsed."

"I should've prepared you for this meeting." Madeline looked down at her slippers. "They can be harsh."

Justain paced. "Do you have any idea how hard I've worked to restore my family's fortune? I've doubled the holdings, secured our finances…worked harder than any of the other earls. Your father and I haven't discussed a dowry. You don't think I agreed to this marriage for money?"

She peered up at him. "You married me to save our honour. Oh, and to keep an inheritance."

Justain backed away from her.

Her gaze darted about his retreating countenance. "I'm not implying anything sinister. I'm stating the truth."

Justain turned and punched the wall, denting the plaster. "Is it wrong for me to attain something from our nuptials?" He shook the dust from his fist. "I wed to protect our family names, but you fail to understand my sacrifice."

"I feel your sacrifice. This wasn't my plan. I should've been reading in my aunt's sculpture garden or venturing amongst the sculptures of Italy, not burdened to a man that swims in burdens."

He pounded his fist in his palm. Flecks of gold leaf shined on his knuckles. "I'm humiliated, Madeline, and if I explain our circumstances, we'll be painted the fool."

"You're so angry. Please stop pacing."

"What? Am I frightening you?" He felt bitterness boiling his skin. "I'm given to strong emotions. Add that to my lists of faults."

"I'm not frightened by you or your self-loathing."

Justain stopped. "What did you say?"

"I'm not frightened, but a self-loathing knight isn't right." She lifted a hand to him. "My neck is stiff from looking up at you. Sit."

Justain adjusted his coat and flopped next to her. "You should be humoured. I deserve this after treating you with contempt. Go ahead with your say. Finish me off."

Madeline threw her arms about him. She pulled him close, forcing his face into her bosom.

Surprised, he pushed his hands in the air. "What is this?"

"When I'm upset, Father wraps me in his arms to soothe me. You did the same at the horrid Gorge."

"I'm not hysterical, Madeline. I'm furious, and I can't even defend myself."

She tightened her grip. His nose pushed deeper into the purple trim of her neckline. "Please don't let the antics of Avington dishearten you. Forgive them."

Justain closed his eyes.

Her embrace felt like a bucket of sand stifling the steam leaching his skin.

"Madeline," he murmured.

"Shush." She stroked his hair.

"Why aren't you more upset? Is this normal treatment?"

She sighed. "At least they didn't throw things."

If he could get to his hands, he'd wring them. Justain stopped fighting and relaxed against her. "This is an effective form of intervention. I won't try to knock a hole in your walls."

"Good. There's no need to give the staff more work. They've had to patch many of Father's. The filigree is difficult to repair." Madeline's fingers trailed the scruff of his neck. They tickled as much as soothed. "Let me request a separate bedchamber, then you'll be able to rest."

"I won't have that harpy you call your step-mother tweaking your nose over this, even if I have to play the lovesick buffoon." He placed his arms about the small of her back and inhaled the scent of her. "What have I walked in upon?"

"Avington Manor at its best, but Father didn't look well."

The last vestiges of his aggravation stripped away as the distress in her voice hit him. "He did look jaundiced. Needs some sun." He tightened his grip. "Well, the St. Jameses aren't a dull people. When we met, you said you were looking for peace. I take it there's none here."

She released him, lowering her arms to the chaise. "When my mother, Lady Angelique died, she took it with her."

"If you'd refused my offer, what would've happened?"

Madeline twisted away.

"Tell me?" Justain whispered in her ear.

"I'd be forced to wed a family friend or the duchess's nephew." Madeline wrinkled her nose in disgust.

He held her fast to keep her from shirking the truth. "Marrying an idiotic stranger is better?"

"Wedding you is better even when you're idiotic." Madeline clasped his hand against her cheek. "I can't imagine being betrothed to someone old like Edward."

"Who's Edward?"

"Edward Lawson is my step-mother's brother. He's a kind gentleman, but he lives to gain the duchess's praise. I know she'd choose someone weak like that, someone always in want of approval."

Justain released her. He tried not to tweak his cravat. He lost. "You're exaggerating, Madeline. It's in our nature to be protective and doting to the women in our lives."

"Perhaps, but there is nothing good about Mr. Kent, her nephew." Madeline trembled, causing her pelisse to flutter as wings. "There's no way to explain his abhorrent nature. He makes my flesh crawl."

"My purple butterfly." He nudged her back into his arms. "You mentioned Mr. Kent before."

"Even when you're boorish, you're better than both." She pushed to the edge. "Let me get you another room. Father didn't look well. We may have to stay longer than a week."

"You'll have the time to see him fit. I'll make camp here. And we've been shamed enough today." He put a palm to her shoulder, stroked her creamy neck. "We united to avoid scandal. Your step-mother reminds me of the high and mighty of Devon. She will pry and spread gossip."

"I've survived worse, Justain."

He tossed her bonnet to the other side of the room and brushed a strand of ebony hair behind her ear. "I'll not give her another reason to hurt you."

Shiny droplets shone in Madeline's eyes. "The loss of my mother crippled everyone. And when Father crawled out of his despair, he married Dana Kent Lawson. He hasn't had an easy day since." Justain took his handkerchief and dabbed at the stream of silent tears.

"Something in my spirit told me to discourage him, but Father seemed happy during their courtship. I didn't have the courage to speak. I could've prevented his misery."

He pulled her tormented form into his lap. "You take too much upon yourself. The duke made his decision."

She wadded the cloth into a taut ball. "I won't do

that to you. I won't make you rue the day we wed. Well, not any more than you already do."

He struggled with the strong desire to kiss away her burdens, but after his bitter words, would she let him? "Let me see what else is in stored for me this evening."

"Nothing more. We're safe in here."

He scanned the room. Thick white curtains, three gilded garniture vases on the mantelshelf of the fireplace. He'd have to be careful not to knock over those delicate porcelain pieces. He glanced up at a picture of a grand woman in a straw bonnet. "Your mother's hat?" He dashed to pick up the straw bonnet. He placed it on a tiny vanity.

Madeline nodded. "It was Lady Angelique's."

"I'm sorry."

She patted her eyes. "Well, I tossed away your wedding pearls first."

He moved back to the chaise. "I'm sorry for more than the hat."

Madeline didn't respond. She wiped her face again with his wrinkled handkerchief.

He wouldn't press her. "Lady Angelique was beautiful. You are beautiful." Justain scooted closer to her. He swept his boot across the carpet. "At least the sapphire rug in here is thick enough to support my bones." He grimaced. "It's hard to imagine growing up in this house. Trenchard was quiet, except for slammed doors. My father found other ways to show his disappointment." The scars on his side. Maybe violent words were better than violence. "Mother just cried. Even today, I can't stand a woman's tears."

Madeline leaned upon his back. "I know you detest sentiment, but regardless of how we got here, I pledge to always honour your sacrifice, my noble Earl of Devon." Her simple expression salved the rawness of his emotions. She did understand him. One fight, one explosion of words hadn't killed it.

Someone knocked upon the door.

Madeline pulled away. "Hopefully, it's my crutch." Her lips seemed so soft, so close.

"I should answer."

"Please do. I need to ready for bed."

He trudged to the door. Being trapped in Madeline's boudoir might not be a bad thing.

❧

Justain closed the door after the last of the footmen bearing their travel trunks left.

"I shall ready for bed." Madeline smiled at him, the first one she'd given him since they started today's journey. She hobbled to her dressing area.

Justain leaned against her bedroom window. Darkness covered everything, not letting a strike of light flourish. Avington Manor could be a fox at the hunt, slaughtered by any advancing rider.

"Your father doesn't have the perimeter lit." He unlocked his trunk and took out his nightshirt.

"You wouldn't see it. The grounds stretch for miles. Perhaps the maze should be lit, but if it caught, the bonfire would illuminate the world."

"A maze?" He disrobed and pulled on the cotton gown and his comfortable robe. "Let me see where I will sleep this evening. The chaise is too short. Humph. Maybe move things about."

"Take care not to disturb the household." The pounding of Madeline's crutch became apparent, right behind him.

Justain pivoted. "I won't drag—" He took his time, drinking in the sight of her.

She wore an ivory negligee, a fragile piece seemingly of another time. The lace sculpted her neck, silhouetting her long elegant frame. The thick wrapping on her leg distorted the sea of vanilla. To entice him further, Madeline had freed her hair from her bun and secured it with a ribbon. It didn't flow freely as in his dreams, but it fed his imagination.

"I've never been a fan of lace, until now. I am sorry to stare, but you're lovely."

"This is another of my mother's. Goodnight." Madeline made her way to one of the largest beds he'd seen. A dozen people could sleep within its berth. The gauzy curtains surrounding the canopied thing didn't obscure her lovely silhouette.

"I have a better idea," he said. "What if we share your boat?"

"Sleep in the same bed?"

"I know it's a radical departure, a husband to share a large bed with a small wife." Justain was a man with normal urges, but he could control himself.

Her eyes narrowed. "You'll take care not to thrash about and hurt my leg?"

Hurt was the last thing on his mind. Stroking her ebony hair and fine figure consumed every thought. If only they hadn't fought yesterday. "I don't believe I snore."

"Then come aboard."

23

The large cedar bed enfolded in woollen blankets and fine woven sheets looked more comfortable than the short pale-pink chaise. All the furnishing bore the same thick feminine paint. Justain approached from the opposite side and opened the gauzy curtains. He slid inside and moved several pillows to make a channel for himself.

Madeline tugged the smooth cloth about her.

The bed seemed a mile wide, and if he had the mindset to avoid his wife, he could. "Do you hate me, Madeline?"

"No." She doused the candle on her night table, but bright moonlight streamed into the window.

Enough light to see her tempting outline.

"Justain, do you need anything? Another pillow?"

What he would give for an offer similar to their wedding night. Yet, as much as he wanted her, something else, perhaps his heart held him in check, froze him in place. "Let's start afresh."

Madeline settled into the covers. The bed swayed with her movements.

Focus on the window, the blank canopy. "Tell me about sculpture. Whose work are you partial?"

"Goodnight, Justain."

His mind flashed between their picnic in the mint-scented garden and wanton embraces of his past. He sat up and scooted as far from her as possible.

Madeline rolled over. Her hair ribbon slackened, releasing luscious tendrils. The ebony swept across her jaw. "Are you all right?"

He shook his head. "I'll go sleep on the chaise."

"You won't be content. Be at ease." She touched his shoulder.

He caressed her fingers, before moving her hand to the mattress. "My mind is not on resting." He tugged her to him.

Madeline didn't resist. Moonbeams revealed pouty lips and a crinkled forehead.

He brushed away the lines.

"It's been a long day," she said. "Surrender to the fatigue."

"Surrender?" Justain chuckled and removed the blankets from his legs. "If I stay this close to you, I'll take you in my arms. Can't face tomorrow with you hating me."

"I'll hate you?" She thinned her smile. "Is it that awful?"

"No, Madeline, but I've seen the lights of hope die when expectations aren't met. For once in my life, I'm going to treat you, a woman, as my equal, not as a mother figure and not as a conquest. I offer you my respect and my protection."

"Then goodnight." She kissed his cheek. Madeline fluttered back down into her mound of pillows.

Justain trudged to the chaise. He didn't know where those words came from, but it felt right. But he still hoped sleep would knock him unconscious.

The staircase was steeper than Madeline remembered.

"Lady Madeline, do you need help?" Meriwether perched on the bottom step.

"I'll manage." Madeline tucked Justain's book under her arm and clung to the oak banister. She made her way down, her stave making the task awkward. "I'm becoming stronger and more capable of manoeuvring." She stopped at the final tread, winded.

The silver-haired man held out his hand. "Where do you want your breakfast?"

Madeline took his outstretched arm. "The patio."

Moving slowly through the twists of the passageways, they passed her hall of bronze and marble figures. Madeline stopped and examined her favourite hewn and cast works of art. She'd picked up a chisel and hammer once to create a figure from marble, a pony. It wasn't bad with smooth lines for its mane. Alas, Father found out and forbade it, not wanting her to risk injury.

"Do you need to rest, Lady Madeline?" The wrinkled hand on her arm felt secure and strong. Meriwether was such a dear man.

"No. Just wistful."

"Someday, my lady, you'll know true joy, and not have to stare at what others have created from stone."

She smiled at the valet. Stone lasts.

They kept on until reaching Avington's flagstone paradise, Mother's patio.

"Thank you. You always seem to be where we need you." She dropped into her chair near the large table. Justain's book fell.

Meriwether retrieved it and put it upon the polished mahogany surface. "Well, now it seems you have an earl to look after you."

Being Father's confidant gave Meriwether more authority than all the other servants could imagine.

"I'll have a service of tea brought to you." He stepped back into the house.

A breeze floated across the reddish-brown bricks of the low wall enclosing the sides of the patio. The cold morning air awoke the blood vessels in her face. The bells of St. Mary's Church rang. Was it a birth, a marriage, or a death bemoaned in the bellows?

Avington's park was lovely. Father's African violets were in full bloom in the close gardens. The breeze wafted their perfume. The distant hammering from the stables created a welcoming melody. Madeline pivoted to the manicured maze. She could look at it now without a sense of dread covering her.

Something crashed to the floor perhaps on the balcony above or in a nearby hall. "Broken objects, I'm home." She glanced down at the flagstones. The patio held many memories of breakfast with Mama.

It also held the fights. Madeline was thirteen, hiding along the knee-high wall, spying on her step-mother and father's argument. Father tried to step past the woman, but Step-mother grabbed him, hit him, and yelled, *"Charles, you coward! Stay and fight."*

He grabbed her arm. His face twisted in anger, drained of all civil emotions, evidence of a marriage lacking faith and kindness. "Name your price, name the place, and I will situate you."

"Death will we separate, Charles. Only by your death." The duchess finished him off with this barb and stormed back into the house.

Even now, bumps flooded Madeline's arm. Violent emotions led to nothing but pain.

"Your tea, Lady Devonshire." One of the maids set down a polished silver urn.

Madeline allowed the woman to fill her cup with the fragrant chamomile, her favourite. The servant curtsied and ventured back into the house.

"Not spending time with your husband. Trouble this soon." Step-mother advanced onto the patio. Madeline wasn't daydreaming anymore. The voice was real and the reference to Justain annoying.

"I wanted to see the morning sun in the garden."

The woman leaned against the table. "What is that you're wearing? Is this the new state of fashion? I knew your aunt had no taste."

Madeline looked down at her rose and white gown. Her fingers dragged over the soft lace gathered about her shoulders. Justain would approve. Father, too. "It's a beautiful dress, Step-mother."

"Tell me. What does Devonshire want from you? He must know your father is well propertied. Was that it? Did you entice him with your father's wealth?"

She shook her head. "Why is my marriage of concern to you? I assumed you'd be happy to know I was settled."

The woman raised a hand to her forehead. "It's a burden lifted." She placed her jewelled fingers near Madeline's cup. "What will be your plans? Will you live here?"

"After a proper visit, we will be travelling to one of my husband's homes."

"He's rich and not here for your father's fortune?" Step-mother's lips drew tight. "What about your plans for this estate? As your father's only child and with the passing of your cousin, the duke's heir, this all will be yours." She pressed her weight on the table. The tea service tinkled.

Poor Thomas taken so ill so quickly, almost like Father. She steadied her cup. "I have no plans for this estate, Step-mother."

"Well, your father may not recover."

"My father will. This conversation has ended." Madeline reached for her crutch.

"I didn't mean to upset you, child. I need for you to be strong in the days to come." Warmth filled Step-mother's voice.

Madeline blinked and refocused.

"I know that I have allowed difficulties with your father to impair our mother-daughter bond." She tussled with Madeline's bun. "You still wear the pins I gave you." She adjusted the silver fasteners. "I was a young bride once, full of hope and promise."

"You never talk about Mr. Lawson, your late husband." She held still as Step-mother took great care undoing sections of her hair.

"I remember his words of love. I was young, dazzled by his mere presence." Step-mother twisted a tendril taut, jabbed her with a pin.

"Ouch." Madeline shook her head.

"I was heavy with my son when I realised that he married me for my dowry. My husband caring for me was nothing more than a silly afterthought."

"That's too tight." Madeline loosened the knot of hair.

"I'm sorry." She released her grip a little. "I believed his soft words and let him break my heart."

"What are you trying to tell me?" Madeline settled back in her chair and brought the china teacup to her lips.

Step-mother stomped to the front of the table.

"Oh, you should've let me choose your mate. Then you wouldn't bear these illusions of sentiment."

No. Madeline would know the alliance was for money. "Pray, let's sit together and enjoy a cup of chamomile."

❧

Justain scouted the land since dawn. Avington's park spread for miles. The gardens and mazes outlined massive green spaces. The auburn trees hugged the grounds, supporting a cloudless sky. He knelt, scooping up dark soil, and inhaled the perfume of the potent ground. "This is good earth. Great-grandfather would be in high ropes to farm here. Even the old man would be happy."

Justain bounced up and shook his hands clean. He trudged past the stables. Groomsmen polished the duke's coaches. Three perfectly glossed chestnut carriages stared back at him.

"The black Berlin would have fit in well." Justain crossed his arms. "Mason would have been proud to have stabled here."

Tilford had taken both his new coach and his most loyal servant. Justain leaned against the whitewashed door. Mason would have approved of the Severn Gorge Parson's trap. But what a bargain, a duke's daughter and a cantankerous clan who looked down upon him. His driver would tilt his nose upwards and say, "Titled gentry trumps respected family."

"Did ye need anything, sir?" one of the grooms yelled through a shiny carriage door. "We'll have one ready in half-an-hour."

"No, I'm admiring your handiwork." Justain

pivoted and started down the path back to the main house. His in-laws were insane but of the highest peerage. His wife, who previously seemed in awe of him, now pretended to tolerate him. "Someday, this stupor will clear and all will make sense."

A loose stone shifted under his heel, causing Justain to stumble. Falling flat in front of the duke would make Justain an even bigger fool. He picked up his pace. The efficient Jonathan Winton waited for him. He rounded the last hill to see his steward perched atop their utilitarian carriage.

Jonathan dropped down from the high seat and stood at attention. "I'm all set to head to Devon, sir."

"We haven't been about our rounds in almost two months. If you find anything out of the ordinary, go back to Trenchard and gather my groomsmen." He patted Jonathan's shoulder. "Are you sure you can handle this?"

"I'll be discreet, my lord."

Justain handed him a fresh stack of correspondences. Reverend Delveaux would love hearing his latest tales of woe. "Take care, Mr. Winton. We must never let another disaster happen, not on my watch."

Jonathan nodded and prepared to mount the box. He stopped and came forward. "Should I send for Masterson or leave this groomsman here to aid you and Lady Devonshire?"

"You will not travel alone. My friend, we'll be fine. The flintlock is in my satchel." He patted his weathered bag. "And the blunderbuss in my trunk. I won't be taken by surprise but return with a few rifles for the stables."

"This Avington is isolated. It would be easy to

attack." He leapt up to his seat next to the groom. "I know you are capable of protecting your wife, but too many incidents have occurred this summer."

"Next to my cousin, you know I am the best shot in Devon." He laughed trying to ease the thick tension. "Jonathan, no one should know I'm here. Keep my whereabouts and marriage a secret. You know how gossip spreads. One slip of the tongue and the wrong elements would seek to take advantage of this remote place."

"Be well, my lord, and take care of Lady Devonshire."

Watching the drab vehicle depart, pedalling along the cobblestone drive, brought Justain an odd moment of comfort. His travelling cell was leaving.

He headed up to Avington's portico. "Take care of Lady Devonshire?" Justain hadn't seriously used Madeline's title. He still didn't feel worthy of his.

Yet, he'd made the mental acknowledgement of Madeline as his wife, ever since that time in the carriage when she kissed him. It felt like what a loving wife would do. Almost everyone else had judged him guilty in the affair. Not Madeline.

How to get back to the comfort of their garden picnic? Though she was still kind, she seemed distant. He missed the easy way Madeline gazed at him, as if he were honourable. "She's spun an ephod of fine silver for me." He'd have to work hard to be worthy of such a vest.

He passed the amiable Meriwether on the top step. The valet in his dark blue coat shuttled down the steps. The man waved but kept on his journey. Did he too dismiss Justain's status?

Soon the landscape swallowed the valet. The entry

became quiet again.

Justain didn't like quiet. He didn't want to be tolerated. He wanted Madeline to adore him, as she did before his temper fouled the air betwixt them. What was he willing to yield? Oh, the way she had melted against him at their picnic. He'd find Madeline and sweep her off her feet. He'd carry her to some darken corridor in this mansion of mazes or the shadows of her favourite marble bust and kiss her until she became delirious.

His fingertips itched at the thought. Justain wiped dust from his soles, before starting into the house. The slick marble tiles spread in four different directions. "West wing, east wing…where do I begin to look for my Maddie in a house this big?"

24

Step-mother clanged her spoon in the cup. It sloshed the dark liquid all over the table. Some splashed onto Donne. "I'm upset. How do I tell Randolph? He loved you. He'll be so disappointed when he returns from checking on Kent mining interests."

Madeline blotted her napkin and captured the tea. Moisture beaded her forehead. That evil man. "No more of this talk."

"Hateful girl. Won't let me be civil to you. Prefer me to rant!" Step-mother stood, loomed closer. "You foolish girl, you're setting yourself up for pain. When Delveaux hurts you, and he will"—the woman closed her eyes and lowered her tone as if struggling with her own memories—"come back to me, Madeline. I'll show you how to regain your life."

"Leave her alone, Dana. My daughter has been home for one night, and you make her homecoming as dreadful as ever." Father hobbled through the threshold on a groomsman's arm. "If you continue this, she'll never visit, preferring the quiet of her new in-laws."

A frozen smile returned to Step-mother's face. She turned to the duke. "Dearest, you should be in bed, not out here catching your death in the chilled air."

Father sniffed and pushed to a chair. "See about

my breakfast."

"Well! Since neither of you will take my advice, I will go pray for your mutual salvation. When judgment comes for you two, I'll know I did all I could." Swishing her burgundy skirts, Step-mother left the patio.

Her step-mother was wrong. They married because they'd been compromised. Madeline had no declaration of love to fret about being recanted and needed to accept the fact that none would come. Her heart could be lost, and Justain would still abandon her. How could there ever be more when they didn't value the same things?

She sipped her tea. "I don't suppose it's possible to show the duchess kindness? It's not good for your health to bear hostility."

He looked over his thin-rimmed glasses and scowled, but then his frown cleared. "You're wearing your mother's dress. Angelique was lovely in rose."

"Everything of Mother's was beautiful."

"You look like her." He patted Madeline's arm. "My dear, I was in the ballroom in Almack's waiting for Lord Chambers. He was late, and I grew impatient with obsequious green girls weighing my pockets at every turn." He winced.

"Father—"

"I'd had enough and was ready to depart when a raven-haired beauty entered the room. Though an escort of Lady Sussex, she captivated me. My eyes never left your mother."

"It's been years since you told the story." Madeline poured him some tea and lifted the cup to him.

He shook his head. "When Angelique entered the room, my breath caught. She was the most beautiful woman I'd ever seen." His lungs raged, filled with bellowing coughs.

Father pounded the table. "I didn't let one week pass before I was at your grandfather's house asking for her hand in marriage. When she accepted me, I thought I'd never be happier. I was wrong."

"Father, you're never wrong. You're a St. James, for goodness sake."

"No, I was. I was happier the day she bore you." He smiled, and his spectacles slipped. "It's one thing for me to live in misery with Dana, but I never should have put you through this. I married the woman to give my little girl a mother and bring some comfort back into my life."

"What's done is done, Father."

"I thought I loved her, but it wasn't the same as what I had with Angelique." He slapped the table, punctuating his pronouncement. The teapot shook. "How would anything compare with the love I had for your mother? If the misery I have now is payment for the borrowed time I had with Angelique, I would pay a thousand times."

She covered his hand. "Father, you're not overtasking yourself?"

"No, child. Meriwether told me you were out here, and I wanted to sit with you as we used to do." His gaze dropped to the vacant seat between them. "If I insisted on Angelique's staying home that day, she'd still be alive. Should've reined in her free spirit and kept her from riding. My heart would be intact, not buried in the St. James crypt." He drank the tea, but his lips thinned. "Where's Devonshire this morning?"

Madeline looked down. "He arose early."

"I'm sure he's out walking the grounds and hasn't

fled. He has more mettle than that." Father coughed and wiped his mouth. He looked jaundiced, as if he'd eaten nothing but lemons.

"When Devonshire wrote me about Tilford…If I had lost you, Maddie, it would've killed me."

"I suppose a marriage of convenience is best." She turned her gaze away from Father's all-knowing eyes to the gilded etchings on her cup. "The joining of the St. Jameses and Delveauxes is a good thing."

"Humph." Father rocked in his seat as if he chilled. "It was a difficult decision. It laboured upon me hard. You're not unhappy?"

"He's kind to me."

"I'd have preferred you find an eternal love, but I'm wise enough to know that occurs once in a hundred years." He mopped his mouth of spittle. The lines of his face set deep. He seemed to have aged ten years since she left. "Lightning struck once within our clan. It seldom strikes again in the same place."

The man didn't mean to crush her spirit with his words, but he so often did. Madeline sighed. "A St. James is never wrong."

Meriwether returned to the patio with Father's breakfast. "Your pills are in the juice. You must finish it, sir."

"Yes, yes, Meriwether. Don't be a nag."

"My duke, do I have to stay and watch?" The valet's tone was firm.

"I'll take it." His hand shook until he downed the laced orange juice.

"Watch him like a hawk, Lady Madeline." The valet left the patio.

"You were telling me about Devonshire." A tremor seemed to course his spine.

She patted his arm. "Justain is industrious and even indulgent."

Father squinted at her. "I'm curious. Explain."

"He's been carrying me though his shoulder was also wounded in the strike. He puts up with my need to read." She lifted the coveted poems in the air for inspection.

"A tattered book. Indulgent, is he?" Her father's eyes narrowed to slits. "Madeline, you're beginning to care for Devonshire."

Madeline yanked the book to her lap, her defences rising. "Shouldn't I care for my husband?"

"You're young and sheltered. I was forced to give him your hand in marriage."

"My heart is my concern, Father." Madeline bristled. "Life matured me."

A pain whipped across his face as he drank his juice. "The oranges don't cover the taste of the ground medicine. These pills are nastier every day, but I get worse without them. The doctors need to come up with bonbons." He slumped in his chair.

"Father?"

"I'm fine, my dear, Ange…Madeline." He straightened. "It takes more medicine each day to bring me comfort."

"Good morning, Lady Devonshire." Justain strolled on to the patio. "Duke. May I claim a moment with my wife?"

Her heart raced. He hadn't left.

"No. Join us." The duke waved him to the table. "You seem winded."

"It takes a number of wrong turns to get here. This is a large house with armies of marble and bronze casts everywhere. I see now what stirs your fondness." He stepped close to Madeline.

She held her hand to him. "Avington's not an easy place to conquer."

"You look beautiful. Reminds me of that enchanting gown you wore when I spied you up north." Justain took his time caressing her fingers before brushing his lips across Madeline's knuckles. His cinnamon coat hung over buff breeches and a striped waistcoat. So handsome.

Madeline turned from his intense sky-blue eyes to her father's tight countenance. "Dearest, please sit," she said.

"The Hampshire air makes young bucks giddy." The duke stabbed at his eggs. "Take a seat."

He didn't budge. "Your grounds are exquisite, Duke." Justain drew his gaze back to Madeline. "Another of your mother's dresses?"

"Yes." Her cheeks grew hot.

"All right, you've made your point. You don't have to act as a lovesick baboon but to the duchess." Father wheezed. "No one should ever know the truth of your union."

He took Mother's seat between them.

"I woke up this morning, and I realised two things. I've married a remarkable woman." He reached for her hand again. "And that I should show her each day she's admired."

Such praise. Madeline should've brought a fan or a shovel.

"Devonshire, are you a horseman?"

"He loves to ride and adores horses." She hid behind her cup for speaking out of turn.

Justain smiled. "Sir, I do enjoy riding. I suppose your daughter understands me."

Father grimaced. He relaxed his furrowed brow. "Please make yourself at home in my stable. I haven't been attentive of the horses lately. They all need the exercise, particularly Derbudon, my Le Perche."

Justain whipped his head toward the duke. "You have a Percheron, the mud horse bred in France?"

"That I do." Father winced and tried to brace, but the intensity couldn't be covered. "I believe I have overdone things this morning. Devonshire, help me back to my study."

"Let me." She put her cup down and grabbed her crutch.

"Sit, Maddie. I asked Devonshire. I want to spend some time alone with my son-in-law. You'll visit me later. We'll play chess. Is that all right with you?"

"Fine, Duke." He wiped a droplet off the book of poems. "Madeline, stay. Enjoy your tea and read your pilfered verses."

"I took the liberty of having your things stowed."

His smile now mocked of shock. "Such a dutiful wife." He took his satchel and placed it at her feet. "I'll find you here. It's the only place I can find without directions."

⁂

Justain aided the duke to the south wing into a room thick with bookcases made into a bedchamber. He helped the man into a gigantic bed with fluted posts. The majesty of the large walnut frame usurped the authority of a Davenport desk and matching cellaret shoved near its headboard.

A shelf stabbed Justain's back. He moved an inch and hoped the frieze-carvings of Cupid's bow and whale-tail drop pendants didn't snag his tailcoat. A stench of cough tonics and wellness elixirs permeated everything. This crowded place couldn't be a sanctuary like Justain's library in Trenchard.

"Thank you." The duke's lungs flooded with coughs. "Devonshire."

He patted the old man on the back.

The duke waved him away. "Not use to being called Devonshire yet."

"It's one of the few names I'll answer to." Justain moved to the side.

The duke's barking roared then subsided. "What are your intentions regarding my daughter?"

"Well, I married her." Justain grew agitated. Madeline was his wife, his concern.

"That's not what I mean. You look at her as if she was choice beef, but you don't love her."

Those St. James's observations were dastardly things. Justain folded his arms. "Is it wrong to admire a beautiful woman?"

"You love Maddie?"

"I care for her."

The man's face fell. A frown framed his drawn mouth.

Justain felt compelled to say more. "Duke, we've developed a friendship. We've a beginning."

He yanked off his spectacles and tossed them to the cellaret. "I'm realistic. You've responsibilities to your lineage, and you'll use my daughter to fulfill them. It's to be expected. But she's never had a season, doesn't understand about the dynamics of life unless she's read it in a book. She's my little girl."

"Madeline is reasonable. She understands a great deal." He'd never praised any woman for her intelligence. "I'll—" Justain couldn't attest to never hurting her. He folded his arms. "I'll protect her with my life."

The duke leaned back against the pillows. "It'll ease my mind to know she's happy." Another round of coughing besieged him. "I'd do anything to ensure it."

"Sir, you must rest. I'll send Madeline in to see you this afternoon." Justain retreated toward the door.

"No, Devonshire, sit and tell me about your life." He pushed his stained fingers through his thick grey hair. "An ambitious man has many sides. I've given you my greatest treasure. I wish to know you better."

❧

Madeline stayed where Justain had ordered, seeking Donne's angels for strength. Meriwether came several times, refreshing her service, bearing teacakes. Yet, her cup grew cold again, and the eternal paradox of the poems hadn't restored her peace. Where was Justain?

The breeze filtered in the familiar scent of vile snuff. The pit of her stomach knotted. She raised her head. Her breath came in tiny gasps.

The virile Mr. Kent bowed in front of her. "You ran off and got married, love. I intended to win your hand and your virtue." Mr. Kent slammed into the seat next to her. "What shall I settle for now?"

25

Madeline couldn't run from her attacker, not with her crutch.

The door to the patio seemed hundreds of feet away. She forced herself to calm. Out thinking Mr. Kent was her route to escape. "Why have you returned to this house?"

"I always catch you reading." He pried the book from her fingers.

"You must go. Now." She controlled every note of her speech, though her knees knocked under her skirting.

"I can't. Not without apologizing to you. I lost my sanity the last time we met. I was filled with jealousy."

"Mr. Kent, you struck me." That awful night his ego seemed to feed on Madeline's screams, so she made her voice plain, no emotion to reveal her terror. "You said you'd strangle me before you let me marry another. If Mrs. Wilkins hadn't—"

"Please don't repeat those ugly words. I know it's no excuse, but I had too much to drink at the gentleman's club that day. I had come here to see my sweet Madeline, but then you tell me you're going away for a season, that your aunt is to choose you a husband." He drummed his fist against the table. "I thought we had an understanding."

Her knees clapped like a gong. "We had no

understanding. And I refuse to be alone with you." Madeline reached for her crutch.

He kicked it a few inches from her. "Please, let me finish my apology." He drew his palms together in act of supplication. "I won't rest until you do."

The Herculean build seemed sincere, but alcohol couldn't explain his ruthless touches.

"You knew I loved you. I thought you felt the same." Kent moved closer, his yellowed thumb slowly inching toward her wrist.

Madeline jerked her hand back. "I never wanted your love, and you tricked me into going into that maze with you."

He leapt to his feet. "That poetry you read. Doesn't it describe the violence of a man's ardour?" The man traipsed around her chair. His fingernail outlined a path about her shoulders. It hurt like a knife's blade. "Doesn't it talk about the lengths one would go to have his heart's desire? I'll go to any lengths for you."

Madeline sat still, silently choking on the smell of snuff rife in the man's crimson jacket.

"Though you protested, you craved the excitement. I still wish that I could have been…" His knuckles dragged harder across the base of her neck. "The first to have—"

"All my affection belongs to my husband." Her chest rose up and down fast, her charade slipping. "Sir, please, stay away from me!"

"You didn't tell anyone of my lapse in judgment." His iron grip tightened. "Admit it, Madeline. You wanted me."

Her shoulder stung. "I thought of you as a friend. Nothing more. Please retake your seat." Her voice sounded small. She would forever only want Justain.

Kent relented and moved away, but her skin ached from his imprint. "Mr. Kent, there will be no way to explain these marks. My husband will be angry." She shouldn't have said that.

Kent smirked. "Pet, if I am to draw his censure, then it should be well deserved." He grabbed her wrist and suckled it.

Madeline struck him with her free hand. "Go away or I'll scream."

"Admit to me that you loved me. The truth, madam. Then I will be done with you." His mud-coloured gaze raked over her.

"I liked your friendship, but that was before I knew your character."

"You wanton thing. You led me on." He released her writhing arm.

"I didn't." Madeline stretched, grabbed her crutch, and propelled away. "Lord Devonshire will be back any minute. He won't be happy to see me upset."

"You tempted me. You shall suffer for your cruelty." The man moved toward her.

She braced along the knee-high wall, lifted her crutch and swung it at him.

He ducked. "What my dear? Trying to get on your broom and fly out of here, you beautiful witch?" Kent knocked it away, and she fell back sliding down the wall.

His hands loomed near her face. Her spirit was cornered, trapped on all sides. "Stop this at once!"

"Aunt says you married a foppish man." He thrust her against him.

The jarring action put pressure on her wound. "My leg, you beast. Stop this!"

He ripped the lace tucker from her neckline,

squeezed, and scratched her as he towed her to the chairs.

"Mother's dress!" She tried to cover her naked shoulders.

"You need a strong man to handle you." He pinched Madeline hard and drew her into his lap.

She kicked and knocked the table. The teapot crashed to its side. "You're insane. Let me go!" Madeline slapped his face, cutting him with her ring.

"You shrew!" He threw her to the floor.

"This is your last warning, you beast. My father will kill you for treating me ill." Madeline started crawling to the door. "I won't be ashamed to tell him this time."

Mr. Kent pulled her backward by the hair. Pins spilled onto the patio floor, jingling against the flagstone. "You've forced me to this. How will I end this passion?"

"Meriwether! Someone help!" She kept crawling to the threshold. "Help!" No one ran from the halls. This side of the grand house seemed abandoned.

Kent's shadow fell upon her as his snuff-smelling fingers covered her mouth. "Yelling is no use, darling. Meriwether went into town on an errand, and I told Aunt that the mirrors were tarnished. With her fastidious habits, she's got every maid closeted away buffing them."

Madeline bit his hand. "God help—"

He slapped her.

A haze of red darted before her, then her vision cleared. "Please—"

He clamped her lips again. "Noisy wench, this place won't do. Someone might come along and disturb us. I will take you to our maze. If the earl finds me ravishing you, it will be easy to convince him of how you pined for my advances."

Madeline fought with all of her might to keep from being lifted from the patio. Justain mustn't find her with him. Her husband wouldn't understand. He didn't trust her. She struck Kent harder.

"End this struggle, love? You've played the coy miss long enough. No one denies Randolph Kent."

He hoisted her high in the air, like a stricken boar after the hunt.

"You'll learn not to disappoint a man inflamed by your beauty." His large palm covered her nose and mouth. "Give into me."

Madeline struggled for air as the beast carried her away.

❧

Justain pushed away from his father-in-law's bedside. "Duke, I'll talk about horses or serving Lord Wellesey forever."

"Such an impressive military career. I would've never guessed. Almost makes me wish I could've served."

"It was short lived. Too short. But I need to find my wife."

"Be gentle with Madeline, Devonshire. She's not as strong as she pretends."

No, his wife was resilient. More strength than he'd ever seen a woman possess. But Justain nodded. "Get some rest."

The duke extended his shaking hand. His complexion waxed pale, and his fingertips were discoloured. "Send her to me in the morning."

"I'll do so." Justain touched the duke's silver signet ring, and then left the chambers.

He roamed the long hall back to the other side of Avington, counting marble tiles. The duke's fingers. Tarnished and yellowed like Mother's, right before she died.

The duke wouldn't get any better. Mother had been ill for months before fading away. Everyone sensed when it was her time. His gut weighed heavy with that feeling now. "How do I tell Madeline?"

After a few more wrong turns, Justain made it to the patio. "Madeline, I lost…What the…?" Pieces of her lace lay scattered across the stones. His book of poems was drenched in spilled tea.

Justain didn't bother to go through the opening. He leapt over the low patio wall and ran toward a strip of fabric caught on the edge of the maze.

~

"Here's our spot. Remember? Before we were interrupted." Mr. Kent tossed Madeline to the dirt.

Her heart pounded as if it would split asunder, and she gulped air. He was going to kill her. She could see it in his eyes.

He reached for her throat again and slipped his stained fingers into her wild chignon. "So beautiful and finally mine."

The wetness spurting from the surgery scar spread to her gown. She gripped her leg to stop the bleeding.

Kent laughed as he hovered over her. "Did I hurt you, Lady Deven?"

Madeline swept aside her tears. "It's Devonshire." Justain would never know how much she cared. Never see God's light in her walk. No one to bolster his honour. She lifted her trembling chin. "You're not even worthy to say the name."

His backhand met her jaw. Stars blended with the water in her eyes.

"Spiteful till the end. Let me tame the shrew. Perhaps you'll be so good I keep you with me a few days."

The hate in his gaze. He surely wouldn't let her live.

Would she even want to go on mired in shame?

He lunged at her.

She braced to feel his heavy body atop her, but felt nothing. Blinking three times cleared her vision.

Justain wrestled Mr. Kent backwards. "Madeline, are you harmed?" Her husband held the man in the air until his body hung like a rag doll. Justain dumped the evil man half into the tall shrub wall of the maze.

"The chit asked for me to have at her. We are old lovers."

She shook her head to the lies. "Abba, don't let him believe this."

Justain grabbed Kent and racked him with punches. "Madeline?"

She held her knees. "Please, Abba."

Justain hit the man again. Mr. Kent's aquiline cheeks now bled; one eye was swollen closed. Justain wiped his hands on Kent's cravat then placed his boot deep into her attacker's chest. "Madeline, did this vermin touch you?"

With a trembling finger, she pointed to her ripped bodice.

Her husband's troubled gaze seemed focused on her ruined skirt. He picked up Mr. Kent, held him an inch from his face. "You blackguard!" Justain hit the worm again and again, crumbling the man's nose. "Steal her virtue!" It was as if something possessed Justain.

"I haven't had her. Just threw her around. It's the leg wound." The fiend squeezed the words out between fist blows.

Justain's hands tightened about Kent's neck. The man turned midnight blue.

"Mercy, Justain. If you kill him, he'll have no chance to repent."

He caught her gaze, then loosened his hold on Kent.

The man gasped. "She's still all yours. Though why haven't you tasted the apple?" Justain's fist blackened the man's forehead.

Kent squealed like a pig.

Justain's knuckles were crimson by the time he dropped the man. "If you look at my wife again, I'll kill you. You breathe a sound of this to anyone, and I'll hunt you. Do we have an understanding?"

"Ya." Mr. Kent fell to the ground unconscious.

"Madeline, I want to take you back to the house. My hands will go around your middle. I don't wish to frighten you."

She nodded and waited to be in her husband's arms.

26

Justain's heart beat so hard it meshed with the rhythm of Madeline's. She quivered as he carried her out of the maze. The beautiful grounds he coveted now seemed tawdry. He marched back to the house and tried to slow his own heavy breathing. He concentrated on each methodical step, but the adrenaline of the moment coursed too hard. Even with the savagery of war, the crimes of Dorset, he had contained his indignation and maintained an air of reason. Seeing Madeline, his Maddie, hurt stole his sanity.

She buried her face in his jacket. Silent tears soaked his cravat. His muscles tensed. He should've killed Kent. As if she heard his thoughts, Madeline shook her head and drew her arm about his neck.

His boots pounded against the stones of the patio. His wife seemed as if she would fly out of his hold at any moment. He held her tighter, wasn't going to let her go.

Avington was deadly quiet. The halls were empty, as if everyone was involved in the conspiracy to harm her. He charged the stairs, pushed open the door to their room.

Madeline's abigail buffed the closet mirror.

He shifted Madeline in his arms. "Miss Regent?"

The maid curtsied. "Sir, I arrived an hour ago and

was told to polish the mirrors in this wing of the house. My lady's hurt?"

"She fell into some trouble in the garden. Attend her. I will wait outside until you call for me." He put Madeline upon her bed and stormed across the threshold.

ॐ

Madeline couldn't make sense of anything. Death had lost again and by Justain's hands. She winced as Anne Regent stripped the shreds of silk from her shoulders.

Anne was a steady woman, and her calm grey eyes exuded a certain measure of understanding. She went about her work in silence. She'd been inquisitive the night of Madeline's wedding, but the maid asked no questions and gently scrubbed the bruises. An hour under Step-mother's direction cured most loose tongues.

Water from the basin splashed Madeline's corset. The warm liquid and liniment eroded the smell of tobacco, which seemed to be everywhere.

The maid left to get a fresh dressing for her leg.

Madeline shivered and drew a blanket about her, but nothing broke the chill. Nothing erased the humiliation, the marks on her chest. Justain's only request was to act above reproach and bring no shame. How would he bear catching his wife in another man's arms? Madeline fell back. Sorrow seeped from her eyes. Her ears rang as she imagined Justain's timbre remarking his shame.

Anne returned with a bundle of cotton wrap in her arms.

Madeline smoothed her face, not wanting to inflame any more gossip. That would happen soon enough, when Justain asked for divorcement.

⁂

As Justain stood guard outside Madeline's bedchamber, Miss Regent tapped him on his shoulder.

"She's ready for bed, sir. She didn't injure her leg too badly, but she's oddly bruised for a tumble."

"Thank you, Miss Regent. Send some food up in another hour. Don't go outside. There's garbage in the garden, and I don't want anyone exposed to it. I've sent the duke's groomsmen to take care of it."

"Yes, my lord." The servant scurried down the hall to the stairs.

Justain took a quick breath and entered the room. His wife was swaddled in pillows. He approached but forwent sitting on the bed, instead grabbing the ottoman. The heft of it gnawed his shoulder, but he'd strain it again to beat the vermin senseless. "Do I need to send for a doctor?"

She shrugged her shoulders and turned away. "Forgive me for causing you shame."

"What?" The word shame should be erased from the earth. Justain softened his tone. "What can I do?"

"A man shouldn't have a faithless wife. I release you from your obligation."

He sighed deep and long. "What are you talking about?"

"Another man's hands have been upon me. This was not the first time Mr. Kent…Mrs. Wilkins said it was nothing."

How could the poor lass think the vermin's actions

were her fault? He rubbed his throbbing temples.

"I don't blame you." Her sobs were thick, her grief no longer silent. "I can't stand to look at me either."

Something very near his heart began to ache. "You're talking nonsense. Get some rest."

"Justain, stop being kind. I saw your face when I showed you my gown."

He struck at his skull, trying to drive away the image of another man atop his wife. A growl launched from his throat. "I should've kill him just for looking at you, let alone for making you feel this way."

She finally held his gaze. The cats-eye jade seemed milky, clouded with doubt. "You don't hate me?"

"I took leave of my senses, thinking someone violated you. You're my wife. I failed to protect you."

"But Mr. Kent will tell everyone of this and harm your reputation. I've dishonoured you."

Justain's throat felt thick, itching with vomit. He'd become the old man, making Madeline care more about disgrace than her injuries. "Kent won't talk. He doesn't wish to be gelded."

"You should divorce this baggage. I won't contest."

"Madeline Delveaux, there'll be no divorce. I won't part with you. I looked at your face, and my gut knew in an instance, you didn't incite his rage."

"You're not angry with me?"

"With Kent." He lowered his voice. "Not with you, my beautiful, innocent girl. Get some sleep."

She lifted from the mattress. Her robe slipped, exposing bruises along her neck.

Justain brought his palms to his face, again attempting to mask his indignation. He paced to the window, hoping to smother the images of Kent's hands on her skin.

"Justain?"

He stilled his fists and walked back to the bed. "Nothing else will harm you. I'll keep you safe."

"Let's go now. Let's get away from here, anywhere but here."

"We can't. We must extend our stay. Your father needs you."

She shook her head. "Please don't tell Father. I can't shame him, too."

"The duke would appreciate it if we were close by. He's quite ill." How to finish destroying her world? "Madeline…he's dying."

The frozen expression on her countenance evaporated. Her lips twisted. Her face paled, showing more hurt than he'd seen in a lifetime. Water poured down her cheeks as she ducked onto her pillows.

27

Justain tugged on the stiff white curtains. He'd seen enough. The groomsmen picked up Kent's worthless hide and dragged him from the property. Now they brought piles of kindling wood to torch the maze. He couldn't wait for the blaze to catch fire. No reminders of this night would exist. The duke wouldn't mind when he learned of this nightmare.

The tapestry slipped through his fingers. Justain seethed. He forced his mouth shut keeping all the apt phrases of sending Kent to the netherworld locked in his mind.

Madeline had mentioned the fool before. In the mineshaft, the poor girl had dreamed Kent hunted her. Why hadn't he taken her concerns seriously?

Flames welled in his veins. He knew why. Justain slow-punched the wall with enough effort to sting his raw fingers but not enough to rattle the hanging mirror. If he hadn't been focused on his own angst…could he have prevented this whole affair?

The scent of charred brush seeped through the window. He closed it and moved from his perch. He didn't want the fumes to wake Madeline. It had taken awhile for the lass to succumb to sleep.

Justain dropped onto the flowery chaise. He'd never spent this much time in a girl's boudoir. His amorous adventures darkened remote inns or the underground pleasures of London. He kicked the pink ottoman shifting it under his feet. This had to be fate's comic revenge.

Madeline moaned betwixt her pillows but didn't awaken. The sound ate at his gut. Even in sleep, her anguish seemed intense.

Her tears, so many tears. When he abandoned his latest conquest, he'd count the seconds for the bucket of sobs to arrive, then toss token words of living for the moment.

His cousin was right. Justain waged a vendetta on any girl who had laughed at his mother or treated him shabbily as a youth. Always had a reason. Never cared about the consequences.

Madeline clung to her pillows as if in a death grip. Perhaps those fluffy clouds consoled her.

He closed his eyes. A parade of faces washed by. Was this how they felt, beyond comfort, betrayed? The scars on his ribs itched. Justain sat up, gazed at the fireplace's dying embers, and picked at his battered book of poems. The heat dried the pages, but the tea left brown stains over the print. "Donne, I've failed to protect you, too."

A light tapping jiggled the door. Justain dashed over and opened it with care to keep the noise from awakening Madeline. Miss Regent entered with a silver platter bearing a bowl of steaming broth and crusty bread.

He motioned for her to remain silent then took the tray from her arms. "Sit with Lady Devonshire. I need to take care of a few matters." He placed the food on the ottoman. "I don't want her waking up alone."

"Yes, sir. But are you sure that I shouldn't see if she'll eat something?"

"No, I want her to rest. Keep the door locked until I return." He took a last look at Madeline and bolted from the room.

❧

Justain beat his knuckles against the door to the duke's study and pushed it open. He didn't bow or acknowledge rank but marched to the headboard."

"I haven't requested an aud"—the duke's cough blew the tail of his nightcap to the side of his nose—"audience, Devonshire."

"This can't wait. I've evicted Mr. Kent from the premises."

"What's going on?" The duke sat up in the bed. His pallor was more ashen than before, a shade darker than his grey shift. "Meriwether hasn't said anything to me."

Justain paced. "He's busy overseeing the mess."

The duke shook a yellowed finger at him. "You needn't fret about another buck under the roof. Your position is secure."

Justain gritted his teeth. "But I promised to protect our treasure."

The duke's gaze narrowed and seemed to drop to Justain's reddened fists.

Justain shoved his hands beneath his coat. "The fool attempted to humble my wife."

"Kent hurt Madeline!" His lungs sounded inflamed from the rounds of coughs.

"She's safe now, Duke."

"Do I need to get one of my muskets for satisfaction, too?" He fumbled with his spectacles and dragged them from the cellaret.

"I've handled things, but I'll be bringing some of my groomsmen. I'll see that the estate's security is strengthened."

"I knew the fool was smitten with her." The duke struck his pillow. "Even worked the courage to ask me for her hand before Maddie left for her aunt's, but I told him no repentant womanizer is worthy of her."

Justain raised his gaze to a crack in the plaster. The man knew how to land a mortal wound. "Kent didn't take rejection well. He attacked her that night."

"What? The crazed fool." The old man tried to rise. "Get the flintlock from the wall."

"You need to rest. With no strength, you'd end up shooting the wrong villain." He patted the man's shoulder. "Madeline doesn't want any more of Kent's blood shed."

The duke grabbed his arm. "I should go to her."

"She's sleeping now. It would be better for Madeline if you focused your energy on recovering."

He passed his signet ring to Justain. "Anything, you need to do, you have my permission. I'll have Meriwether notify the staff and the duchess that you'll be making changes."

"Hold on to this." Justain flashed his own onyx and ruby band. "Inform the duchess and Meriwether that I have your confidence."

"Don't hold this over Madeline. She'd never willingly disgrace the St. James name."

Justain glanced again at the ceiling crack. "Sleep well, my dear duke." He pivoted, flung the door open. It rattled on its hinge.

Madeline looked out at the grounds below. The groomsmen would be circling again, coming over the ridge. "Every hour on the hour."

"Lady Devonshire, you're up." Anne approached her footfalls quieter than sprinkling snow.

"I've had two days of lying in bed. I'm eager to see Father." She moved from the window and warmed herself by the fireplace. She waved good morning to her mother's portrait, the pastel painting of Mama opening Avington's orangery doors. The candlelight reflected from it, making a heavy shadow drop from the thick frame. Madeline would often stand in the outline and pretended Mama was close enough to hug.

She turned, but stayed near Mama. "The late duchess was brave. Lady Angelique carried supplies to Spain during the Peninsula War. Mother never forgot to support our kinsmen. She was strong and took courage in the Lord."

The candle dimmed, and Madeline shivered as the shadow retreated.

"You must be careful, Lady Devonshire." Anne's brows drew together. Her lips thinned to a slim line. "His lordship will be cross if you fall." She wrapped a shawl about Madeline. Her maid looked as fragile as the garniture vases on the mantel.

Madeline stepped closer to the painting. Would Mama be proud of her? No, not as long as Madeline hid in the shadows, never risking, never trusting. "I'm not a vase, not anymore."

"Excuse me, ma'am?"

"Mother lived for purpose." She shifted her weight to improve her balance on the crutch. "It's time for me to do the same."

Anne lowered her chin. The maid's grey hem

floated over the thick sapphire rug. "I think his lordship wants you to rest. He's concerned."

"My husband is protective, but I have to take some control of my life. I need to press forward."

Anne raised her head, her gaze blank. "But the master's been in a foul mood as of late."

Madeline tugged the soft wool tighter across her shoulders. Though God spared her, Death would still visit, and like Mama, Madeline must make a difference. Father and Justain needed her witness.

"I've let my fears control me long enough. It's time for me to be the woman Providence calls me to be." Madeline would tell them, show them, shower them in His peace. If only her men were close enough to God to call Him Abba, to know the freedom of His love. Madeline ventured toward Anne, stilled the woman's fingers. "Help me dress."

"Yes, madam." The maid shook her head as she strolled to the closet. "Do you know what you wish to wear?"

"My butter cream dress, something fashioned for me."

28

Justain steadied his mount, the satin Derbudon, the silver Le Perche of the duke's stables. He firmed his seat, and they jumped a fence, sailing over the high wall as easily as a breeze traversing the moors.

Yet, the speed couldn't speak to his troubles. For the past three days, he got little sleep in Madeline's room. The conscience he had believed he left gathering mould in the wine cellar of Trenchard had found its way to Hampshire, making him on edge, second guessing his actions.

At last night's family dinner, between the duchess's taunting him over the tragedies befallen his family and the duke's bluster of his Spanish connections, Justain longed to be back at war.

At least the last of Mr. Kent's belongings were gone. Miss Regent found bags of Dover pills. Opium drugs were the rage of the Ton. Mother had fallen victim to them. Justain wanted to punch someone. Kent had to be addicted to those things to think he could run amuck at Avington.

Justain loosened his tight grip on Derbudon's reigns. Hard to become a better man when the past kept washing his face.

Jonathan's crumbled note, the harbinger of bad news, smouldered in Justain's breast pocket. "My world has become an asylum." He pointed Derbudon past the woods behind St. Mary's church and to the stables.

Like the main house, the stables were a work of grandeur. Constructed of the finest cedars and millwork, the building would house at least sixteen horses. The thick thatch roof could provide a haven for Wellesley's corps. The storage area in the back contained enough barley and oats to feed the King's mounts. Like Justain's stables at Trenchard, this place remained tranquil, far from the commotion of his in-laws.

Derbudon slowed to a trot.

Justain bounded down and opened the iron-framed door. With all the duke's groomsmen on patrol, he had to secure the Le Perche himself. It was a task he didn't mind.

He led the stallion to its pen and brushed his silver coat. Mud plastered the horse's legs. Muck covered Justain's trousers. He'd need brushing out as well. At least riding brought him joy. Without drowning in brandy, Justain needed something to keep from exploding. He unfolded the parchment, held it up to the light, and read the horrid scratch again.

My Lord,

No signs of Barrow have been found. I ordered the groomsmen to be more vigilant and sent warnings to the tenants and the orphanage. The Duke of Dorset is asking we report our movements but seems to have no true interest in helping.

Roderick tracked rumours from the Severn Gorge to Hampshire, but it proved fruitless. He's returning to Devon to join the hunt for Barrow.

Trenchard looks well. The painting is nearly complete. Furnishings will start arriving before the month's end.

Your servant,

J. Winton.

He stuffed it into his pocket and avoided the urge to rip his steward's letter to shreds. Gossipmongers were on the hunt. The Ton already alleged Justain's tactics were heavy-handed. He took a deep, cleansing breath, grabbed his knife, and stabbed a bale of hay, cutting it free. Then, he forked fresh straw into Deburdon's pen. "Here you go, boy."

Manual labour would ease his spirits. It reminded him of Mason. Of listening to his driver's stories as the man worked the stables.

Justain inhaled the perfume, the straw, the lathered horseflesh, the cedar of the pen. It calmed his warrior heart. But the rhythm in his head cried, "Join the fight. Be about the chase." He leaned the fork against the wall. Death was on the duke's heels. When her father passed, Justain would need to be here to support Madeline. He sighed.

Deburdon nudged his hand.

"Let's take another turn about the grounds. What do you think, old boy?"

The stable door banged shut. No one else should be here. The hair on his neck prickled.

29

Footsteps neared.

Justain's pulse raced. His satchel with his blunderbuss pistol lay on the far side of the troughs, his flintlock in a trunk in Madeline's room. He'd have to overwhelm the intruder with sheer strength. Justain coiled his fist and braced along the wall.

A blur of butter slid past the corner.

He sprang forward and pinned the assailant against Deburdon's railing.

"Egad, Madeline!" Justain removed his forearm from under his wife's chin and eased her to the ground cushioning her atop a loosed bale. "I'm sorry. Are you all right?"

"Yes." She caught her breath and shifted into the mound, flinging twigs of hay. "My crutch?"

"It's in Deburdon's pen." He crouched beside her and tested her elbow, her ankle and searched for signs of distress.

She chuckled. "That tickles." Her face reddened.

He let go of her kid slipper and brought his hands to his knees. "I told you not to leave the main house or go anywhere by yourself. What are you doing here?"

"I came to find you."

"You found me." He stayed near, craned his neck to the thick beams girding the roof as a long, slow blast of frustration fled his nostrils. He could've hurt her.

She leaned over and tugged the buckle of his boot. "We need to talk."

The lass would pick a day he bore low patience. "This isn't the time." He reached for her to lift her from the straw.

"No more delays."

She avoided his help and brushed a few ebony curls back into place. Must be important for her to defy him.

"Step-mother has Anne consumed with polishing. Meriwether's with my father. Everyone has someone to confide in but you." She intertwined her fingers with his and pulled the fist to her cheek.

Her skin felt smooth like Devonshire cream, but she must still be too fragile for his attention, his ardour. "What is this?"

"I've left you to face Avington alone." She kissed his thumb.

He freed his hand. "Spend your days with your father. Ease his pain."

"What about yours?" She leaned into him. "Your steward's away. Who's here to jest with you?" Her strawberry fragrance blended with the smell of the fresh hay.

His heart raced; the draw to her now undeniable. He swallowed the dry lump in his throat. "The filly hasn't been good company as of late. Jealous of my outings with Derbudon."

"I've always been jealous of your union, your masculinity and her dark beauty."

"Your delicious turn of a phrase." Justain strummed the lace trim of her cream pelisse. "You've more things to come to terms with than my riding habits."

"You can say his name." She straightened his cravat. Her fingers graced the taut muscles along his neck. "I won't crumble talking about Kent."

"I don't know how to help. And I'd hate to make things worse."

She tossed pieces of hay into the air. "I approve of your chopping down the maze."

"The duke approves, too." He stared at the broken yellow straws. The sight of the lush maze being cut into bundles and set ablaze gave him great pleasure, but it was a poor substitute for killing the man who had attacked her. "Your father's given me free rein to make this better for you."

"Look at me." She touched his cheek. "You barely look at me anymore. You're not Kent. Being around you is different."

He leaped to his feet. "I'm glad we've progressed." He retrieved her crutch then paced.

"You haven't. You're afraid to share the same room, staying out here in the stables until you're sure I'm asleep. You won't hold my hand. I haven't heard a story in ages."

The calm acknowledgement of his frigid behaviour pricked his gut. So much for the Lothario of Devonshire. He leaned against the wall.

"I'm not panicked when we're together. God has put you in my life. I have my own sovereign protector, right here on Earth." She motioned to him. "Please, sit." The confident set of her chin, her steady gaze. Did she really want him near?

He eased down next to her. "How am I a protector when I left you to danger?" For a second, he glanced away from her jade eyes. So many tears had included those gems. His fault. He tapped the heel of his mud-sodden Wellington. The grey dirt hardened about it, ruining the boot's meticulous shine.

Madeline clutched his shoulders and held him as if he'd disappear at any moment. "You didn't know about Kent. I was too ashamed to tell you of his trickery. If I'd trusted you, he'd never have been allowed back at Avington."

"I couldn't protect my own brother, Madeline. Barrow is still out there. What if my wars hurt you, too?"

She squeezed him tighter. "You didn't kill Richard." Her lips met his cheek. "I'm alive and unharmed because of you." His wife never seemed more beautiful, even with straw poking out of her chignon. She took his mouth, tasted of chamomile. "You're my knight."

Why did this innocent creature believe in him? He was no better than the grey mud.

❧

Madeline wanted their peace to return. "I won't break if you embrace me."

"You've nothing to prove." His voice sounded raspy. "Let me help you back to the house."

"Don't dismiss me. After all we've been through, I should've trusted you." She burrowed deeper, popping the silver buttons on his waistcoat. She pressed against him hoping to feel the beat of his heart.

Her shifting weight must've unbalanced him. He fell back upon the hay. His arms wound about her waist, but then he flung his hands to his sides.

She clung to his navy-blue lapels. "Tell me I haven't shamed you."

"You haven't." For a moment, his gaze shot past her. His sky-blue eyes clouded with emotion, but Justain rarely spoke of his feelings. Maybe today would be different.

He stroked her shoulder with feather-light circles and sent waves of heat through her muslin sleeves. "I made you dread my reaction. That's what the old man did. He made Mother afraid of her own shadow while he became embroiled in scandal after scandal." He shook his head. "You said you didn't want me to rue the day of our wedding."

"Yes."

"Maddie, I don't want you to rue that day either."

Her heart clenched. Maybe their connection lived. "I wanted nothing from Mr. Kent. I fought him. And you stopped him from—"

"I know." He took a piece of straw from her hair and cast it to the ground.

"Please know I didn't want him, but he said I drove him to this."

Justain growled, low in his throat. "Kent lied. There's nothing that you could ever do to deserve that."

"Then hold me. It's the only way to know nothing's changed. That you still care." Madeline refused to exhale and awaited his response.

Seconds, maybe minutes spun away. Then a wave of fingers pulsed down her back, cinching at her waist. The grip was firm, secure, but she longed for more. Madeline laid her head upon his neck and savoured the sandalwood scent on his skin. "I've prayed for the courage to find you, that we could restore our intimacy. Your touch is a window."

"You saw me become violent, begged me not to

kill. You should never see that."

"You saved me." Her heart welled. She wasn't sure what this surge of longing meant, but the strength of it tingled her toes.

Sunbeams from a distant window danced upon his sable locks. Justain brushed her knuckles across his mouth.

Blood rushed to her face.

"I should finish examining my wife and ensure she's uninjured." He tilted her countenance, combed her skin with his fingertips. It jolted like lightning. "Your neck may redden. Your abigail will think I'm the brute."

"Then I'll become violent. No one will ever bemire your character. I won't stand for it."

A tiny smile blossomed, and he elevated her elbow. "I have muddied this magnificent gown."

"Miss Regent helped me make Aunt Tiffany's creation more modest. The lace covers a multitude of sins…the bruising on my chest."

His jaw tensed. "You may speak of this, but I can't. I'm not that well-adjusted."

The wind whistled, flapping the stable door. Justain sat up, fists clenched, jaw tightening.

Madeline pushed at his chest, forcing him back to the ground, then she hugged him again.

He stuck an arm under his head. "You want me flat on my back, madam?"

"It's harder for you to run away. Now tell me what has you anxious. Something's bothering you other than the antics of Avington."

"A nagging problem. It'll be resolved soon."

"If you won't unburden yourself to me, I'm not much of a helpmate." She turned away and smoothed the crushed muslin of her gown. "This isn't going to work."

"What?"

"Nothing." Madeline would always be his wife in name only. "You want me as a fragile treasure, something to admire upon occasion." She pinned up a loose tendril as if the action would contain her disappointment. "I shouldn't keep hoping, wanting us. It wouldn't last. What lasts?"

"Never say!" Justain swept her close, pressed her to his bosom. "You're my wife, and something's changing. We're building." He slowed his words. "Never give up on us."

"I have to make you angry for you to choose? To be held securely, you must be ready to chew horseshoes?"

"I'm wrung through." He threw his hands up and fell back into the mound. "I don't know how to reassure you."

"Make things as they were." She hovered over him, stroked the tender flesh behind his ear. "I believe you were courting me."

He caught her fingers. "What are you doing?"

"Softening my wild puppy."

"I'm not a pet." He closed his eyes. "But it's peaceful here."

Madeline tucked her chin onto his shoulder. "I used to hide in here when I was a child. Some of my books are in the loft over the pens. Mama stayed with me there during a terrible storm. What a sight, her train and kid slippers steeped in straw. This is a great place to forget the world."

"So it is." Justain stretched out in hay.

She was in his embrace, with arms intertwined

and feet tangled. He gazed at her. "What will you do now that you've softened me?"

"Let me see. I was taught a proper kiss, but it's been a while."

Derbudon brayed, probably amused at the humans frolicking so near his pen.

Madeline didn't care. She rubbed her cheek against Justain's. "Kiss me."

"I'm glad I shaved." He placed his lips to her forehead, then pulled back. "Now, let me get you back to—"

"Shh. I want to enjoy the smell of the bales and hear your heart beating fast."

Justain drew her closer and took her mouth. The touch was soft at first, but her skin hummed as it deepened. He'd long since branded her mind with the flames of his passion, filled her with dreams only he could tame. He moaned, nipped her jaw. "I've missed you, your gentling spirit."

Her hands glided against his shirt numbering his ribs. "Are these scars from Tilford? My poor puppy."

He moved her fingers, pushing them to his chest. "If your thoughts wander, I'm out of practice." He petted her eyelashes then rolled to his side. His palms roamed beneath her pelisse. Heat spread from her stomach to her spine. He framed her face. "You make a man believe he could be anything. That he's honourable and fine."

"You are, finer than gold. God has made you so beautiful, sculpted you with the best marble."

"I lo—" He cleared his throat. "This won't be a marriage in name only."

"Never hoped for that." She sought her favourite ear, then leaned into the breathless dizzying haze of his affection.

He descended upon Madeline and sheltered her. Desperate and wanton were his lips, his caresses. His gentle touch seemed to offer the words he couldn't express.

Words she so wanted to hear, but nothing mattered now, just the heavy beating of his heart.

Justain kissed her, even as the wind pounded upon the door and the horses bickered.

ꕥ

Horse hooves pounded outside. "Maddie," Justain whispered, "that's one of the groomsmen making the rounds. It's time to get you back to the house."

"Yes." She took a small gasp of air, but her smile lit the dark recesses of his heart.

Justain towed her upright, propped her staff under her arms. "Let me finish with Derbudon. Then I'll escort you."

Madeline smoothed his jacket. "I don't want you rushing your chores. I'll go sit with Father."

Justain touched his lips. He could still taste her sweet kisses. "How's the duke?"

"He had a rough night, but he's faring better. I don't know if he's getting the right dose. He won't take his medicine unless it's minced up and drowned in juice. Who knows if the kitchen gets it right?" She shook her head. "Maybe, you'll join us?"

He brushed straw from her hair. "It's cramped in his study."

"Thank you for this time with Father. I'm working up the courage to talk with him, too, but he's so imposing. I still feel like a child in his presence."

"My persistent wife will find a way to soften him." That old dog needed softening.

Madeline removed a piece of straw from Justain's cravat. "I can make it back to the house by myself."

"Your dress." He swatted the mud from her skirt. He didn't want to rankle the duke. His father-in-law needed his strength. "There…the duke won't think we played in the dirt. Are you sure you don't want my help?"

"I refuse to be a burden." She stroked his cheek. "The groomsmen are patrolling. I'll be safe." She moved to the pen and patted the Percheron. "Will I see you for dinner?"

Rubbing his jaw, he missed the warm caress of her fingers. "Perhaps."

She waved and left the stables.

He soothed the horse's nostrils. It took the fool Kent to help Justain see Madeline. She was a treasure, his treasure. "After all she's been through, my wife seeks me out." Resilient woman. Had he in some small way aided this metamorphosis? The edge of his mouth tingled. His fingers itched. He'd have Miss Regent ready dinner in their room tonight. They didn't have to wait to reach Innesfrey to consummate their marriage.

30

Madeline studied the chessboard. The squares seemed endless. Usually, a battle plan would illuminate in her head, but her husband filled her thoughts. They'd found each other again. The sandalwood smell of her father's sheets reminded her of Justain.

"Hesitant, my dear?" The duke settled back against his pillows. The massive fluted headboard shadowed his face, almost hiding the bags under his eyes. He tried to straighten his arms, but the tremors in his hands continued. "Maddie?"

"Here's my selection."

He rubbed a jaundiced cheek. His fingers shook like the flutter of a fan. "Terrible move."

"Is it terrible because you're in check?" She smothered a gloat.

He dragged a worn bishop in front of her king piece. "No, you've allowed me to win. Checkmate." He muffled his cough. "I trained you better than that. What's preoccupying you?"

A giddy sigh left her lips. "I was thinking about the lengths Justain goes to keep me…us safe."

"You're thinking about the good earl?" His nose wrinkled. "You've complaints of his tactics? Has he laid down the law to you?"

"No, he hasn't." Something in Father's tone wasn't

right. Was he feeling sicker? "Father?"

He looked over his thin spectacles. "It seems romantic now, but he'll stifle you."

"His rules are no stricter than yours. And given the circumstances it's to be expected."

"I knew he'd laud this over you. I knew it." His tired gaze trailed to the door. He waved a ragged hand and made a welcoming motion. "Come in, Devonshire. I see you skulking in the hall."

Her breath caught. Justain looked immaculate. His cravat seemed whiter than a dove. His hair had been brushed until it shined. He dressed in a jet-black coat, turquoise striped waistcoat, and buckskins.

"Good evening, Duke. Lady Devonshire." He bowed, then kissed her hand and didn't let it go.

Her fingers felt so warm meshed with his, never warmer.

His sky-blue eyes seemed more open, more filled with joy than she'd ever seen. Her statue now breathed with life and vitality. "My dear duke, we'll miss the family dinner tonight."

"We will?" The heat of a blush singed her face. She lowered her gaze and met Father's crinkled forehead.

Madeline dropped Justain's hand and regretted the sudden chill to her skin. She held up the shiny silver walking stick. "Look at the cane Father got me."

Justain nodded as he spun it. "The handle's minted with the St. James crest. Nice." He leaned it against the bedpost. "Good evening, Duke." He helped Madeline rise, his strong arms surrounding her to steady her.

"Humph." Father's spectacles slipped an inch down his thin nose. His shaky hand waved them back. "No, I've been waiting for you. Sit."

Justain eased Madeline back into her chair but remained standing.

"Have you finished battle hardening the place?" Father cleared the chessboard.

"Yes." Justain gazed at the marble. "Chess is an odd game for a female to learn."

"She'll beat you, Devonshire." The duke wheezed a long octave before clearing his throat. "She's almost as good as me except when she's intent on losing. Would you know why that is?"

"Father, please." Madeline reset the board.

Justain cocked his eyebrow but didn't answer.

"Do you play chess?" Father fluffed a pillow trying to better support his back.

"No, Duke, I don't. I'm an avid card player."

He cleaned his lenses. "Given to gambling? Your fortune's intact?"

"I wager what I can afford to part with, and I'm no fool with money." Justain shifted as if impatient. "I consider my miniscule losses alms to the poor."

"I won't have my daughter being made to beg in the streets because of a foolish investment or grieving an extravagant excursion to Bath or Lancashire."

"No." Justain seemed unsettled by Father's words, adjusting his perfect cravat.

A shiver skirted her spine. Something definitely wasn't right. "I'm sure that my husband is diligent in all matters."

Father barked another serious of coughs. His wobbly fingers pointed to a water goblet.

Madeline stretched to get it. She tried to hold it for him, but he seized it with his shaky hands.

"Duke, the Delveauxes have a doctor that's very good. He was instrumental in Madeline's recovery.

Should I send for him?"

"No more doctors, and I sure don't want a country medicine man like Dr. White poking me."

Justain's eyes narrowed. "You know Dr.—"

"I've read about Samuel White."

That haughty tone. Madeline pushed the board closer to her father. "It's your turn."

"Mine." He captured a pawn and dangled it in the air. He held his arm steady and flashed the St. James crest forged on his silver band at Justain. "Elegant, aye Devonshire. To know Madeline was happy, I would pay such riches."

Her pulse raced. How to end the tension between the men? She turned the board. "I'll win the next one."

Father tossed the pawn into the air.

Justain caught it without effort.

"Good Devonshire." He laughed. Father sat ramrod straight and seemed strong again, as if sickness had never touched him. "There are several documents on my desk, Devonshire. They make for an interesting read."

31

Madeline touched her heated cheeks. The duel was on.

Justain handed the pawn back to Father and made his way to the mahogany desk stashed in the corner. Two piles of paper separated by a bottle of liquor splayed the bevelled marble top. The thinner stack contained maybe a couple of pages; the other had an endless supply of stationery.

His finger traced the outline of the crystal flask. "Duke, you shouldn't have. I recently abandoned brandy. What brought on the need for gifts?"

The old man coughed. "Read the papers, Devonshire. You may change your mind."

Justain held the first paper up to the light of the candelabra.

His countenance changed, growing dimmer as he scanned it. Justain took his time flipping through the stacks. He crumbled one tawny piece of parchment and packed it into his fist.

"I thought a summary would make things easier for you." Father used the same awful tone he reserved for Step-mother.

Justain cast a look to Father over his shoulder. His eyes seemed vacant. "Why all the questions of my intentions, the surprise at my military service, if you investigated me?"

"Did you think I'd give my permission to wed Madeline based upon your station and a fancy letter? I've been looking into you since your first correspondence. I'm glad you didn't take my agent's bait and desert my girl to follow a fool's trail written in red ink."

"You've investigated him?" Madeline's grip tightened about a queen, as if it were a restorative. "How could you?"

"Maddie!" Father scolded. "It was bad enough to leave you in his care, but then Devonshire wanted your hand. I had to weigh the foolhardy advent of Dorset and his womanizing versus his stewardship and military record."

"You have a letter from Lady Glas-Glaston." Justain's rich voice seemed stilted and choppy. "I'm sure she ripped me to shreds."

"On the contrary, she's taken a fancy to you. She told me you were an honourable man worthy of Madeline. That's why it's to your left, one of your three recommendations."

"Three. So many." Justain tore a white paper in half.

"The Duke of Wellington decided the matter. He said to overlook the foolish pursuits as the lusts of youth."

"The Duke of Wellington? You contacted Lord Wellesley!" Justain scanned the door as if seeking retreat. He fluffed his cravat. "Why show me this now?"

"Madeline has become attached to you. I'd hate for her to be broken-hearted by scandal, like your mother, Lady Beatrice."

"Don't men-mention Mother's name again." His nostrils flared. "Her heart might've ached, but it was the poison of the high and mighty Ton, rubbing her nose in the old man's messes that killed her."

The air felt thick. The gilded sword above the mantel could slice the strain between Justain and Father.

"Struck a nerve. Fevered blood does course beneath the foppish ties." Father forced his quaking arms to fold. "See, Madeline, how the perfect warrior crumbles."

"Father, please. Don't do this!"

He waved her silent. "I could've found another man to marry Madeline, but I trusted the hero of England's words. Wellesley told me to see past the gambler, the scourge of his father's boot."

Justain coddled his side for a second. "I'm not proud of some of the things I've done. And my father is dead."

The duke reared up, pushing aside the chessboard. He seemed powerful again, akin to a yellowed cast of Zeus vanquishing an uprising. But Zeus threatened her *David,* and just when the sculpture seemed to breathe life. "I decided to set a final test with your cousin's help."

He gazed at Madeline. "Devlin betrayed me, too?"

"No, my men never found the reverend. Jodest Montgomery, the heathen of Bath, the one spending all of the Duke of Dorset's money. Montgomery mentioned our mutual acquaintance, Contessa Salvatore. Her late husband and I are old friends."

"Spanish connections? That's why Emillae was in Leicestershire on our wedding day." Justain brought a hand to his mouth. His face paled.

"When she told me you didn't take her bait, I saw my gut was right. Lady Glaston and Wellesley were right. You could honour my daughter. Or was I wrong? Were you done with Emillae or still mooning over Lancashire?"

"Please, relent. Justain doesn't deserve this." Madeline's heart beat a hundred times a minute. "Everything in those papers is well in the past. You know he's a good man."

Father ignored her. His gaze never strayed from Justain's. "Will you always protect and covet Madeline as I do?" He held his insignia ring to Justain. It swayed in the air with each tremor. "Swear to me your allegiance, that you'll never let your baggage like Gallows—"

"Barrow." Madeline seized the outstretched hand. "He doesn't need to prove anything."

Father shook free and extended his vibrating fist again to Justain. "Swear to me that you'll do all in your power to keep Madeline safe and faithfully make her happy. Then I'll sign another copy of the writ you shredded. All my business interests from my trading in Africa will be yours. That's eight thousand pounds a year. It'll end the dependence on that queer inheritance foisted on the Delveaux line."

That was Father's game. He, of all people, should know he couldn't force someone to do his bidding.

Justain picked up the bottle of brandy and held it to the light. The facetted glass reflected a rainbow upon his hand. "In some perverted way, I'm flattered you've gone to such lengths, hunting and bribing people to know more about me. And now I've won your approval." A wry smile twisted on Justain's lips as if he was humoured by this dark affair. "I understand that you're trying to gather your affairs, put things in order before you expire." He set the brandy back onto the desk. "I've spent one lifetime seeking approval, another trying to drown the need. I won't change to please you." He started toward the door.

Madeline held out her hand to him.

Justain ignored it. No warmth filled his eyes. All the tenderness disappeared. "There's nothing I can do for either of you." He bowed and left.

She stared at the hall, watching Justain's shadow grow smaller as he soldiered away. A pain swept through her. It cut like a knife's blade slicing her heart. She needed to go to him, convince him to forgive Father's arrogance. Struggling on wobbly knees, Madeline propelled to the door.

"Don't follow him."

She pivoted. "Why would you humiliate him and in front of me?"

"I don't want him holding this Kent business over you. I evened the score for you, Maddie."

"Evened the score?" She wanted to scream. "He's been respectful and decent."

"The way you idolize his footsteps. Your eyes brighten at the mention of his name. At least the truth will show you he's mortal."

Her chest felt as if it would burst. "Do you see my profound disappointment?"

He started coughing. "You'll get over it and learn how to use it to keep Devonshire in his place." The spite in his raspy voice was thick.

She rubbed her throbbing temples. "My disappointment is at you, Father. He's told me of his failings."

His brows flew together. "Really?"

She slipped back to his bedside. "And he hasn't lauded anything over me. He's been so kind. Did your report tell you that he'd rescued children from Barrow? Or that his commitment to honour drove him to propose."

"Maddie, I know you feel deeply for him. Pushing him to commit his life to making you happy in exchange for my wealth…it's within my right to do so."

"Why would I want him to have it, when the lust of money has made everyone here unhappy, maybe even crazed?" She towered over him, hoping to see some signs of the father she loved.

He lowered his gaze to the chessboard. "He's an ambitious man. The right incentive will make him the man you want."

She wiped away a dripping tear. "He is the man I want. Justain was beginning to open up his life to me. He started to trust me. And I…I could've been his Angelique."

He looked down and spun the board to assume the opposing colour. "Come let us play chess."

"For once, Father, say you're sorry. Chess won't fix everything. I'll send Meriwether in to sit with you."

"Maddie—"

She left the room, now understanding the blight of the St. Jameses' pride. They could be wrong, very wrong.

❧

Icy water, not hot blood seeped through his veins. Justain barely made it back to the main hall. The map in his mind disappeared, replaced with piles of shame-filled paper. Even Richard's widow had put her hatred to words. The woman repeated her accusations that Justain had intentionally killed his brother for the title.

Justain leaned against a marble warrior. If only the point of its spear were real. It could run him through.

He wrested the parchment from his pocket and smoothed its creases. The list of his sins numbered the clouds. Memorable passions were on the paper. Passions he wished to forget were there as well.

"Emillae has no loyalty." The contessa meant to betray him, her next act of revenge.

The duke must've bribed Devon. Even worthless cousin Jodest sold his secrets for silver. Only Dr. White, Wellesley, and Lady Glaston recommended him. He crumbled the note, making a taut ball. What did it state that wasn't correct? Every inked word illuminated truth. The duke was right. Justain did battle both sides of the bit.

He swatted his sweating brow. Strawberry fragrance laced his palm. Madeline had sat in that room for hours. She didn't warn Justain. Must be complicit. Why else was she accommodating, forgiving of his dark moods? His wife didn't expect better.

He'd almost bought her missionary act, almost ceded her power. Did women possess a middle ground between weak and conniving? "She's better than Caroline at getting her way."

He trudged further down the hall, paying no attention to where his feet carried him. Feisty old bird, the duke. In his gut, Justain admired the duke's loyalty to his daughter, envied the fatherly pride. Though the man spoke with vigour, his pallor seemed worse. The duke tried to cover the shakes of his hands "He's trying to make things right for Madeline before he dies."

Two months ago, Justain wouldn't have been able to make that concession, to be charitable to someone who slighted him. He struck at his forehead. Madeline affected his opinions even when he wanted to draw blood.

He turned down the main passage and tried to count marble tiles to calm down before his thoughts started to stutter. The duke pestered Wellesley. "At least my old commander spoke well of me. If he hadn't, vibrant Madeline would be married to an old man or that skunk Kent." No scenario seemed winning.

Another ride? He'd already exercised the duke's stables to their limits. He wouldn't be reckless with them. The wine cellar? That wouldn't do. If anyone found him in the cups, it would confirm to all his stature as a man given to excess. His aimless wanderings led him again to the patio. He edged forward and sat on the low knee wall. Justain cast pebbles at the lawn. He should've saved one of the horses. They'd be on their way to Devon, away from this lunacy.

"I fancy Avington right before sunset." Meriwether stood at the door. "It's quietest then. Sir, may I get you something?"

A gun or tall glass of brandy. "Will you retrieve my satchel?" Justain asked. "It's upstairs."

The man nodded and soon returned with the leather bag.

"Thank you, Meriwether." Justain took it and slung it to the ground.

"The sun's about to set." The reserved man pointed to the tree line. "The colours foretell the ending of one day and the promise of the next. A new day with new mercies."

Justain fiddled with the straps upon his boot. "Mercy's a good thing."

"It's God's miracle." Meriwether straightened the wrought-iron chairs about the table. "Do you want something to eat?"

"I look that bad. Humph." Justain launched forward then dropped into a chair. He started rummaging through his bag. "No."

"Very well, sir." Meriwether moved to the doorway. His onyx coat flapped like a regiment's flag. "With each new day, we get to decide who we are. A new man with new mercies. Our choice until there are no more days. The duke is running out of choices. Good evening, sir." Meriwether left.

Mercy. Running out of days. Justain sighed, opened his satchel, and removed his writing set. He wrote to the one person who never abandoned his trust, the one person who'd understand.

Avington Manor, 25 October 1821

Reverend Devlin Delveaux

Sourton Chapel, Devonshire

My Dear Cousin,

No new disaster has occurred, unless you count my daily life. I remember the time Richard taught me to ride. He pushed me to hold my seat firm until I got the horse to obey. Lately, it seems no matter how hard I try, I cannot keep my seat firm. I cannot get my life in order, let alone obey.

I would be in your debt if you visited Avington soon. My father-in-law is near death. I have no words to comfort Madeline. I know you will.

Very respectfully,

J. M. D.

He curried one more taste of mercy and wrote Madeline's aunt. Then he rose from the table to find Meriwether. These letters needed to be sent right away.

32

The horses jumped about in their pens after sharing the water trough. Justain took Derbudon's stiff brush and beat his pants free of mud. This place had become a second home to Justain, and busying himself out here was a great way to keep from Madeline and her falsehoods. Those jade eyes wouldn't fool him again.

Jonathan Winton hustled through the doors of the stable.

"My ally is back. What news of blessed Trenchard do you bring?"

"Some of the furnishings have arrived." He dropped a large sack onto the floor. "Sorry for the delay, but it took three days to get back on track from trying to root out Barrow."

Justain shook his steward's hand. "Winton, I need something to lift my spirits. Tell me you know where he is and my men are following his every move."

His copper eyes lowered. "I can't, my lord, but Dorset is running well. The new tenants are preparing the land for winter melons."

Justain gripped the bristles so tight, he surely strangled the handle. It wasn't fair Barrow remained free, and Justain remained a prisoner of Hampshire.

His steward untied the tan sack. "I think Devon is proud of your care of the orphans. The renovations to the orphanage have been finished. The children love the book room."

"Good." Someone should enjoy Justain's earnings.

"I ran into Mr. Montgomery in Devon. He's lookin—"

"I don't want to hear of my evil cousin. Jodest Montgomery is seeking new pockets." He pounded his fists along the stall, spooking Derbudon. Justain rubbed the horse's ear to calm it. "Bully. Hope he's broke and miserable."

Winton yanked one of Justain's favourite saddles and his long mud boots from the bag.

He took the perfectly worn leather implements from Jonathan's hands and began stripping Derbudon. "Nice of you to remember."

"Lady Devonshire sent a note and insisted that I bring you these from Devon."

Justain dropped the saddle. "You take orders from her now?"

Jonathan picked it back up, dusting it with a handkerchief. "Well, your wife is my countess." He handed it to Justain. "You seem upset, my lord."

He snatched the saddle from the outstretched hands.

His steward wrinkled his forehead and craned his red mop to the thatch roof. "I thought it was a reasonable request. Her request didn't seem out of the ordinary."

"No, she'll kill you with kindness while her father dives in with his knife."

"Sir?"

"She wanted me to believe that she's different. It's one of the faces she possesses."

Jonathan shook his head. "That's not what this

was."

"Winton, don't protect her. She reminded you of her title! Finally showing her true colours." He attempted to belt the horse's girth, but his hands slipped. He thrust the saddle aside.

"No, it was a simple note, and she even thanked me for watching over the two of you during our travels to Hampshire."

"What's she up to? What's she doing?" Justain rubbed the throbbing vein in his neck. He didn't mean to let his temper get away from him, but Madeline's betrayal raged like flames in his gut. If Athena had reared from his fumbling, the filly couldn't hurt him worse. What a fool he was to let down his guard and allow the blasted girl into his heart.

"My lord, she thought that you'd be more comfortable with your own things."

"I don't care what they do or how they try to coerce. I'll not alter my plans. She'll be sent to Innesfrey. I've made my decision."

Jonathan glared at him. "What's the matter with you, Justain?"

33

Every noise stilled. Even the horses stopped. "Well, Justain?" His childhood friend rarely called him by his Christian name. The situation must warrant it. Jonathan stepped back and leaned against the pen. "What has upset you this day?"

Justain tried to relax his stance, but every muscle coiled tight. "A week ago, the duke propositioned me to secure Madeline's happiness with more money than I've been able to generate in a year."

"Yes, I see the evilness of their hand."

"Here." He tossed Jonathan the parchment list of sins. "They had me investigated. They're trying to manipulate me. It's been her game all along."

"Just one page?" Jonathan crumpled up the note. "Did my lady admit to this?"

"Didn't have to. She's been acting, plying me with sentiment to get her way." Making him want her love. How could he be so stupid falling for her deceit? He took a deep breath. "She'll be in Innesfrey where I know I'll keep her safe. Nothing will change my mind on that."

Jonathan rubbed his forehead. "You don't see that Lady Devonshire is genuine in her concern for you?"

"I let my guard down, and they attacked my flank. It may not have been Madeline's notion, but she'll side with the duke and use her charms to trap me into her way of thinking."

"Sir."

"I'm sick of the whole manipulative lot."

The colour in Jonathan's face drained. "My lord, please."

"No, I'm not going to let you convince me differently. I hate them all. When will I be freed from here?"

"Sir, stop!"

The air filled with the light scent of strawberries. Justain winced and turned.

Madeline leaned against the stable door. The silver St. James crest flashed from her new cane.

"I didn't mean to interrupt." Her voice was low, and she fanned a letter. "A courier dispatched this from Reverend Delveaux. I thought you'd want it right away." Her cheeks burned scarlet. She must've heard every bitter word. "I'll put it here." She placed it on the rail and pivoted away.

"Madeline, let me help you back to the house." Justain dashed to her.

She shook her head. "I'll make it on my own. By myself." She tramped out of the stable.

"Blast it." He marched back to his steward, grabbing at a stabbing pain in his neck. "Why didn't you warn me, Jonathan?"

"I tried." He shook his head. "Well, you won't have any problems settling her in Innesfrey now."

"This is no time to joke. If I follow her, what should I say?"

"You've succeeded in convincing my lady you're a blackguard. But, sir, that's what you wanted."

Justain stiffened his shoulders. "What are you saying?"

"With everyone but Miss Lavis, the minute you find a flaw, you dismiss them. You treat them untoward."

"Call me a perfectionist. Since I've restored the family holdings, everyone pretends to want my favour. No one's been genuine; only my childhood mates, you, Devlin, and Miss Lavis are consistent."

"Why do you want to suspect malevolence on Lady Devonshire's part? She might be innocent of her father's plans."

"You want me to believe that as her father lies dying she thinks of bringing me comfort. No, it's been a careful orchestration to soften me on Innesfrey."

"If you don't see her Christian walk, you need to spend more time with Reverend Delveaux. You've married a woman who's not ashamed to live as Christ. You're fortunate."

He scowled. "Fortunate, Jonathan? I don't see that."

"You're on the path to be one of the most successful earls of Devon, yet you revert to trying to earn acceptance from others. Look at the energy you expend to perfect your life for those who are unworthy. You shouldn't live as this. You deserve better."

"That's not what this paper says."

Jonathan lit a match and burned the paper. "If you don't forgive yourself, there's no hope for you." He saddled Derbudon.

"If it's no act…" He rubbed his ear and remembered Madeline's many words of encouragement. "How do I keep her good opinion? She hasn't asked for baubles. She's not obsessed with receiving compliments." He opened his palm, remembering the peace he drew the last time he held Madeline's hand. The ache in his gut moved a little higher, right to his heart. "I'm a fool."

"Give me your boots. I'll put a polish on these while you ride." Jonathan pointed for a swap. "She's your wife. Make amends before the sun sets."

"I don't know what to tell her." Justain pulled them off and tugged on his high boots. "But haven't I always loved Caroline? There's not room in my heart for two."

"I don't think there are two." Jonathan bit his lip.

Justain climbed aboard Derbudon. "I'll find my countess when I know what to say."

Madeline trudged into her favourite hall and collapsed at the base of the Grecian warrior, her substitute for Michelangelo's *David*. Hot tears drizzled down her cheeks. She splayed her fingers across the marble-carved sandal. The cold stone should cool the blood pulsing within.

How could Justain suspect her as being part of Father's conspiracy? Had their time together meant anything?

The venom of his words rang in her ears. She wanted to smash her head against the statue to silence them. Her chest stung, and Madeline struggled for air. "Father of Heaven, why do I always put my trust where it will be broken?"

She brought her palm to her face, dabbed at the streams of tears. "Abba, gird me with strength. I don't want to hurt like this."

After Mother died, years of being caught in Father

and Step-mother's battles made it so easy to bottle up her emotions. Not anymore. She wept aloud, emptying her soul upon the unbreakable marble.

*

The shadows moved. The sun must've ascended to its highest point as Madeline lay prostrate at her statue's feet. She stood, dusted her purple skirts, and trudged to her father's study. With a deep breath and straightened shoulders, she entered his chambers.

The duke rested, but even asleep, his face looked strained.

Each day as her father declined the headboard grew larger. Madeline scanned the beautiful wall of books near the east window. One of the thick auburn curtains hung open.

He awoke. "I still remember getting you up and watching the sunrise, Maddie."

"Father, go back to sleep. I came to—"

"Angelique didn't like that. She'd say, 'Beloved, our child needs her rest, or she'll grow up…grow up…'" He covered his mouth as his lungs roared.

"Nervous, lacking your fearless strength." Madeline could quote their statements of love, but maybe it, too, was transitory. Her heart sank, possibility hit the floor.

Father stopped coughing. "Yes, that's what she'd say, but often she would join us to watch the great paintbrush of nature illuminate the skies."

She tried to force a smile. "You opened a window. After Mother…you always had them closed."

"My sun had gone, and I didn't want to view an imitation. Today, I had Meriwether tie one curtain back."

A round of shakes besieged him. Madeline raised a cloth to wipe dribble from his chin.

He took it, patting her hand. "How's Devonshire treating you? Is he still miffed?"

She looked away. "Fine."

"Maddie, you were never good at hiding things from me." He seized a gulp of air. "When a man of Lord Delveaux's stature is compromised into marriage, there'll be resentment. I tried to fix it for you."

She pulled the carved set from the shelf and put it on the blanket. It was pointless to discuss Justain. Father wouldn't understand this whirlwind swirling in her stomach, the ache in her soul. When was the last time he felt anything but contempt? "I came for chess."

Madeline filled her lungs with the room's stagnate air. "Do you want the light or dark pieces?"

"I'll be the black knights." He stopped her from spinning the board. "You're level-headed and reasonable, but inexperienced. I was happy when you kept to your books. We men are peculiar. We make choices at night that have no meaning in the day."

She steadied her knees and arranged the marble pieces.

"I tried to make him be faithful to you. Women don't have many options. You'll keep his house, share his bed for as long as he wishes it, and bear him an heir…while he may never share your fidelity."

A renegade tear welled in her eyes. Only a miracle could change things, and Madeline wouldn't be that lucky.

Her father winced. "I'm sorry, Maddie."

She blinked and patted her ears to unstop them.

"Shouldn't have intervened." He shrank back

upon his mound of pillows.

Meriwether entered the room. "It's time for your medicine, your grace."

"No more of that horrid stuff."

"Father, please. Your pain eases when you take it."

"Put it on the table, and both of you out. I need a nap to restore my energy."

"Very well, sir." Meriwether placed the tray on the cellaret, then extended his arm to her, and they ambled from the room.

"Lady Madeline, I don't think he'll make it beyond this week. You must be prepared."

She tightened her grip on his elbow. "I know, Meriwether. I heard it in his voice when he spoke to me. Father never apologizes."

34

All the curtains hung open. The sunshine ripped through the clouds and warmed the chill of the book study. Father was up three games to two, but Madeline cornered him for the win.

"Not this time, my dear." The intrepid man castled his rook and slipped away. He started laughing, but the chortle gave way to his horrendous coughing.

"Should I get the doctor?" She grabbed Father's hand to soothe him.

"No more doctors." He shook free and threw the sable blanket off his chest. "Are the game pieces disturbed?"

"They're fine." She tucked the cover around his lap.

"Good. I've a new topic: my funeral. I need you to be brave in the days ahead."

Madeline looked away, her eyes burning. Death would soon take the only thing left in this world that loved her. Justain wouldn't accept such foolish talk. She straightened and gazed into his tired hazel eyes. "You must fight, Father."

"I'm a realist. I'm getting more tired every day. The medicine's making me sick. With my nephew gone, you're all I have to count on to make arrangements."

"Me? I'm just a woman?"

"You." He patted her hand. "I want a traditional Irish burial. Make sure the wake is covered in food. Good food, none of Dana's specialties. I almost wish I could see the bands gather for me. You think they'll gather?"

"Hampshire loves her duke. You've been good to many."

"Yes, but not to you." He heaved a heavy breath. "Notify the vicar and send announcements to your step-brother and my barrister. Write these things down. You won't fail me?"

"I won't." Father would choose now to believe in her when he determined not to recover. She swallowed hard. "Father, if you're set upon this course, have you regarded Christ?"

He looked over his thin spectacles and pinched his smile tight. "Is this some new tactic to distract me from winning?"

The girl who left Hampshire would've abandoned this discussion, but Madeline had learned from Justain to take risks for what she wanted. "This isn't about chess. Have you regarded Christ?"

"I haven't." He dropped his gaze to the board. "End that look of pity."

Her skin warmed as if Abba hugged her and pressed in her to win Father to Him. Madeline moved her hands from the chessboard to command his full attention. "I know you blame God for Mother and Step-mother."

"No, only for Angelique. I was well on my way to hell when I met Dana." The duke laughed an empty hollow laugh.

"Father, be serious. Do you know Mother wasn't going to Almack's that night? She meant to stay at home, but she was overcome in her spirit that her destiny waited at Almack's. I believe the Lord foretold that her love was there."

"She was so lovely. Let me tell you the story. I was—"

"Do you think if Mama knew she'd be with us for a short time, she wouldn't have married you?" Madeline searched his face for comprehension.

"No, she was brave."

Madeline felt the energy of their love hover in the air. "Mama would have fought anything, risked everything to be with us for a mere moment."

"Yes, that was Angelique." He turned to the window as if he hoped to see Mama standing there.

Madeline leaned forward. "Why are you risking eternity? Why would you miss the chance to see her again?"

His gaze snapped back to her. "You're formidable in your logic."

"Father, I know your heart. No one was more hopeful. We live, we're in our right minds, and that you'd even try to love again is a testament to Christ. It's the power of His grace."

"You've found your voice, but it's not the noise of a child. It's the voice of a strong woman. You sound like Angelique ministering to me."

"I believe I've aged a great deal. I was at Death's door. Justain never told you how close I came to succumbing. I clearly heard that my work wasn't finished. I had to live."

Father touched her face. "So like Angelique."

Madeline gripped his hand. "I had to come back here to remind you of yourself. As much as I love you, Father, I love your soul more. Set that precious spirit free. You must repent. End the hate and remorse you battle."

"It's too late for me, child." He looked over Madeline's head to the window.

"There's still time. No one's taken this day from you. Father, you have said you've lived in agony for the past eight years. Don't condemn that soul to live there for eternity."

"I'm old and tired. Does it matter?"

"It matters to me, to God. You didn't kill Mama. You didn't injure me with Step-mother. You have to forgive yourself. Let's pray, now."

"Later, Madeline. I'm too tired." He closed his eyes and coughed again.

She took a goblet of water from the cellaret and lifted it to his lips. "You'll consider what I've said?"

The duke wheezed, tugged on his covers. "I will. You'd have made a great priest or barrister."

"I learned my fervour for Christ at your knee." She grasped his hand.

"Let me rest for now. I don't want to be pressed further."

"I love you, Father."

He closed his eyes again. "I know, dear. We'll take up chess later. Put away the pieces."

Justain leaned against the polished oak threshold of the duke's study. He had never heard such boldness and conviction pass Madeline's lips.

Meriwether stopped next to him. "Sir, join them."

"No, it seems my wife and her father are having a private moment." Justain didn't want to eavesdrop, but he couldn't help it.

He'd avoided her for two days. Justain didn't want to see the hurt his foolish words had inflicted, but she seemed to have recovered well and without his aid. A sigh fled his mouth. "I mustn't intrude."

"Nonsense." Meriwether carried a tray with the duke's juice. "They've no walls from the good or the bad." The informal crow started into the room.

Justain grabbed his shoulder. "No, tell Lady Devonshire I'll see her later."

"As you wish, sir."

Justain walked away and headed out of Avington. He trudged beneath the overcast skies to the stables. How he longed for it to rain and wash away this new shame.

Two of the duke's grooms polished the coaches again. He looked away, not wanting to see his reflection in the sparkle of the three carriages.

This time he'd ride up to the ridge and wait for mercy to leak from the clouds.

Silence painted Avington. Candlesticks lit the main halls, brightening the twists and turns. Justain had never returned this late. He passed the red dining room. His stomach rumbled, but he felt good about missing another awkward meal with his mother-in-law. The biting words between courses did nothing for his digestion.

He steadied his hand on the mahogany rail and climbed the carpeted stairs. Justain opened the door to Madeline's bedchamber. The room glowed. Candles and the fireplace burned.

His wife lounged on his chaise, reading the well-tattered book of Donne's poems. She wore her peach negligee with her feet adorned in pink kid slippers.

"What are you doing up, Madeline?"

She dropped her gaze back to the book. "Take the bed tonight. I'll be joining Father in a few minutes."

"You should rest. I won't have you sick." He moved to the ottoman.

"I've become more resilient." Her gaze remained on the print.

"Resilient?" Justain cleared his throat. "Then let me apologize for my tirade."

She didn't budge.

He rubbed his jaw. "At least look at me."

She closed the book. "I don't want to argue tonight. Get some rest, Justain."

"What you heard..." He undid his cravat. "It was unkind and unfor—"

"It's your truth, what's in your heart." She held a small smile. "I understand."

His heart? That useless organ wasn't speaking to him. He bounced to his feet and strolled to the bed. His dressing gown and brocade robe lay folded atop the sheets. Her night table bore a covered dinner tray. He lifted the lid, expecting frogs, but discovered sliced lamb and bread with a dish of mustard. Madeline remembered.

Could he feel worse? Pharaoh pulled back the sheets. No locust or plagues splayed the linens. Was that her game, to kill him with kindness? Justain picked up his garments and headed toward the changing screen. He stopped and divested his clothes.

Madeline never looked up. She missed his peacock strut. Some women swooned from his manner of dress or his athletic build. Madeline was different and now seemed impervious to his charms. He finished dressing and sought the attention of the lamb. Seasoned with cloves, each morsel danced on his palate. "Thank you, my dear." He downed a goblet of tart lemonade.

She poked her head above the pages. "Goodnight."

He sank onto the soft mattress, but leapt back up. "Do you ever get mad?" He paced back in front of her. "Say things you regret?"

"What would you have me do? You won't believe me. I've no way of ever gaining your trust." She stretched her limbs. "I don't want to play this game."

He folded his arms. "You intend to act the coy maiden for the rest of our visit."

Madeline picked up a hair ribbon and marked her place, then took her time sliding the abused book on the ottoman. "Our visit will end soon. I need to go to Father."

"This won't be put off. We've done a dance this past week. It ends now."

"What do you want, Justain? Tell me what you'd have me do."

He claimed her hand and kissed it. "Stay with me tonight."

35

Madeline tightened her grip on the cane. Justain should be deemed the master of confusion. He said he hated her, all the St. Jameses. Now he wanted her again?

Justain stepped closer. The light from the oil lamp streaked highlights in his rich sable hair. "Stay in my arms tonight."

"Why? Concerned I'll stab you in your sleep? Never know what treachery a St. James will wreak."

He smirked then bent forward and put his lips onto her forehead. "I haven't forgotten your nightly kissing ritual."

"Let's not pretend." She sighed and tilted away from his handsome face. "That token meant something to my parents."

"It means something to me, too. It means we will start over, Madeline Delveaux."

She eased to the floor, but her cane made an ominous thud. "Only time will ease your mind." Madeline patted his lapel. "I'm going to go relieve Meriwether."

Justain put his hands upon her shoulders. He smoothed the fabric of her robe.

Madeline's muscles tensed, but he worked a gentle path down her back.

Her reserve waned, and she leaned into him. Why

couldn't he be her rock, someone to depend upon when…"Please stop." Her voice was a mere whisper. "This sweetness will disappear with the next bad wind."

"I want you in my arms." He brushed his knuckles along the nape of her neck. His rough skin sent shivers through her.

"You've been riding a lot and still haven't worn gloves." Madeline pulled away and started for the door.

Justain blocked her exit. "There's something intoxicating, feeling power beneath my fingers." He traced her sides with his palms.

Her knees felt weak. Why was he doing this? He'd just shred her heart to ribbons again.

His arms wrapped around Madeline, and he tugged her against his chest. "I've fouled up too many words. I need to show you how much I care. You've infected my soul, Madeline, a fever I shan't resist."

"Now I'm a sickness?" Madeline pushed at his hands. "You'll recover well enough. Nothing lasts." She shook her head. "I don't have the strength to watch your favour disappear again."

Justain spun her around and whipped her up into the air. Her cane fell to the carpet; the sea of sapphire muffled its impact.

Madeline clutched at his robe. "What?"

He swept across the floor. "I'm putting my wife to bed." Justain nestled her amongst the pillows and joined her near the mattress's edge.

She tried to sit up. Her thumbs stumbled across the sleek linen of his nightshirt. Madeline snatched her hands back. There had to be away to escape caring so much, of wanting his strong arms about her. She moved away from him. "Please, get me my cane."

Justain flung one arm behind his head and with the other, he clasped her hand. "Something should be painted on the canopy. Maybe a mural of stars, or perhaps sheep jumping over the moon."

She rolled her eyes. "No more delays. I need to go."

"I need you."

She sat up and gazed at him.

His jaw quivered as if he struggled to choose the right words. "I need you, Madeline. I'll shout it to the rooftops; make a spectacle of myself, if that's what it takes for you to believe me.

"No riddles. Not tonight, Justain."

"You're the wordsmith, not me. It frightens me to think of you hating me." He thumbed his chest. "You've dug somewhere up in here, and I'm a coward to run from these feelings."

She shouldn't look into those woe-filled eyes. She melted against him as his hands tightened about her, as he towed her close.

"Rest in my embrace." His lips met her cheekbone, and a line of fire washed across it. "Forgive me in spite of all the foolish things I've said." Justain nibbled his way to the hollow of her throat. "Tell me we still have a chance, Maddie." His shallow breaths tickled. He nuzzled the cut of her chin.

Madeline didn't know what to do with her hands. They tangled in the folds of his robe.

He nipped her jaw with his teeth. "I won't disappoint you again."

"We do find ways to be at cross purposes." She touched his side, numbered his ribs. "But Father needs me."

Justain rolled onto his back and expelled his breath. "Then you must go to him." He trudged over to the chaise and retrieved her cane. His countenance was blank save a tight smile. Was he wounded by their disagreements, her lack of trust?

"Don't over task yourself." He lay back down on the mattress.

Madeline pattered around the bed. She put her hand on the crystal doorknob, but didn't turn it. "Why do you make everything a test of loyalty?"

He sat up with his long legs draped over the side. "I'm not asking you to choose."

"Yes, you are. If I go through this door, you'll always believe I'll side with Father over you."

"I won't, but it's easy for me to think the worst." His gaze lowered to the carpet. "Madeline, I know I don't deserve you."

Her heart ached. She slipped to the headboard, picked up a pillow, and with all her might, hit him across his face.

He grabbed her hand. "Must I make you angry for you to choose me?" Justain enfolded her in his arms and lifted her to his chest. He bussed her forehead. "Rest, in my arms. I'll wake you in a few hours."

This mood of his might pass, but right now Madeline wanted to pretend Justain loved her, that she had one person in this world on whom she could depend. She laid her cheek against his lapel and savoured the sandalwood adorning his neck.

The bells of St. Mary's awoke her. Sunlight streamed through the window. Such a solemn noise for what appeared to be the beginnings of a beautiful day. Sleeping with Justain's strong arms around her felt so nice, so perfect. Where was he?

She rubbed her eyes.

Justain perched at the edge of her bed. "Madeline."

She stretched and pushed away the linen sheet. "Have two hours past?"

Concern filled his watchful gaze. His sky-blue eyes seemed sad. "More than two. I let you sleep."

"Oh." She sat up. "I'll have to hurry to join Father for breakfast. Send for Anne?"

"I will." He stood then paced on the rug.

"Justain, you're dressed." His intricate cravat adorned a navy jacket and a dark green waistcoat. "How long have you been up?"

The bell tolled again.

"There's no easy way to say this." He took her palm in his hand. "Madeline, your father passed during the night."

36

Madeline couldn't speak. She dropped back down and stared at the blank canopy.

Justain sank upon her bed and reached for her fingers. "I know you'd been hoping he'd improve, but he grew weaker each day."

"Justain, he's not gone. We were supposed to pray. You're mistaken."

"I wish that I was. He succumbed to his palsy." He rubbed the soft flesh between her knuckles. "At least he will be in no more pain."

She snatched her hand back. "I suppose you'll give me the next platitude that my father's in a better place."

Justain pushed to his feet. "I don't know what to say. This anger must be part of your grieving."

"When did he pass?"

"Meriwether said it was around midnight."

She touched her lips. She had been kissing Justain, and her thoughts were far from her father. "I failed him. He's no longer in physical pain, but Father has traded that lot for eternal torment."

"Let me comfort you." Justain reached for her.

She gazed at his outstretched arms. They'd stirred tender feelings within her; they had distracted her from her vigil. "No."

Justain leaned in close. "Maddie."

She touched his cheek before letting her hand fall to the coverlet. "It's punishment for being too timid. If I could have the last few hours, days back, I'd press Father. I'd beseech him to make amends."

"Madeline, it's all right for you to mourn. I'm here for you."

Justain wouldn't understand, never would. "I need you to do something." She opened a drawer in her bed table. Madeline gathered the notes she'd written that afternoon as her Father instructed. Her thumb trailed the heavy parchment, her father's stationery. She inhaled, filled her lungs. "Please dispatch these for me and send someone for Father Williams. Have him meet with me this afternoon to discuss the service."

"I could handle things. As your husband I could…"

His gaze met hers, then he looked to the carpet.

He must see her determination. She would cede Father's request to no one.

"Fine. I'll do as you wish." Justain took the letters from her hand. "But you won't give yourself time to grieve?"

"I failed him where it counted, but I'll perform Father's last wish, the coordination of his funeral." She pulled her knees up to her chin and wrapped her arms around them. *Abba Father, why?*

"I'll see to these tasks, but is there anything else?" Justain put the letters into his pocket.

She turned to the threshold.

"I'll go now." He waited for another silent minute then left the room.

The door closed, and she waited for his footsteps to fade. Bitter tears wet her bedclothes.

❧

Justain set out as Madeline's servant, doing her bidding. He walked the long corridor. If he'd made love to Madeline last night, she'd never forgive herself or Justain. Thank Providence. For once, he didn't act selfishly.

Madeline looked forlorn. The duke's death was expected. A few kisses and earnest sleep shouldn't be blamed. Yet she wouldn't let Justain console her? "My wife's stubborn."

Justain entered the duke's study. The proud man had been shrouded in his bed linens. His hands were folded to his chest with his insignia ring poking through the cloth. The last time he was in this room, the fiery duke brandished that band about his yellowed fist.

Meriwether sat in a chair presiding over the body. The light of a solemn candle highlighted tears on the valet's creased face.

The day Mother passed, her room felt cold and he'd sat just as Meriwether, waiting for life to stir. Thick bandages and salve bound her hands. They'd been burnt in Trenchard's fire. Justain watched over her until his legs grew pained in the caned chair. Richard had to force him from the room.

"I'm glad you were with the duke, Meriwether. You were his constant ally."

"His friendship…" The man sputtered a deep sigh. Sorrow etched the lines in his face. "It was something to treasure. He should've had more years. Should've lived to see grandchildren. He was healthy as much as six months ago, just like his heir." The man yanked a handkerchief out his pocket and mopped up the rivers of water collecting at his chin.

Justain trudged to the infamous desk. The chess set was stacked, ready for a challenge. "Madeline loved this game with the duke."

"Yes, the world disappeared for them when they played." Meriwether refolded his tear-stained cloth.

Justain moved a pawn. "I wish I knew how to play." Madeline seemed so distant. Once he got these letters to Jonathan, he'd go look after her. Mustn't let her be alone. "And you must carry on. The duke would want that."

"His grace would. Very well, sir."

Justain crossed the threshold, took six steps, and then stopped. "I'm not up for this task." God's shoulders were. "Lord of Heaven, please bring peace and comfort to my wife." *Please grant this request from a stranger.*

❧

Father's body laid in repose in the parlour. Madeline stayed in the hall and stared at the pine coffin. All his power and wealth housed in a wood box.

She wandered down the corridor to Father's study. The bed was gone. Meriwether had brought the room back to order. The mahogany shelves glistened with polish. The varied book spines shined.

The room felt big again and became the study she knew as a child. Madeline opened the velvet curtains of the great windows. She let the sunshine flow through the leaded panes. Maybe the warm light would burn away her sorrow.

She plodded to the desk and enfolded pieces of the

chess set in brown paper. Her fingers lingered on the indentions of the carved rook. No more games. She'd never see Father again.

The sound of Justain's boot heels became clear. He stood behind her, put a hand on her shoulders. "Everything you've requested has been done."

"Thank you." Madeline kept wrapping the pieces.

"I brought something to cheer you." He draped an arm about her shoulder and gave her a small yellow bouquet. They were similar to the flowers from their wedding. "I hope you like them."

"They're beautiful." She put down the chess pieces to covet the gift.

He nudged her. "Meriwether says you have the house in a terror, getting things underway. I don't want you overexerting yourself."

"I'm fine." Madeline tucked the flowers under her arm and moved to the centre of the desk. She splayed paper over a queen.

"Lady Glaston has made it to town."

"Aunt's here? How?"

"I wrote to her two weeks ago. I thought it'd be easier for you with her near."

"Oh, I thought she swore never to return. I guess that's why she's not at Avington now." Madeline shook her head. "Thank you."

Justain stopped in front of her. "Are you avoiding me?

She slipped to the far edge. "There are many things to do. Please hand me another piece of paper."

He flipped a piece of brown parchment to her. "You won't even hold my gaze."

Madeline rolled up the bishop.

Justain dropped his hands to his side. "You didn't

do anything wrong."

"There are many pieces."

"Don't place a wall between us." He raised her chin. "Whatever this wall is…I want it removed."

She jerked away. "Is that an order, Justain?"

37

Madeline gathered the remaining pieces, pushing them into a circle. She wasn't in the mood for puzzles.

Justain massaged his neck. "The study smells of mustard liniment. When you were sick in Much Wenlock, your room smelled of this same treatment."

"I wish it was sandalwood. That's how I want to remember Father."

"The duke's death shouldn't take us away." He raised his hand to her face and caressed her cheek. "Let me support you."

Madeline gritted her teeth. "Another command, my lord?"

His forehead crinkled. "If that's what it takes, so be it. I order you to talk to me."

Madeline moved backwards. "My father told me of my obligations to you. Not one was to be a maudlin, weepy child." She traipsed toward the door. The train of her black dress slapped the floor.

He intercepted her. "I know you're angry."

"I appreciate your concern, but I won't cry to you or anyone about things I cannot change."

"Lass, I'm not asking you to cry. Hit at me. Strike at me, but show me more than this veil you call a smile."

"Why? I'm not so green to think that kisses in the dark mean anything. This is a compromised marriage.

We're not of one accord."

He blasted air out his mouth. "Things are different."

The light streaming through the windows made her squint and obscured her view of his eyes. "Different? If only I had gone to Father." She leaned her head on a bookshelf. The tart perfume of ink brought her comfort.

"You regret kissing me?" He tugged a loose strand of hair as if to draw her back to him. "You've done nothing scandalous."

She rubbed her forehead. "Perhaps, I should be scandalous instead of the one always left behind."

"Everything will be fine. Come to me, Madeline." He stroked her arm.

She shook free. Nothing she counted upon lasted. Hadn't Justain proved that?

"You're hurting, Madeline, and it's keeping you from admitting the growth of your feelings. It's not selfish to have one moment of pleasure in this gilded mausoleum."

Wetness streaked her cheeks. Why was he doing this when she'd hurt that much more when he again stomped on her heart? "I won't do this now, assess my feelings. Leave me be."

He bit his lip as if she'd slapped him. "I'm saying this all wrong."

"In your own way, you're trying to be helpful, but I'm fine." She swatted away a renegade tear. "Please find Mer—"

"I don't ack-acknowledge my feelings, and I'm even worse at showing them." He took his handkerchief and trailed the droplets. "When I said I needed you, I meant it."

"I'm not pathetic, Justain. I'm not crumbling. My thoughts are ordered. There's no need to reassure."

"This is beyond obligation, more than friendship. I care, Madeline. I ache because I know you're in pain." Justain moved to her and swaddled her in his large open arms. "The duke, more than anything, wanted me to make you happy. Let me hon-honour that request."

Did he stutter the truth? Madeline slumped against him. She couldn't fight both Justain and the loss of the only man who ever loved her.

Justain held her as if she were fragile, like fine porcelain.

She wasn't unbreakable marble. The dam holding the swollen river of her grief burst free, and Madeline wept aloud.

❧

Justain wished he could hold his wife a little longer, but Meriwether entered the room.

"Lady Madeline, Vicar Williams is here. He's waiting for you on the patio." The valet's countenance dimmed as he gazed about the room. "Years of special confidences. Now no more."

Justain stood straight. "Should we move the minister to a drawing room, Madeline?"

"The patio?" Her gaze floated toward the grand window. "No. I will meet him there." She retrieved the flowers.

Justain touched her hand. "I know you won't let me orchestrate this for you, but may I be at your side?"

"If you wish. Thank you for the acacias." Madeline left the room.

"They're mimosa," he corrected. His attempts at

helping seemed temporary. Blast it.

He caught up to her as she entered the patio and pulled out a chair for her.

She pulled a folded bit of paper from her pocket. Smoothing the tear-stained paper, she laid it flat on the table. His poor girl. How could he be of help? His wife leaned close to Vicar Williams and pointed to her list of instructions.

Justain always regarded her as intelligent, but now he saw her as a dutiful taskmaster. She'd handle the duties of Trenchard well, even giving his dictatorial butler a run for it. He was proud of his wife.

The grandfatherly man wrote in his book. "You intend to be there? Lady Madeline, that's not proper."

"It's Lady Devonshire, now." She refolded the paper. "I will be there."

"I'm Madeline's husband, Lord Devonshire." Justain leaned over the man. "She is determined to do this."

The vicar shook his head. "I see."

"It's a church service." Justain gazed at Madeline. "You couldn't stop any of the women in this family from doing as they pleased."

"Well, it's settled. Thank you, Reverend. Father's service is set." Her voice crumbled.

The grandfatherly man closed his book. "I'll lead the funeral, starting at nine o'clock in the morning."

She didn't respond.

Justain laid his hand on her shoulder. "That'll be fine."

"Good, my lord. I must run along to prepare St. Mary's for the service. The chapel will do right by the duke."

Justain shook the vicar's hand and escorted him

from the patio. He saw the man off from the portico at the front of the house then followed the tiles back to the patio.

Madeline's chair sat empty. She'd vanished.

He pounded the table. The mahogany wobbled. Where did she go? He thought he had made an impression upon her in the study, but now she left to be alone again. "Why is it so difficult for her to depend upon me?"

"Perhaps, she doesn't know how, not having an older cousin to lean upon."

Justain pivoted to see Devlin Delveaux standing at the threshold, Meriwether beside him.

The valet swung the reverend's sack. "I'll prepare a room for you."

"By the garlands on the doors, I take it I've arrived too late." Devlin removed his dark-grey cape and claimed a seat at the table. "I'm sorry for your loss."

"Which? My wife's or mine?" Justain gripped his stomach.

"You don't have ailments similar to Richard's. There are no tumours in your gut?"

"What? No, I didn't eat breakfast."

Devlin reared back in his chair and sighed as if relieved. His fingers combed through his salt-and-pepper hair. "If I know my cousin, there's not a problem you can't fix or a female you can't charm."

Justain sighed. "You remember when Mother died. I've been thinking about her lately."

Devlin lost his grin. "I do. And I think about my parents upon occasion."

"It feels like all hope is stripped away." Justain slouched in his chair.

"You became close to the duke?" Devlin leaned

forward. "I thought that your letter—"

"Mother never got the chance to be proud of me."

Devlin shook his head. "Aunt Beatrice liked you in your regimentals."

The bells of St. Mary's tolled again. No soul in Hampshire could miss the death wail. Justain slapped the table. "Devlin, Madeline's withdrawn, scurried off."

The reverend propped his boot up and retied his laces. "Her father died. It'll take some time for her to come to terms with her grief."

"She's pushing me away." He yanked his cravat free.

Devlin chuckled. "She's mirroring you, Justain. She's picked up your bad habits. You shouldn't expect her to give of herself, to be vulnerable to your whims, when you offer her nothing in return. The law of the harvest, cousin. You're reaping what you've sown."

Justain slumped against the table. "This is all a ploy to get me twisted up. I didn't see that. I'm growing soft."

"No." His cousin shook his head. "Give her time, and she'll trust you. That's what you want from her?"

"Devlin, I should go find her, and let her know that you're here."

He caught Justain's shoulder and stopped him from fleeing. "What do you want from Madeline? You've been trying to convince yourself that she'd be better off in Innesfrey and she hasn't worked her way into your heart. Thou dost protest too much."

"What do you know of matters of the heart? No one but God has touched yours."

His cousin's indigo eyes glazed over. "I'm flesh and blood, Justain. I've loved deeper than you've ever known."

Justain dropped back in his seat. Dubious claim, but Devlin never lied. "I love my horse, Athena, too. That doesn't count."

"No, Justain. A woman whose beauty still haunts my dreams when my mind is undisciplined."

It was true. "Who? Do I know her?"

Devlin picked a stray piece of lint from his cape. "Her name's unimportant. Our union would've brought unhappiness to our families, hurt those closest to me." Solemn, soulful, like the moaning of St. Mary's, Devlin's voice sounded heavy as if he felt the pain anew. "I'd rather be miserable than to bring you or the rest of my kin sorrow."

"She was of common birth. I would not have cared. The old man would've allowed you anything."

He took a seat, stretched out his long legs. "She'd never be happy as a vicar's wife, so I let her go." His indigo gaze rose to meet Justain's. Pain burned in those orbs. "The thorn in my flesh runs deep, but I live to be Providence's servant. And your keeper."

Devlin was Justian's blood-brother in so many ways, but how could this unflappable tower of strength carry a flaw?

"I'm always too caught up in my sphere to notice anything else. Devlin, I know dozens of lasses who would do anything to gain your attention."

"They aren't the memory of a summer storm in Trenchard's heather." He leaned back in his chair. "Delveaux men are as the vole. Either we mate for life like the country vole, or we're never satisfied and keep looking for endless comfort similar to the town variety."

"A vole? Devlin, I'd never guess you'd be a rat for

love."

St. Mary's bell tolled again. Devlin looked toward the church. "It was the right thing to do to free her from an unfulfilling promise."

Justain twisted his signet band. "I should let Madeline go?"

"Devonshire, you need your countess as much as she needs you. Sacrifice your healthy pride and offer to share your life. Allow yourself to be happy." He yawned. "You're a country vole, too."

Justain stood. "I need to go find her. Meriwether should have your room prepared. Rest up from your latest camp meeting. Please conjure up some Bible verse to give her solace."

"While I'm at it I should get one for you!" Devlin shouted as if to make sure Justain heard him.

Country vole? Devlin's words haunted him. The old man was a town rat, as was Richard. Wasn't Justain one as well, switching his fancy from woman to woman, from Caroline and now to Madeline?

❧

The sun began to set before Madeline headed into her bedchamber. She eased the door open and slipped inside.

Justain sat by the fireplace with his feet up and his muscled arms folded. His cravat was undone, his sleeves wrinkled and rolled up to his elbows. "Decided to make an appearance before dark?"

"I thought you'd still be out riding." She closed the door, sat on the end of the bed, and readied herself for a lecture.

"Did you lose all track of time? I've looked

everywhere. I even had some of the groomsmen leave their posts to search for you."

She took her shoes off and lined them near the footboard. "I'm sorry. I assumed you wouldn't release the hounds until it was pitch black outside."

"This isn't funny. Do you want me alarmed? Does it bring you satisfaction of some sort?" His boots stomped the floor as he paced in front of her.

"It brings me no comfort. I needed to do something before tomorrow." Madeline stared at the fireplace and watched the flames dance and shed embers.

"What did you have to do that I couldn't help you complete? You're still recovering, Madeline. There are villains who may want to hurt the wife of an earl or the daughter of a duke."

"I won't disappear on you again, and I'll take more notice to insure that you know of my whereabouts." Her voice pitched as she struggled not to be baited.

"I'm not trying to scold you. I want you to understand my concern is genuine. I'm waving a white flag and surrendering. You're not making this easy."

"I do understand, but how do I make you comprehend my feelings without alienating you?" She gazed in his eyes. "You've told me how you hate Devlin's pestering about faith."

"I don't hate it. It makes me uncomfortable because of the life I've led." His sky-blue eyes darted. The fork in the conversation must've surprised him.

"I don't know how to make you happy." She turned back to the fire.

He leaned forward. "I overheard your last conversation with your father. I didn't mean to, but no one could have done a better job at trying to get him to make peace. Not even Reverend Delveaux, with his many gifts."

She rubbed her leg.

"Devlin arrived today. I should get him to talk with you. The reverend's good at empathy."

Madeline swallowed hard. "You really don't understand how I feel. What if I had that conversation with Father the night we arrived? What if I talked about faith the day I left? I'll never know what might've happened."

"Some things even the great Madeline cannot change. Why do you try to take upon the weight of the world? You did your best."

"If I keep quiet, and I let another person I care about lose the opportunity for true peace…I won't bear it."

"Madeline, I want you to be free to talk with me about anything, even if it is spiritual in nature. If you're going to let it eat at you, forget the consequences. Proclaim your faith."

"This won't work." She lowered her head and tugged at the fringes of the rug with her feet. The truth overwhelmed her; he'd never see her point of view. "As soon as this is over, let's make haste to Innesfrey. I'll make no more complaints."

38

Justain's soul ached for his wife.

Her eyes rimmed red. Her voice sounded raw. Madeline must've hidden herself to cry alone all afternoon. Why didn't she give him the chance to console her? "All is not lost," Justain said. "Tomorrow, the sun also rises."

"No more platitudes." She moved the carpet fringe with her cane.

"I'm trying to be generous to your pain. There's no need to run off." He wanted to hold her, but she'd probably retreat if he advanced.

She set down her cane against the footboard. Madeline tugged at her high onyx collar. Her hair blended into it, making her appear wrapped in darkness. "You're not listening."

"Madeline Delveaux, if you flail yourself for every soul you cannot save," he finished unbuttoning his waistcoat, "you've already lost."

"What if death knocked upon your door tomorrow? I'd feel this anguish again." Her voice trailed off.

"It won't."

Madeline dropped on to the mattress. "I will not bear Barrow or some mishap to take you from me, especially when I know you haven't made peace with God. I need distance to regain perspective."

He wiped his neck with his palm. "Your Father was right. You would've made a fine barrister."

"You were right about a marriage of convenience. I've grown up, and I want the peace of Innesfrey."

Justain eased closer to the bedpost. "You're failing your poets; everything is worth the chase, the victory." He wiped his mouth, trying to blot out the hollow sounding message. "Oh, Madeline, don't lose courage."

She straightened and faced him again. "I've admired your strength. I wish that I could fight and win, but with every victory, there's someone who loses, someone who's left behind. I won't be that person again."

Justain sat beside her. He pulled her head onto his shoulder. "You'll be at Innesfrey for a few months. Then, maybe a trip to see your sculptures?"

Madeline kissed him.

Justain revelled in the feel of this woman pressed against his chest. Yet, there was a bitter sweetness to her lips. He tasted the salt of her tears.

She relented. "Tomorrow, you will stand up for me in the procession."

Justain touched his mouth. "Why does this feel like good-bye?"

"We will practice our official duties as man and wife, but bind me to Innesfrey. It's what I want."

"I know you love me, Madeline. You mustn't deter your heart."

She bounced to her feet. "You insufferable man! How dare you say such things?"

He stood and smoothed her dress of wrinkles. His hands pressed down her sides. "Tell me I'm wrong."

"Everything that I love leaves me or dies. Why

would I sentence myself to that pain again? Aunt never ventures back here for eight years. Mama and Mrs. Wilkins are at rest. At least I have peace because they knew peace." She shook her head. "Not like Father. He's gone and is in torment. You'll be the same."

He pulled her back into his embrace. "I'm alive and plan to be so for some time to come."

Madeline pushed away. "I see why Step-mother remains detached. She learned from her aches. It's time for me to be that wise."

Someone pounded upon the door.

"Not now!" Justain rubbed his temples.

"It's me, sir," Jonathan replied. "We found weapons along the tree line. An old rifle and a silver pistol."

"Silver?" Justain's gut vibrated, but this wasn't time to hunt danger, not with his marriage crumbling. "Winton, I'll find you later."

"You should go and review the objects." Madeline turned away and headed for the threshold.

"Don't go, Maddie."

"You and Father are so similar." She patted her heart. "I won't hurt like this anymore. I won't lose what little peace that remains." Madeline brushed her face free of tears. "I need to check on the cook's progress. All the dishes for the repast in the orangery must be perfect. I'll be in the kitchen for an hour."

The door closed behind her. If it had slammed, Justain would've felt better. He could toss this mishmash as part of her grieving. It didn't slam. She was resolved on the matter.

He eased himself back onto the chaise and stared at the fire. He tried to smother the flames in his nostrils. "I should be happy; Madeline wants to be away from me." Wasn't it his plan to settle her in Innesfrey?

Justain huffed a tight breath. The burning oak in the brick fireplace wafted a rich scent. It smelled akin to the woods after the rain. His tattered book of poems rested on the ottoman.

"Yesterday she had you." He picked it up and reared his hand backwards to fling it into the flames.

He didn't fling Donne into the hearth, but laid it on the floor. Seeing the tattered book burn would be emblematic. Madeline should be as one of these poems. The fragile heroine who clings to her knight, fighting with all her might for their love. "I've lost her." Justain picked at a button on his waistcoat. The soldier should go inspect the grounds.

Mason's silver flask. Justain kept it hidden in his trunk filled with brandy for emergencies. He dug it out and swirled the bottle. The brandy burped inside.

The door swung open. "Madeline said you needed me?" Devlin gazed at him, shaking his head, frowning. "She was right."

Justain winced. "I haven't touched a drop since Leicestershire."

Devlin took the flask and uncorked it. "Is this the smell you crave?"

"She doesn't want me. Wants some mewling Methodist…some angelic An-Anglican. That's not me."

The man flopped onto the ottoman. "There's always an excuse." He spun the bottle. "I suppose this is the answer. A pint of spirits to absolve you of guilt."

Justain jerked it back and threw the flask into the flames. The leaking alcohol made a bright fireball before the fire tamped down. "She won't twist me up. She isn't Caroline." He ground his fist in his palm.

"Does every woman need to swoon in your presence, Justain? You're not that shallow."

Justain grabbed the poker and fetched Mason's tarnished flask. "Madeline doesn't think I'm worth the risk."

"But what are you sacrificing for her, Justain? You don't claim to love her, though I think you might. What are you offering her?"

He stabbed the embers to rekindle the fire; the shiny band on his finger sparkled. The badge of honour for the married Earl of Devon. "Until her father's death, Madeline did want me. She wanted to be of one accord. I've been running." The way she kissed him with the intensity of the sun, sought him out as if the day began with him, and made him believe he could wrestle the moon. "Devlin, what am I to do?"

"You've been on a path to reform your life. When we lost Richard, you told me you wanted to be a better man. You've changed the surface, but what about the inside?"

"Caroline made me want to be better, but Madeline makes me a better man." Justain put down the poker. Why hadn't he realised how special Madeline was before it was too late.

"If you base your hopes on anyone, man or woman, you'll always be disappointed. If your self-worth is based upon opinions, you'll continually be reduced to rubble." Devlin handed Justain a small onyx book, his travelling Bible. "Let me show you how to bolster your foundation."

The sun of Hampshire absented its station, leaving thick grey clouds to cover Avington like a mourning shroud. Today, the duke would be laid to rest.

Justain stood on the portico with the mourning party. The intermittent call for atonement and remembrance, the spiking of the bells of St. Mary's, mocked the grouping, the belligerent widow, and the bewildered son-in-law.

The duchess wore fine black satin trimmed with onyx pearls. The woman must have ordered it in advance for the occasion. "Where is Madeline? She could at least watch the procession from here."

Justain turned to the hills. Something shined in the distance. Metal? He blinked to clear his eyes. "I had my steward seat her at St. Mary's chapel. She didn't want to impede the procession. Lady Glaston's with her."

A frown painted the duchess's face. She twisted the bangles on her arm. "At the church with that guttersnipe? They've no regard for tradition or respectability." She shook her head. "What a poor showing for the family. My son couldn't make it, and you wouldn't let Randolph Kent attend."

"My dear Duchess, Mr. Kent's not welcome." The skunk found living more important. Justain waved Devlin near. "Also, my cousin is here, to help represent our families. Reverend Delveaux, this is the Duchess of Hampshire."

She pinched her brows.

Devlin bowed. "My cousin says you have a modern view of forgiveness. I'd love to discuss how a woman of your stature sees mercy being dispensed."

Her countenance dimpled, and she accepted Devlin's arm.

The desperate wailing of bagpipes cried at a

distance. The procession would pass the house soon. Then he and Devlin would follow.

Justain searched the tree line. Nothing unusual, but his gut still tingled. He'd spent too much time chasing bandits. Time to focus only on his duty to his wife and his Hampshire family.

The funeral caravan herded the faithful of Hampshire to salute their duke. Like a flood, the people poured down the path approaching the main house.

The breeze picked up, but his long greatcoat braced him from the chill. The family followed behind the horse drawn caisson bearing the duke's casket. Derbudon, the silver stallion, looked well high-stepping in front of the parade.

The bells of St. Mary rang loud and strong. Justain led his cousin and all of Hampshire into the brilliant chapel hewed in marble and coloured glass.

❧

Justain shrouded Madeline's view of the crypt.

She and Aunt Tiffany couldn't come any further, but Madeline wasn't ready to return to the house. She needed to know Father's interment was complete.

Yesterday, she'd viewed the opening in the wall, ran her fingers in the fresh dirt. She'd placed Justain's flowers on the cast plaque bearing her mother's name. At least Father would be laid next to Mama.

A bird whimpered in the distance. The moan brought a lump to Madeline's throat. She wiped her eye. No more tears. No more losses.

The vicar led the men from the crypt.

It was over.

Justain said nothing, but wound his arm about her. "Let's go back to house."

She nodded and allowed him to help her over the uneven ground.

Slicing through the air, a shot rang out separating the crowd. Mourners ran behind the crypt or dove behind trees.

Her heart beat fast. Her formerly stiff knees felt like jam. It was happening again. Death was coming. God couldn't wait until tomorrow.

Justain towed her behind a maple tree. He surveyed the line of fire.

Devlin dragged Lady Glaston behind a massive stump.

Another shot flew past.

Madeline's pulse pounded. "No, not Justain, too. Please, Abba Father."

Justain scanned the hills as he worked a small gun from beneath his coat. "There are at least three or four fiends shooting."

She bundled Justain in her arms to shield him from the bullets.

Working his hands free, he pulled a second pistol from an inside pocket. "Everything will be fine! Trust me. I have to do this, Madeline. Please let go."

A shot hit the maple; sap spat onto his sleeve.

The noise, the screams of the crowds, the thunder of blood coursing her ears. She filled her lungs. "No more." Then threw herself in the direction of the bullets.

39

Justain caught Madeline and yanked her to the ground. A single slug whipped past. It would've killed her for sure.

"Are you mad, lass?" Another spray of bullets hit their maple tree. Fire pumped through his veins. "Are you trying to get killed?"

"Yes, if it will save you."

"You aren't sacrificing yourself." Justain shoved Madeline low among the knurled roots. "Listen to me; I need you to stay put. Will you do as I ask? This is a command. Will you?"

She nodded.

He loaded his blunderbuss and secured the hammer. Then he rotated and showcased the flintlock to Devlin. Would his cousin put down his ministering to take a life?

As if hearing Justain's thought, Devlin raised his hands. "Toss them."

He pitched his trusted flintlock, along with a sack of bullet packets. "Devlin's the best shot in Devon. He'll protect you and Lady Glaston if things get out of hand.

"You mean when you're killed." She dropped her head to her knees.

More shots assailed their tree.

Justain raised her palm to his chest. "You won't be

a widow today. I intend to have a long complicated life with you. Cheer, woman. Life with me won't be so bad." He sucked in a deep breath and leaped into the tall grass. Justain drew his weapon.

Another bullet exploded.

Justain smashed his chest flat to the ground. He took cover behind a rock and refilled his gun. The blunderbuss proved excellent for fast close-range skirmishes, but unlike his flintlock, this small gun's long-range accuracy was questionable. He needed speed and luck to fulfill his promise to Madeline. Even with Devlin, he was out numbered.

Justain waited thirty seconds and then fired. He felled the rampaging man less than twenty feet from his head. "I'm winning this fight." He crawled up a mound and shot again.

A cursing yell cut through the tense breeze. He had cut down another bandit.

A boom sounded across the wide part of the clearing, attacking their tree again. "Please stay where I left you."

As he pivoted to check on Madeline, the pepper of a bullet flew past his ear. Someone had marked him. He rolled, sinking down behind a tree root. If Justain hadn't pivoted toward his wife, the bullet would've penetrated his temple. He would be dead.

He glanced back at Madeline. Her onyx mourner's shrouds bulged from the bottom of the tree. His wife remained unharmed.

Another gun sounded. It was Justain's flintlock. He knew the music of that barrel. Devlin struck someone in the far tree line. A burly man stumbled forward, brandishing a silver musket. Barrow.

One arm drooped to Barrow's side. Devlin had

wounded him, but the villain hadn't been put down. The blackguard drew his weapon and aimed at Justain.

"This ends now, Barrow." Justain waited for his sight to fill. *Concentrate*. It would take too long to tamp and reload. *Steady.* If he missed, his promise to Madeline would be broken. *Aim.* His finger hovered over the trigger.

Fire. The bloated beast dropped backward, from the impact. The lead shot hit him between the eyes. The mighty goliath fell.

Another weapon discharged—a rifle's belch.

"Lord Devonshire!" Jonathan ran from a thick grove of trees. He had blasted a bandit. The body slipped down the slope.

Justain searched for his cousin. "Devlin, get my wife, everyone to the main house!" He didn't recognize his own voice.

The area cleared as the faithful of Hampshire, the poor sheep, disappeared from Avington's rich land. If another bandit existed other than the four felled, he could've easily disappeared in the confusion. "Well, at least you're done, aye, Barrow."

Jonathan waved the all clear signal. "No one's hiding in the brush, and the ridge is being scoured by Masterson." He met Justain near the first bandit. "I sent a groom for the constable." His hands shook as he yanked at his navy coat.

"Are you injured, Winton?"

"All these people?" His copper eyes seemed glassy. "This could have been worse than Dorset."

"Jonathan, are you wounded?"

He rubbed his face. "No, sir."

"We handled this, Jonathan. You, Devlin, and I, we prevented Barrow from claiming another innocent shield."

Justain took the rifle from him, secured the hammer, and slung it over his shoulder. "Let's drag this man down to the others."

A scar wrapped the dead bandit's forearm, a hot-ore sear.

"Look, Winton, if you had any doubts about Barrow's involvement with Tilford, the proof is here, another ore miner."

They pulled the fiend to his mate, two more to go.

"Let's get the one in the tree line and save Barrow to the end. It'll take us both to move the load of evil."

A breeze picked up, dissipating the odour of gunpowder. Justain tugged out a handkerchief to wipe his brow. He put his boot on the third bandit's stomach and rolled him over. "Mr. Kent!"

"What's he doing here? How did he know Barrow?" Jonathan stooped down and pushed Kent's silver flintlock away. The St. James crest shined on the metal. "Maybe he heard the commotion and decided to join in the rout."

Justain rubbed his forehead and pictured the battle, squinting, seeking Kent's vantage point. "He kept shooting towards Madeline, even when I was away from the maple." Justain stood, scratching his head. "Even when I proved a closer target."

"Well, you said Kent was crazed." Jonathan grabbed an arm and tugged.

"He came from up north when Madeline and I arrived at Avington. That's what the duchess said…Jonathan, undo his cuffs."

Justain pushed Kent's cinnamon coat sleeves up as Jonathan unbuttoned the cinched shirt fabric.

The fiend's arms held a tiny melt scar, a miner's

injury.

They dragged Kent to the line now making three.

"Kent's in league with Barrow? How would they know each other?" Jonathan shook the dust from his hands. "Doesn't make sense?"

Justain took up one of the bandit's guns. "They all bear silver muskets. Muskets with the St. James crest. They used the duke's own weapons?"

"You suspect a larger conspiracy?" The steward's mouth shrank to a dot.

"We'll know in a minute." Justain straightened and led his steward to the last assailant. The events of the past three months sifted in Justain's head. "This butcher, Barrow, knows every lowlife in Mother England."

The two men rolled the portly fiend onto his back. A fatty-cheeked man with a melt scar on his jaw and lifeless eyes stared ahead.

It wasn't Barrow. The size and girth of the man was similar. From a distance, Justain had thought it was the murderer. But up close, this wasn't the smooth face of his brother's killer.

"Another miner?" Jonathan picked up the man's silver musket and pointed it to the trees. "Barrow's got to be around here somewhere."

"Put the gun down. This isn't Barrow's handiwork." Justain sighed into his palm. "I suspect none of this was Barrow."

"If it's not Barrow…" Jonathan plopped onto the ground. "What does this mean?"

Justain wiped his brow again. "It means my personal demon still lives. Let's search the rabble." He bit his lip. Richard's death still hadn't been appeased.

Yet, the puzzle in his head stood complete.

"Jonathan, when I ordered my Berlin carriage, how long did it take for delivery?"

Jonathan stooped and checked the pockets of the decedents. "About two months."

"Madeline said the duke had three shiny chestnut carriages. One was stolen from the Tilford Coaching Inn."

"That leaves two." Jonathan reared back on his heels. "But there are three parked near the stables."

"Kent brought it back after the attack. The duchess said some of their family mined." He grabbed his steward's arm. "This is about Madeline. This has all been about Madeline."

Jonathan's copper eyes grew wide, then squinted. "Sir?"

"Kent was jilted by Madeline. He must've followed her from Hampshire. Planned to kidnap or kill her…at Tilford. If I hadn't." Justain cleared his throat. "Hadn't invited Madeline into my carriage, she would've been in this madman's clutches. She'd be dead."

"Good thing you were there looking for the informant."

His chest tightened, and Justain looked to the peaceful hills. "I was meant to be there. Meant to be a part of her life."

"Sir, are you all right?"

Justain kicked Kent's arm. "Look at his stained fingertips. The man is hopped up on opiates. When I evicted him, I found a ton of Dover pills." Stained fingers. The duke's fingers. Mama's fingers. Opium! Kent poisoned the duke with opium. That's why he hadn't dreaded detection. Kent knew the duke would die.

Justain wanted to darken his own daylights for being so blind.

❧

The wild tones of rampant gossip vibrated through the walls of the orangery, the grand ballroom of the west wing. At least the duke's service held some dignity.

Meriwether had taken his guns and greatcoat and refreshed Justain's face and hands with lemony water. Justain trudged inside, hoping he wouldn't stand out.

The duchess passed him at the threshold. "You made a mockery of my husband's funeral."

"No, Mr. Kent did. He decided to show up after all." Justain whispered to keep from feeding the rumour-hungry crowd. "He's responsible for everything."

"Are you sure?" Her black eyes didn't flinch.

Justain nodded.

"I suppose you must tell everyone and further shame us." She twisted her bracelets. Her coal-black eyes darted. A chill seemed to exude from her stone countenance.

Did she care at all? Could bitterness push one to that place? If it could, Justain needed to flush his system of it.

"I'll be in my room." She waltzed past, her shiny satin skirt swishing down the hall.

He pressed further into the gilded room. A perimeter of silence surrounded Justain, as mourners ended their conversation to give him their full appraisal. The gawking, open mouths and whispers were worse than the violet lines of Almack's.

But where were his wife and cousin?

40

Every inch of the orangery shined of gold trim. Its ceiling mural of the heavenly cherubim stretched the length of the room at least eighty paces. Justain stepped lightly on the glossy floor. The hand-buffed mahogany planks were slick enough to slide all the way to Devon with the slightest push. He planted his feet; Justain didn't need a clumsy moment to further tarnish this day.

The lit crystal chandelier cast rhombus reflections everywhere like shooting targets. His pulse raced, and he craved his blunderbuss.

On the other side of the expansive room, Devlin leaned against a cream-coloured wall, holding court, but his watchful eyes drifted to the corner.

Madeline sat near him. With chin lifted high, she chatted with two old men, probably exchanging condolences. Her dark grey frock contrasted the rose of her cheeks. No one could tell by her gentle countenance she'd been the target of a war.

Providence had chosen for him a wife from Hampshire, away from the expectations of Devon and the complications of Dorset.

For the first time in his life, Justain felt lucky to be gifted with a treasure. Time slowed to a crawl as he watched the grace of the woman, his Maddie, as she slipped her gloved hand to her face. Lady Glaston's bear hug about his shoulders ended the trance.

"She's not fragile, young man." Lady Glaston released him and smoothed his cravat. "Go to her."

Justain smiled. "You broke your promise and came inside of Avington."

"Sometimes you have to stop being pigheaded to show people how much you care. Excuse me. I must see what happened to Gunter. He went to fetch me some punch."

Justain straightened his shoulders and marched to his wife.

"Lord Devonshire, this is Mr. Widenmere, a long-time friend of the St. Jameses."

The man twitched his shaggy moustache as he shook Justain's hand. "That was some mighty happenings at the crypt."

"Maybe the duke would've liked the commotion." Justain returned his gaze to Madeline.

Windermere chuckled a hearty laugh. "That he would."

"May I steal my wife from you for a moment, sir?" Justain didn't wait for the fellow to respond. He took Madeline's cane, pocketed her arm within his, and propelled her to the hall outside the orangery.

"Justain, the guests?" Her face held a tense smile.

"There's no new terror, Maddie."

Her shoulders slackened. "It's over. Barrow won't threaten us again."

"I promise to always keep you safe." Justain navigated to a nook beneath the staircase and cloistered her there. "Are you injured?"

"I'm fine." She touched his cheek, stroked the cleft in his chin. "You're alive."

Madeline was the target. The reality hit him hard

like a sucker punch to the gut. "I…sorry…" He couldn't string together a coherent set of syllables, so he pressed her deep within his bosom.

"Justain? What's the matt—"

He hauled her high into his arms and kissed her.

❧

His mouth took hers, parting her lips, stealing her breath. Bands of iron gripped every part of her as if he tried to recover Adam's missing rib.

She lowered her chin, slipped to his throat. "Justain, we're—"

He put his finger to her lips. His hand trailed her jaw and drew her towards him. The ruby ring smelled of wax and gun smoke. "I should've forgotten about me and focused on you." He claimed her lips again, sculpting them to respond. Flame engulfed her at his touch. What was he trying to say? Her thoughts dissolved in the magic of his hands. The world spun around her, and she gripped his neck to keep from floating away.

"The trust you exude, never ques-questioning my motives, fighting for my soul." Justain kissed her harder.

She pushed at his shoulders. "All is fine, Justain."

"What of us?"

"You and Devlin, you've saved everyone. We're all fine."

He shook his head and brought her hands to his mouth. "Keep me a better man."

Her heart beat fast, but this couldn't be real. Devlin pounded into the hall. Her gazed drifted over Justain's shoulder.

Devlin coughed. "We need your help with the guests. They are leaving, and I suppose the duchess is too ashamed to return."

With his palms, Justain soothed her crushed bodice. "No more talk of shame."

She sighed. "Let me go see everyone off."

Justain's smile dimmed, but he placed her cane in her hand and allowed her to return to the orangery.

41

The final guest departed. Madeline dipped her chin to Justain and left the room with Lady Glaston. He followed, hungering for the scent of her hair.

Devlin stepped in front of him and blocked his path. No avoiding his cousin now. The confessional was open.

"Is it over? Is Barrow dead?" He pulled Justain's flintlock from beneath his waistcoat and handed it to him.

"The murderer's still out there. With all these tongues, Barrow and his forces could be here by morning."

Devlin sighed. "He got away?"

"Barrow wasn't here." Justain checked the hammer of the gun, and ran his palm along the short barrel. "There've been threats under my nose which I've ignored."

"But you suspected something would happen today at the duke's funeral? Under ordinary conditions, you only smuggle spirits under your cloak."

"I'm never without protection. I've carried weapons since Dorset." He poured the last of the cold coffee from the buffet and gulped it. "Randolph Kent did this."

Devlin's brows lifted. "The scourge that attacked

Madeline?"

Justain nodded. "The blackguard poisoned the duke with opiates. I could've saved him and spared Madeline this agony. No wonder I've been thinking of Mother."

"We focus too much on the past, and we miss what's important, the blessings we have right now in our lives."

"My wife…everything was to harm Madeline. I've been so blind." Justain's chest hurt as if a boulder sat upon it. Everything he cared about could've been taken away. Was this Madeline's burden? He downed the coffee, hoping it had enough heat to melt the lump in his throat. "I could have cost you your life."

"Well, your eyes are open now." Devlin hummed *Amazing Grace.*

Justain set down the cup. "Well, I have been blind."

"You should come to one of my camp meetings. You might find Newton's hymn comforting."

Justain wrenched his gun on to the buffet abandoning his temporal protection. It dropped with a thud and spun upon the glossy surface. With trembling fingers, he gripped his cousin's hand. "Reverend, help me surrender to this grace. I need it. I don't want to live like this anymore."

❧

Madeline sat on the edge of the chaise, moving her slippers over the rug.

Aunt braided her hair. "You've tree sap on this section. I'll brush it out." A hundred more strokes and the torture ended.

"Anne did a good job of packing. I should lock the portmanteaus." Madeline tried to stand and force her sore muscles to obey but couldn't.

"Don't you dare move! I'll not have you falling on the floor. Lord Devonshire will be beside himself. Let him lock them up. His guns are atop that one."

"It's a miracle he wasn't killed." Tears rolled down Madeline's cheeks.

Aunt traipsed to the picture of Lady Angelique resting near the footboard. She fingered the ribbons of Mama's dress captured in the textured paint. "It's finished, dear sister. Your duke is buried, and your girl will leave Avington."

Madeline dampened her sleeves while trying to stem the flow of her weeping.

Aunt returned to her side and rubbed Madeline's back. "You and the earl will have a rich life together."

"He'll take me to Innesfrey, and we'll start our separate lives."

Aunt chuckled, the laugh turning into a full-belly rollicking roar. "There's no way that young man will ever leave you to build a life without him. He's besotted with you."

"I can't make Justain happy. He's too much like Father. I keep picturing Father crying out for a drop of water to cool his singed tongue. I can't watch Justain die in bitterness, too."

"I'm sorry you didn't restore the duke. His love for Angelique never died, and it clouded his opportunities. He never understood how a loving God would take your mother from us. The duke didn't release his pain. But you need to release yours."

Had Madeline released her pain? She leaned back onto the cushions. She pulled Justain's satchel from beneath her. The broken book of Donne's tales spilled out.

A page tore free. She picked up the poet's *A Valediction Forbidding Mourning*. Underlined on the paper—*'So let us melt, and make no noise, No tear-floods, nor sigh-tempests move.'*

"Melt with no noise." Madeline had perfected crying without a sound. At least in Innesfrey, she'd be free to voice her emotions without fretting about Justain being made to feel guilty.

Aunt smoothed the streaks from her cheeks. "You tried to protect your husband today, but he wouldn't let you. He cares for you too much."

The door creaked open. Anne stood at the entry. "Lady Glaston, Lady Devonshire, I tried to follow your packing instructions."

"I'm sure your work is perfect." Madeline leaned back into the padding, hoping the dim light of the room concealed her sorrow.

Anne curtsied and left the chamber.

The glow of the hall lanterns crept around the hinges of the closed door. Her spirit illuminated. "I did try, Aunt. I tried to follow His instructions. Abba Father, help me to forgive myself for falling short."

"Get some rest." Aunt Tiffany helped her crawl onto the bed.

Madeline closed her eyes and cradled a pillow.

"His grace is sufficient. Find the strength to love your husband. Treasure him and every day God gives." Aunt kissed her forehead and left the room.

Madeline sensed Providence's ministering angels whispering to her. The last vestiges of her grief released. "Abba Father, You kept Justain safe. Thank You for all that I do have."

Peace fell on her, and she closed her eyes.

❧

The glow of a dying lamp lit the room. Madeline focused on the windowsill. The filigreed carvings above the thick pane glass tried their best to reflect moonlight, but the clouds of Hampshire still mourned.

She turned toward the chaise. Justain slept there. His head drooped against the cushions. His hands, which had fired a gun over and over again, now rested with Donne. His bare feet dangled over the edge of the ottoman.

She should douse the candle so Justain could get a better portion of rest. Madeline grasped the handle of her cane and quietly made it to his chair. As she leaned over him his eyes opened.

"Sorry, Justain."

He smiled and brought her hand to his lips. The warmth of his breath tickled her wrist. He released her and eased the book from his lap to the floor.

"A page tore out of Donne. I wasn't borrowing it; it fell out of your satchel."

"Well, it's part of my worldly goods. It belongs to my wife, too."

She turned from him and poked the logs in the fireplace. "The book's taken a battering."

"But it's withstood. Sit with me, Madeline."

She pivoted and lowered to the edge of the chaise. "Are there a lot of books in Innesfrey?"

"There are…but there are more at Trenchard."

"You'll have to start boxing them for Innesfrey. I've a great appetite for reading."

He seemed amused. His handsome face hadn't

held a grin for quite a while. "Why would I do that?"

"Do you think I'd settle for this?" She picked up the book from the floor to wave it under his nose. "This isn't Donne's poems." Her fingers caressed the worn leather cover. She flipped open the parchment inked with scriptures. "You were reading the Bible?"

"Devlin loaned it to me. If the words in this book cause my wife to sacrifice her life for mine, it seems fitting that I investigate them. That I commit them to my heart."

A smile bloomed in her spirit. "It'll make a great study."

Justain arched an eyebrow. "I'm going to need help interpreting these passages."

She smoothed a lock from his temple. "I'm sure your cousin, the good reverend, could be of assistance."

He put the Bible in her lap. "No, I want my missionary with raven hair, a heart of gold, and soft lips."

She caught his gaze.

Justain stroked her jaw. "We may have to sleep on blankets until the furnishings arrive at Trenchard, but I'll make the adventure fun. Then maybe a wedding trip to Italy?" His voice turned serious. "The Countess of Devon should be at her husband's side. Your place is at Trenchard, Lady Devonshire."

"I should be for Innesfrey. There, we'll start afresh, without guilt and resentment. We'll learn to trust each other, absent tragedy."

His sky-blue eyes radiated. "I trust you with everything within me, Maddie."

She looked away.

"I need you to trust me again." Justain put his

hands along her shoulders. He rubbed her muscles until she sank against him. "I know you're tired, but it's time for me to fight for this union."

He drew her into a kiss. His lips seemed to plead for their marriage, his fingers upon her waist numbering his reasons.

She settled near his ear to catch her breath. "At least this Barrow mess is over."

"My chasing after Barrow is over. But this attack was Kent's doing. You did hear his voice when we hid in the mineshaft. He's tried to take you from my arms ever since, but he won't hurt you or anyone else, anymore. He's dead."

"Kent?" She inhaled deeply. The tiny bloom of hope withered in her spirit. The battles weren't done. "Then Barrow is still after you."

"Once we're in Devon, I will make it plain that my plan for vengeance is no more. I'll let the Crown deal with him. I intend to have a long life with my own personal missionary." He stroked her hair. "You must be at my side. I need you, Maddie."

"Justain, I don't know."

"I'll even desecrate Trenchard with a sculpture room." He moved his hands away. "I finally see what I want, and it's not revenge."

She wanted a life with him, but her stomach quivered. "The risk is too much for me."

Justain closed his eyes for a moment. "I've no more defences. You and God. You've slain my heart, and I can't live without either of you." The words were quiet in tone, but the most powerful things he'd ever said.

Madeline batted away a tear then tugged his palm to her cheek. "You never fight fair."

"I fight to win, but I've a task for you, my countess."

She lowered her head onto his shoulder. "And that would be?"

"In the mineshaft, you enchanted me with a few wicked tales. The prophet and the harlot was my favourite. Please retell it, but keep it exciting or you'll lose my interest."

"I'll try." She hugged his neck, sought the warmth of his mouth.

"Oh." He groaned. "This is a good beginning."

Madeline forgot her fears and rested in Justain's arms until the morn.

Thank you for purchasing this White Rose Publishing title. For other inspirational stories, please visit our online bookstore at www.pelicanbookgroup.com.

For questions or more information, contact us at titleadmin@pelicanbookgroup.com.

White Rose Publishing
Where Faith is the Cornerstone of Love™
www.WhiteRosePublishing.com
an imprint of Pelican Ventures Book Group
www.PelicanBookGroup.com

May God's glory shine through
this inspirational work of fiction.

AMDG

CPSIA information can be obtained at www.ICGtesting.com
Printed in the USA
LVOW101334010513

331820LV00003B/61/P